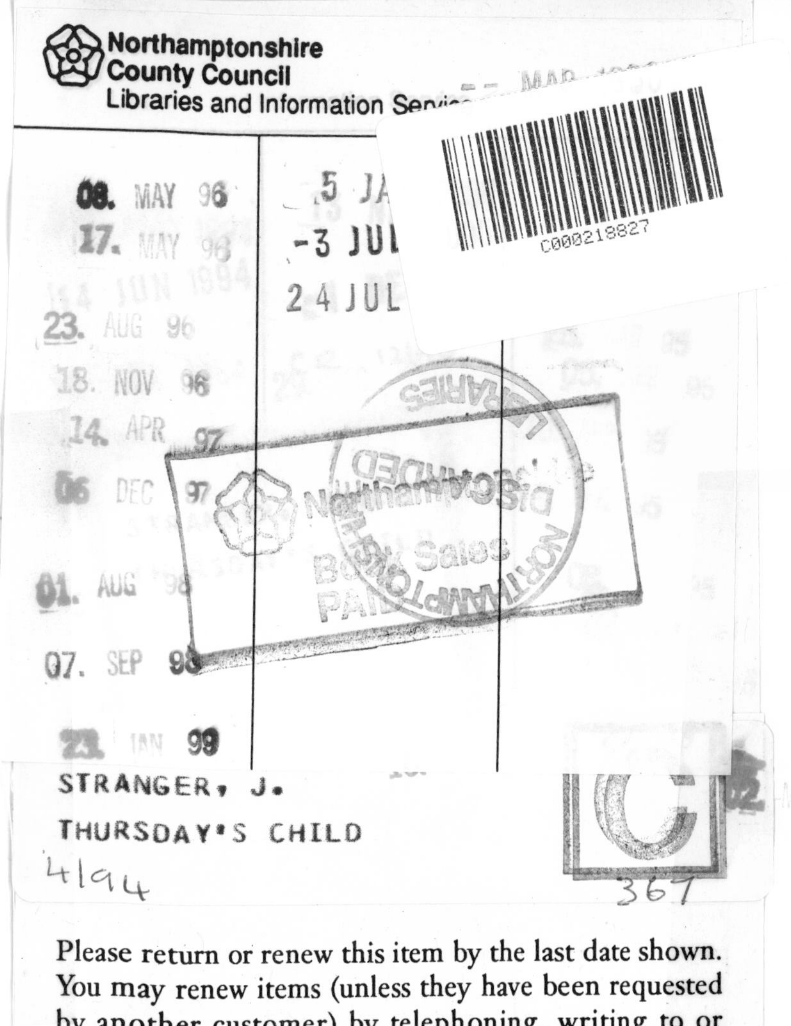

Northamptonshire
County Council
Libraries and Information Servi
08. MAY 96
17. MAY 96
23. AUG 96
18. NOV 96
14. APR 97
06 DEC 97
01. AUG 98
07. SEP 98
23. JAN 99
5 JA
-3 JUL
24 JUL
C000218827
DISCARDED
NORTHAMPTON LIBRARIES
Book Sales
PAID
02 MAR 96

THURSDAY'S CHILD

By the same author

THE HILLS ARE LONELY
THE RUNNING FOXES

THURSDAY'S CHILD

Joyce Stranger

SOUVENIR PRESS

First published 1994 by Souvenir Press Ltd,
43 Great Russell Street, London WC1B 3PA
and simultaneously in Canada

ISBN 0 285 63179 9

Photoset by Rowland Phototypesetting Ltd,
Bury St Edmunds, Suffolk

Printed in Great Britain by
Biddles Ltd, Guildford and King's Lynn

This book is dedicated to all police dog handlers everywhere. Very few people realise what an incredible effort goes into making the dogs.

It is also dedicated to my past dogs, Janus, Puma, Chita and Josse, and my newcomer, Troy, and to all those who came to my dog club for teaching over the past twenty years; and to German Shepherds Sam and Timber who, with John, Bob, Brian, Bill and Eddie, and of course Bryn, have recently given an intriguing direction to my teaching.

AUTHOR'S NOTE

Lee Valley Police Dog Section exists only in my imagination. Its methods and characters are all imaginary.

I owe thanks to so many men who are still either training police dogs and their handlers, or have now retired. I met them while competing with my own German Shepherd bitch in civilian trials in which many police dog handlers take part.

Among them are Les Edwards, who helped me enormously with training my own dogs; his wife Denise, who was once a woman police constable; Bini Moehler, Clive Ferries, Graham Mabbut, Wilf Chadwick, whose book on dog training and long phone conversations have been invaluable, Marlene Jordan, who was a woman police dog handler and worked in prisons, and others too numerous to mention.

The more we learn about dogs, the more we are aware we have only touched on the fringe of knowledge and that there is far more to training a dog than can ever be acquired by reading a few books.

Very few of those who meet police dogs realise that at the start they were boisterous animals knowing nothing, and that the most enormous effort is needed to make them an asset beyond price, able after only thirteen weeks to pass a complicated series of tests at a very high standard.

One

Joe Gulley, kennelman for Lee Valley Police Dog Section, was used to nursing each new group, and to nursing Josh Thornton whose duty it was to shape the trainees into competent dog handlers. He gentled them, he coaxed them, he made time to listen to them. But he had never had a team like this.

The weather did not help.

Rainstorms alternated with biting frosts. The hard ground meant that none of the dogs could be jumped. It was tough on human and animal alike.

'It's never been as bad as this,' Josh said, that Tuesday morning. It was the second week of February and the fourth week of their thirteen-week initial dog training course.

'The men say it's because we have a woman on the team for the first time. They say Brier Morrey's a Jonah.' Gulley pulled at the ragged end of his grey moustache.

'You believe them?' Josh looked down on the little kennelman, with his quiff of grey hair. Gulley, he thought, looked like an angry rooster defending his hens.

Gulley's look was more eloquent than voiced disgust.

'I've warned them about the date. An unhappy anniversary. Brier needs gentle treatment.'

'Not too gentle,' Josh said. 'Could drive her over the edge. She's still sore. It takes time, you know that. The man who killed her husband will be out, alive, in a few years' time. That galls her—that Tom should be dead and her family suffering, while the man who shot him will one day walk free.'

Two years ago today, he thought as he went into his

office. There had been flowers that morning on the pavement where Tom had died, from people who remembered. Josh had seen them on his way to work and had hoped that Brier would not drive that way. He knew she usually added two miles to her journey rather than pass the place. Memories were bitter.

Brier had learned to endure.

'You have the children,' everyone said.

It had been a good marriage. Tom could laugh at the world and laugh at himself, and had taught her to laugh at herself.

Laughter had died with him.

That morning she had to persuade herself that these were just another few hours in a sequence that had lost all meaning. The day escalated into disaster.

They had suffered from two weeks of incessant rain, but even so Josh insisted that today they must work out of doors. There was a limit to the hours that could be spent on theory and time was short: just over nine weeks left out of thirteen to the final tests, and they all needed to cram in much more practice. The six German Shepherds were young and raw and the handlers were new to dog training. Brier's dog had been handed over by his owners only three weeks before. He was totally undisciplined, a real handful, and she was finding him extremely hard work.

Josh drilled them and chivvied them and, unusually, almost lost his temper. He was overtired and overworked. A man they had spent a year hunting had been given a derisory prison sentence the day before. For the moment Josh felt uncharacteristically disheartened.

His mood was aggravated by a throbbing headache, and by the sight of Brier's tense face. Her dog, Kim, in spite of his boisterousness, was one of the best dogs he had had in a long time. She was the most competent handler on the team but her feelings were affecting the dog.

It was difficult to concentrate.

'Can't we take a breather and get out of this appalling weather?' Tony Spence asked, blowing on his hands as he eased his soaked dog into a sit. Neither he nor the dog was yet in harmony with one another. A spoiled and unruly pet, given to the police in despair because he was so wild, Jacko resented discipline.

Tony had tried to change the dog's name but the animal would answer to nothing else. Tony wanted a dignified name and this sounded more like a monkey's. He was aware it was a minor and silly objection, but it still needled him.

The dog himself was a handsome fellow with a bright and mischievous expression, and a very strong will of his own. Make or break, those two, Josh thought. Tony was a prickly customer and he wished he knew why.

'Tony never did like getting wet.' Rob Jacobs was the oldest man on the team. Tony at times seemed to him little older than his eldest son, who was causing problems, as was his daughter. Tony, irritated at being made to feel like an unruly teenager, glared at him.

They were working in the large yard that separated the small one-storey office block from the two police houses that faced them. Gulley had opened the doors of all four garages, so that they could take shelter in the worst downpours. The large grass compound, surrounded by eight-foot chainlink fencing, was sodden and Josh was afraid that the constant passage of men and dogs would turn it into a mud patch.

The kennels were empty. They were only used as temporary accommodation, unless one of the men was on holiday. The dog stayed there then, and Gulley took charge of him, feeding him and exercising and cleaning his kennel.

The place was isolated—neighbours would have been likely to complain about barking dogs. Headquarters were four miles away, along a narrow, high-hedged lane, connected by a road through the housing estate to the motorway that bypassed the town.

'You needn't think crimes only occur when the sun's shining.' Josh Thornton was colder than they were, as they at least were moving with the dogs, while he stood still. 'It's like mountain rescue. People are more likely to get lost in evil weather with snow on the ground and ice in the air and a howling gale blown all the way from Siberia.'

'Thought we'd break early,' Gulley said from the side of the field, pulling his cap down and his scarf up. He at least was dry. 'Not fit weather for man or beast. We'll all feel better after a hot drink.'

Derek Mott took a towel from his van and rubbed Spike as dry as possible. He pulled the dog's ear and Spike whirled in a happy circle, trying to tug at the towel. He was a merry dog, still with a mind of his own.

Derek blew on his hands before walking into the office. Josh noted his care of Spike, and that Brier had also dried her dog before sheltering. The other men had merely handed their dogs over to Gulley. Need to be told that won't do, Josh thought. Derek lived with his widowed mother. He had not yet settled down to marriage. The members of the team were already taking bets as to how long Sue, his current girlfriend, would last. Policemen needed wives who would accept the unsocial hours, the broken appointments, the sudden calls to duty. Most of Derek's girlfriends were speedily disillusioned.

Gulley produced scalding hot soup instead of coffee and they drank it thankfully, but there was little conversation. Not even Tony resorted to his usual ribbing. Every one of them had the same thought in mind: they could end up like Tom, a day's wonder, a headline in the newspapers. They were all painfully aware of their late colleague's widow, working her dog with a set face, avoiding them all, avoiding even Gulley when he went over to speak to her. Tom had not been in the dog team, but then, at the time of his death, none of them had. A friendly man, they had all known him, worked with him, and enjoyed his lighthearted approach to life.

Josh, watching Brier unobtrusively, sighed. He had wanted her on the team because she was a good handler. He had not realised that her daily presence would affect him in quite a different way. It was eight years since his own wife had died of cancer. He was healed and ready to start again. But Brier needed time, and he could never show his feelings for her lest the other men noticed. He treated her with reserve.

The break did them all good and afterwards they began to make more progress. Soon Kim was responding so well that Brier felt a stirring of excitement, an emotion long forgotten. Things would be easier when the weather improved, she told herself when they stopped for lunch, and she turned with enthusiasm to Gulley's egg and cress sandwiches and scalding coffee.

Gulley had married a woman who took odd hours and difficulties in her stride, and believed that if you fed people well, then they could cope with anything. She adored dogs. She owned three Tibetan Terriers which she bred and showed, and Gulley had his own Jack Russell. Alice was a grand cook and would have loved to run a small tea room, but she felt that Gulley needed her at home.

Brier finished eating, then called Kim and went off to work on him by herself before the men came out. The first hour of the afternoon would be practice of everything they had learned. The dog began to respond and the faint stir of excitement returned.

Then Josh called her into his office. She thought that he wanted to discuss the dog, and so he did, but not in the way she expected.

One look at him and she knew he had bad news. There were two people with him. They were very young, the man dark, his hair in a pony tail. He wore one heart-shaped ear-ring. The girl could have been a model—long legs, long blonde hair, and one of the shortest skirts Brier had ever seen. Not long married, she guessed.

The man, his face embarrassed, looked at his young wife as if wanting to disassociate himself from the scene.

She must be frozen in this weather, Brier thought, knowing she was being uncharitable. She suddenly couldn't bear to look at a woman who was young and beautiful and had a husband who was alive.

'I can't live without Kim,' the girl wailed, tears flooding down her face. 'I thought I could, but I can't. It's dreadful without him. Please can we have him back? Please?'

They had no choice. They had paid nothing for the dog and the owners had the right to change their minds. Yet they had handed him over so blithely three weeks before, and left without even a backward glance.

She watched Gulley leash Kim and lead him to them, and turned her head away when the dog looked back at her, pulling to return to her, unable to understand this new change in his fortunes. He had not greeted his first owners with enthusiasm. A quick tail wave, and then he had returned to sit at Brier's side, his brown eyes watchful.

The day dragged on. She stood, envying the men. They had dogs. She was now a spectator instead of taking part. By five o'clock she felt bitter, as well as angry and miserable.

People had no right to change their minds.

She knew as the thought came to her that she was being unreasonable.

Josh took her home. The empty dog van stayed in the police garage: no need for that now. He drew up in front of her house. Yesterday she had driven her own van, Kim in the back of it, a newborn fragile excitement mastering her as he was beginning to learn so well and, at last, to concentrate. She had worked hard to be part of the Police Dog team; now it looked as if all that effort was wasted. Unless Josh found her a dog, and soon, she would be back on the beat. Thoughts about Tom, suppressed all day, began to overwhelm her.

Josh looked at her, knowing she needed comfort. She sat stiffly, her head turned away from him, and he felt it unwise even to touch her hand, to say he understood, to try to assure her that the pain would go, in time. He and Tom had been friends of long standing. He missed him too. They had fished together. He had known Brier for even longer, although he had never known her well.

Brier's mother, a professional breeder of outstanding German Shepherd dogs, had given him pups, always willing to donate one from a litter to the Police Force. Lee Valley, like many other Dog Sections, did not buy its own dogs, but relied on free gifts from the public of unruly teenage animals that had become unmanageable.

Brier did not want to get out of the van. She looked at the house that she had loved so much when Tom was alive. They had chosen it together, furnished it together, lived in it for nearly twelve years. The children had both come home to that house as new babies.

The children. They would be waiting eagerly, not just for her, but for the dog. Kim had made them laugh, had relaxed them, had begun to bond them as a family again.

Street lamps shone on rainwet paths. The distant hills were hidden. The dreary winter garden glittered with a few early snowdrops. Lamplight cast long shadows. She had been looking forward to longer daylight hours. She had seen daffodil leaves thrusting through the earth that morning, a promise of spring, when she trained her dog before driving to the Centre for their lessons.

No more Kim.

A dreary January had given way to a miserable February. That morning, in spite of the date, she had felt more hope than she had known for a long time. Nearly four weeks into the training course of thirteen weeks and she had already lost two dogs. The first she had had for only two days.

X-rays had revealed bad hips: he could never work. He had been lucky as a couple had just lost their own dog and were delighted to have Sabre, who would be the fifth German Shepherd in their lifetime. The vet had put them in touch.

She hadn't missed him, as Kim had come in the same day and she had brought the new dog home. The children were as yet cautious with Sabre, who would probably not have made the grade even if his hips had been sound. He was over-boisterous and difficult to control, with a mind of his own that made teaching him a chore rather than a pleasure.

By contrast Kim was a delight, in spite of his exuberance. He was far more responsive than Sabre, who had been surly. He settled in as if he had lived with them all his life. Brier and the dog soon developed a greater rapport than the rest of the group had, as yet, with their dogs.

His loss was a disaster.

She would have to start again, from the beginning, nearly four weeks behind. If they found her a dog. Good dogs were few, though many were offered.

She would have to face the children, to tell them they had no dog at all now, just as Dana was becoming fond of the animal and getting over the prickly tempers that had plagued her for the past two years.

'I don't know how to tell the children', she said. 'And what kind of life is that dog going to have? He has brains and needs to use them. That couple's problems arose because they spoiled him. Let him have his own way all the time and they hadn't taught him a thing.'

'Gulley's taken care of that,' Josh said. 'You know how protective he is of all the dogs. He told them that if they didn't join his dog club and work on Kim, he'd see that he was taken from them, as they weren't fit to own a German Shepherd.'

In spite of her misery, Brier laughed.

'Gulley's impossible. I'll swear he fills that club of his by sheer blackmail. How did they take it?'

'Like lambs, apparently. It's a pity people grow old. Gulley was one of the best of us, and a good PR man. The Force lost a major asset when he had to retire. Alice helps him with the dog club. Takes the money, does the register, brews tea and sweeps up afterwards. Like him, she's one in a million.'

'The Force's loss was our gain,' Brier said. Gulley had hated retirement and jumped at the chance that Josh gave him, of looking after the kennels and the dogs. He had expanded his own duties. Alice had been delighted. There was nothing worse than a man sitting miserably round the house, without anything to get up for or go out for.

Gulley came home happy, and told her about his day. She felt she knew the people on the dog team as well as he did. She already knew Josh, as he called in often and was regaled with pies and flans and quiches, with cakes and scones, and was always given a tin of goodies to take home. Alice, whose own two sons were grown and living abroad, mothered everyone.

She had reminded Gulley of the anniversary that morning at breakfast.

'Two years to the day since Tom Morrey was killed,' she said. 'Take care of Brier. It'll be a bad day for her.'

Gulley had eased Brier's day, had tried his best to rouse her from the memories that came unbidden and threatened to overwhelm her.

'We're his family,' Josh said. 'He and Alice always did have room for everyone in their home. Gulley took five of us back one day unexpectedly and she didn't turn a hair. Just grinned and brought out the cake tin, which was always full. Still is, for that matter.' He smiled in happy reminiscence.

'I can't imagine Alice without food,' Brier said. 'I took the children to see her last weekend. They've never been so spoilt in their lives. I think they'd have happily left home and gone to live with her, just for more of her apple pie and cream. It was out of this world.'

Behind them, in the van, Spark, Josh's treasured German Shepherd, heaved a deep sigh, wishing that something would happen. He was one of the best dogs they had ever had in the Lee Valley dog section. Beside him Lim, the little Springer Spaniel, trained to detect explosives, shook his head and his ears flapped against the metal side of the van.

There would be no dog in Brier's house tonight. No dog to greet her in the morning, to take outside and teach, to watch his learning, and revel when he understood a new command.

'It's not fair,' she said.

Josh ran his hand wearily through his thick dark hair. The grey just above his ears added to his distinction. He was a tall man, not yet over-burly. He looked down at his passenger with concern.

'It's bloody unfair.' He had worked on the dog too, teaching Brier to the best of his capacity, rejoicing in their progress.

He knew she had no idea how he felt about her. He was aware of dark eyes, amber-shot, of the sleek cap of shining blue-black hair which her son had inherited, of lines of strain that had not been there two years before.

He had heard of Tom's shooting almost as soon as it happened and had stayed with the little family that night, helping Brier's mother. Tom had been a good friend, and Josh, like his colleagues, had found it hard to control his anger.

It had been such a stupid way to die. A terrified teenager, with a gun he had no idea how to use, on a botched post office raid. Tom had interrupted it and the lad had panicked. Afterwards he had sat in his cell in tears, but that didn't bring Tom back. Nothing could.

Josh looked at the patched lights of the house that Tom had bought when his parents died and left him their money. He knew Brier needed time to rally herself before she went indoors.

'I took flowers to Tom's grave before I came in this morning.' Brier looked at the shadowed garden. 'I wasn't the only one. At least six others had laid flowers there too. Gulley said people had put flowers on the pavement where he died, outside the post office.'

Josh had not told her. He wondered if Gulley were wiser than he.

Brier needed to talk. If she had had Kim to bring home, to feed, to watch as he stretched himself on the rug, it would have been different. The dog would have helped to ease the hurt.

'Did the flowers help?' Josh's voice was soft. The darkness of the van invited confidences.

'To know he was remembered? And with affection? That they cared enough to make the effort? Yes, it did help. One bouquet was from the mother of the lad who killed him, Gulley said. She came to see me after he was sentenced . . . it was very difficult.'

'You didn't tell me. What did she want? To explain away his action?'

'No. To say she and her husband were devastated; that they could never forgive him. That he had ruined the family, affected the other children, and they couldn't understand why he had turned rotten.'

'It happens,' Josh said. 'Maybe society as such is to blame. The way we live, and the prizes only available to those who have money. Videos, cameras, cars, designer clothes . . .'

Brier was not in the mood for philosophy. Her mind returned to that afternoon.

'I thought I had a dog that would be a credit to all of us,' she said, her voice flat, damping down all emotion.

'That was quite a scene, wasn't it?' Josh had been dismayed, hating histrionics, though his calm behaviour had finally quieted the girl.

'She was acting.' Brier had disliked the woman on sight and she knew that was unreasonable, too. 'If they loved the dog so much why did they hand him over in the first place?'

She contemplated the evening ahead.

'Are you coming in? It would help me tell the children.'

'Better not. Gulley and I have a list of people to phone, in the hope they might have a dog for you. We haven't much time to find one. Though maybe we could fit you into another county's training course.'

'None locally?' Brier asked, but knew the answer.

'I'll find you one. We can try Stafford, Manchester, Essex, Yorkshire, Derbyshire. We've helped all of those out in the past. They owe us favours. If we find one Gulley can collect him.'

They both knew it was a forlorn hope at such short notice. There might be a suitable dog in one of the Rescue organisations, but they had to have a stable, sensible animal that had not been ruined by abuse or ill-treatment.

'I need a dog,' Brier said. 'It helps to have him beside me, to have a goal in life again. I don't want to leave the dog section. I've been coasting for the last two years, in a fog.'

Josh gave way to his own feelings and covered her hand with his.

'I know,' he said briefly. 'I've been there too.'

'I'm selfish.' Brier opened the door, and jumped out. 'Never thinking of anyone else.'

'Give it time,' Josh said. 'Want me to pick you up in the morning?'

'No need for you to come out of your way. I'll use my own car. No dog to mess it up.'

He watched her walk up to the front door and insert her

key. Sighing, he drove away, his thoughts already busy on the calls he would make in search of a replacement for Kim.

Ben and Dana raced out of the sitting-room where they had been watching *Star Trek*. Brier looked at them, at Ben, small and compact, with her own blue-black hair and amber-shot brown eyes; with Tom's nose and chin. Dana, a slender, dainty child, with a tumble of chestnut curls inherited from her father, stared at her now with Tom's grey eyes.

'Where's Kim? Why haven't you brought him in? Can I go and get him out of the van?' Ben had inherited his grandmother's passion for dogs. Both children spent a great deal of time at her kennels.

'I haven't got him any more. His owners wanted him back.'

There was no way of breaking the news gently.

Ben, who was ten, had already built a rapport with the dog. He looked at her with stricken eyes. Dana, only seven, began to cry. Brier felt panic build in her. She was too exhausted to deal with any more grief.

'Why did you let them have Kim back?' Ben asked.

'He was their dog. They'd bought him and paid for him and had him from a puppy and they loved him.'

Kate Bird emerged from the kitchen and gathered Dana into her arms. Dana had rejected her mother since her father died—almost, Brier, thought, as if she felt it were my fault. The child pushed her away.

Kate, who was widowed, had come as housekeeper when Brier was left alone. Her husband had been a policeman, too. The police had suggested the arrangement, trying to ensure that all that was possible could be done for the little family. Kate knew the background, the irregular hours, the problems likely to beset Brier.

The children had soon stopped calling her Mrs Bird and christened her Birdie. In no time the name was used by everyone who came to the house.

Kate sighed as she looked at Brier. She managed them all with a firm hand, and with lots of laughter, but she knew, only too well, the significance of the date, and had hoped that at least everything would go well at work. The dog was beginning to help Brier recover her lost equanimity. The situation was now worse than she had expected. Sometimes she felt she was looking after three children, not just two.

'There's a coffee for you,' she said.

The kitchen was warm. Brier picked up the mug. The hot liquid was welcome. Her head was beginning to ache. The effort of keeping her temper with the dog's owners had cost her more than she realised.

'They can't have him back. He's our dog now.' Ben's voice faltered. He felt everything passionately, but seldom revealed his feelings in words. 'They didn't love him.' His small face was set. He stared at her out of enormous dark eyes, fighting tears. 'If they had they'd never have given him to you in the first place. They couldn't have.'

She couldn't bear to talk about it. She felt near to tears herself. All that work wasted. All that time. The dog had been responding so well.

Kate looked at her, reading her mind, as she so often did. The loss of the dog was a small disaster and the children were going to be difficult this evening. Better for Brier to be out of the way. She tightened her arms around both of them. Ben and Dana were very dear to her.

'It isn't fair,' Dana wailed. 'He was a nice dog. Why can't we keep him? I want him back.'

She looked at her mother, who realised the noise was all there was. Dana was dry-eyed.

She broke free from Kate, stamped her foot and shouted at Brier.

'I hate you. You take everything away from us. You don't care. You go away every day and leave us with Birdie. You don't even want us. I want Daddy back.'

It was more than Brier could bear. She ran upstairs. Ben, saying nothing, walked out of the kitchen into the sitting-room and switched on the television set. He sat, his small face concentrated, refusing to take part in the family problems. It was his only way of coping with any situation—to pretend it was not happening and remove himself physically whenever possible.

He knew that Dana didn't understand. He sensed his mother's misery and shared it but did not know how to help her.

Kate, her mouth set, tried to comfort the child, and finally took her upstairs and bathed her and put her to bed.

'Your mother has to work,' she said, as she tucked in the covers. The room was bright with the strong colours of the vivid pictures that Tom had painted on the wall. Thomas the Tank Engine, and Bambi and Dumbo. 'If she didn't, we couldn't live in this house and would have nothing to eat.'

Dana turned her back and closed her eyes, refusing to hear.

Half an hour later, Brier came downstairs. She had changed into corduroy slacks and an Aran jersey.

'I don't think I can cope,' she said, sitting at the kitchen table. 'I can't make Dana understand.'

Kate spooned sugar into a second cup of coffee. She understood the pressures only too well. There was nothing she could say. They had both discussed Dana's problems endlessly and neither of them knew how to deal with the child.

'Birdie, that dog was keeping me together. If Josh can't find another I'll be out of the dog section again. The thought of changing to that has kept me going for these last two years.'

Kate looked at her with concern. Brier rarely used the children's nickname.

'They'll find you a dog. Things'll turn out right, in the end.' Her voice was reassuring.

'Do they? Have they for you? You know what it's like. Your husband was killed on duty, too.' That was something they never mentioned.

'Twenty years ago. I had Susan to keep me sane. She was fifteen. Not the easiest of ages, but she was supportive. It made her grow up, as she did realise I was devastated too.'

She stirred her own coffee and sat down, moving awkwardly so that Brier was aware that rheumatism was troubling her again. She had a sudden fear that Kate might soon not be able to cope. Kate, unaware of Brier's worries about her, continued to stir, as if the action would help both of them.

'The trouble with me began when she went to America and they settled down there. I was very alone. Coming to you saved my sanity. You need me. My daughter doesn't.'

Brier smiled at her and walked round the table to give her an uncharacteristic hug.

'Bless you, Birdie. Working in this madhouse helps?' Brier drank and then reached out again for the sugar bowl. 'I've a craving for something sweet. Any cakes?'

Kate walked across the room, and fetched a large tin from the cupboard beside the big Aga. She took out three rock buns and put them on a plate. She looked at the pattern and put it back in the cupboard, reaching for another. Brier knew she had used the plate with the dog's head on it, that her mother had given her for Christmas.

'I've never said.' She bit into the bun with satisfaction. 'I could never have coped without you. Do you really enjoy being here?'

'It's given me a new life. A family to care for. The grandchildren I never had, as they're thousands of miles away. Also my pension is small and household expenses very high. Don't you worry about me. Just wait for your own time to come. It will get better.'

'What can I do about Dana? If I go up to her she'll only rage and work herself into a passion.'

'She's scared you won't come home one day, like her Dad. It's taken her oddly. She's a different type from Ben. She was Tom's little treasure. I think she feels that Ben's yours, and she lost her place when her Dad died.'

'I can't convince her,' Brier said. An enormous weariness mastered her, so that even making a small decision was an effort. She was aware of silence from upstairs. She ached for her small daughter, wanting to hold her close and comfort her, but Dana stood stiffly, rejecting any advance from her mother.

The constant background of voices from the sitting-room irritated Brier: she longed to turn the set off, to go to her own room and shut the door and shut out the world. Ben was seeking his own comfort. She wanted to be free of the need to think, to cope, to work out what was best to do for herself and for the children. To be free of worrying about Ben's inability to share his feelings and Dana's too ready sharing of hers.

Birdie took the cup over to the sink and washed it under the tap.

'You go to your mother's. You haven't been near her for almost four weeks. You haven't forgotten it's her birthday?'

'All taken care of.' It was a double anniversary, which made it worse. It had been her mother's birthday the day Tom died and they had planned a party for her; just a small one, her and the children, a cake with candles, a dinner at home. A happy day.

But by six o'clock Tom was dead. He had phoned at lunchtime to say he had remembered to buy the wine. They had joked and laughed.

'See you,' Brier had said, as she rang off. She had never seen him alive again.

She felt the familiar rage flood over her as she thought of the lad who had shot him down so callously. He was alive, and prison was a small penance for what he had done. He would come out and resume life again. Tom was gone for ever.

It was a feeling she had to control, or she would lose her job. The useless rage returned whenever there was a killing of any kind. Policemen and women weren't allowed to have passions.

Kate interrupted her thoughts.

'Stay with Helena for supper. I can cope here. Girl, stop standing there like a pot cat and get on with you. No use brooding.'

Brier grinned in spite of her misery. Kate's forthright manner amused her. 'I sometimes wonder if I say thoughts out loud when you're around.' She slung her bag over her shoulder. 'I'll be off.'

Kate handed her a gaily wrapped package. A small woman, she bustled everywhere, her greying hair often in an untidy bush, but her brown eyes were always ready to light up when the children made her laugh. She was easy to live with and rarely took offence.

'Can I have a special supper?' Ben asked, coming out of the sitting-room. Behind him guns chattered and men shouted. Brier went in and switched the set off.

'You've had your tea.' Kate was rinsing out the two mugs.

'I'm hungry again.'

'Hollow legs,' Kate said, and Brier grinned at him.

'Was tea so long ago?' she asked.

'We gave Grandee our presents and had a special tea. Sausages and beans and birthday cake and dog biscuits.'

Brier laughed.

Her mother had bought a cutter for biscuits in the shape of a dog, and there was always a store ready for the children.

'It sounds like a feast for little pigs,' she said.

'Pigs don't eat dog biscuits.' Ben was doing his best to lighten the atmosphere.

'Good boys can have tea and supper,' Kate said. 'Scones and jam and maybe a slice of my very special cake.'

'You'll make him fat,' Brier said.

'With all that energy? He's hardly ever still.'

Ben was looking thoughtfully at the cake tin. Brier knew that she could safely leave him with Kate. Dana would sleep now, and maybe feel happier in the morning.

The empty dog's bed in the corner was a poignant reminder. His bowl of water was still on the floor. She went out into the freezing dark.

Two

Although they were separated by only four fields, it was over two miles by road to her mother's home. The housing estate had grown round the farmland, isolating Helena Grant's house and a few of the meadows.

Brier drove slowly, aware of icy patches. The lanes were deserted. She drove savouring peace and silence and the lack of a need to make any kind of response to anyone. A cassette played music from *Swan Lake*, a dreamy sound that soothed her.

Her childhood home welcomed her, so that she felt like a schoolgirl, returning to sanctuary. Even here, at Willowbank Farm, there had been change and her father was no longer there. His memory was still strong and she almost expected to see him come out of the kennels and greet her, just as she so often turned when a door opened at home, as if Tom would come through it and envelop her in his bear hug.

She uncoiled long legs. She removed the keys and slammed the door. She stared at the car, Tom's last purchase before he died. She frowned, and then remembered. She unlocked the door again and took the brightly ribboned parcels from the passenger seat.

Light spilled from uncurtained windows into the yard. She stood for a moment, her cap of dark hair brushed by a faint wind. Icy fingers reached from the north, and she shivered. Her mother glanced through the window, waved and turned away.

Brier always needed time to unwind after a day's work. She looked at the farmhouse with appreciation. Not many people could return to the place where they were born and find it almost unchanged.

It was a warm, friendly building, the red brick softened with age. The house had grown over three centuries. The old dairy had become the kitchen, the barn had been converted into a wing that housed an extra bedroom, a bathroom and her father's den.

The Virginia creeper was almost dead now, but a few scarlet leaves clung round the window, glowing in the spilled light. Cobbles had been replaced with paving, and Brier was not sure that that was an improvement. She was always afraid her mother would slip and fall on winter ice.

Was it a false memory? Had the cobbles been as lethal?

The bare trees shimmered with a coating of frost. It was bitterly cold.

The dogs were restless tonight. The new block was a big improvement: there was far more room, and it was possible to stand erect in each compartment. Much easier to clean.

She did not want to see the boarders, only her mother's dogs, her own friends. Her visits were too rare. She missed the busy life of the kennels and whenever she could still came back to help, bringing her children with her. Ben was good with animals. Dana . . . she sighed. Dana was, at present, very difficult to live with.

She had never been an easy child. An impatient toddler, wanting to do everything her brother did, she had screamed with fury and then held her breath when thwarted. Terrible at two, she had been tiresome at four. By the time she was five years old even Tom, who could handle her better than anyone else, had found her unpredictable. Her sudden flaring rages left everyone exhausted.

Brier opened the door and went in, switching on the light. This block housed ten kennels, not all of them occupied. She was greeted by a vociferous chorus. Nothing much had changed. This eager greeting had been part of her life from the time she could toddle on her own across the yard and talk to the dogs through the wire mesh. She might have been coming home from school instead of calling in briefly before she resumed her adult roles. Except that the dogs were all different.

Tara was nursing her pups who must be almost six weeks old and due to go in a week or so. Brier went into the kennel and knelt down, accepting the thoughtful lick as the bitch nosed a puppy towards her. Brier lifted the small body, admiring bone and substance. Her mother always bred wonderful stock.

The tiny animal snuggled against her and a trusting tongue licked her hand. The pup smelled delicious, a warm and familiar scent that was part of her past. The white rug on which Tara lay was immaculate. She was sprawled to let the puppies climb over her. One was still sucking, though they must by now be almost weaned.

Brier sighed, painfully aware that tonight she would not fall asleep feeling lucky because she had the pick of the year's intake. Kim was so clever. She knew his real owners would never appreciate his intelligence or realise what an asset they had.

She buried her head in the soft, warm fur and the puppy licked her face and then cuddled confidingly against her. She needed her mother's brisk consolation before she went back to face the family.

Her father had died the year before Tom. A major stroke took him away from them, very suddenly, one autumn weekend. She still missed his sound guidance. He had been told to rest, to take life easy, but he never took advice. She couldn't imagine him creeping around, careful of every movement. He had run instead of walked, and enjoyed every rumbustious moment.

He was a big man, full of ready laughter, loving his family and his animals, always there to listen and console. He was a miracle with dogs, who all trusted him, and obeyed him without question. If only she had inherited half his skill.

If only he were there now. If only Tom were there now. If only she had her dog. If only . . .

Her mother had kept the farmhouse and sold the land, reserving forty acres for her own use. The money had rebuilt the kennels.

The four fields that separated Brier's home from her mother's had not yet been developed. They were still grass fields, now neglected and overgrown. The first buyer had gone bankrupt and sold to the council. They had sold on, and there were rumours of a hypermarket, but so far no one had made any move to build. It might have been better to keep them and rent them for grazing, Brier often thought, but it was easy to be wise afterwards.

Also, they had brought in much-needed money, as farming no longer ensured prosperity and her father's last few years had been very difficult indeed. He farmed the land and her mother bred the dogs, but they were also his passion.

She had a sudden vivid memory of him walking the fields, his latest German Shepherd pacing quietly by his side, never dreaming of running off and exploring on his own unless given permission. His last dog, old Dante, who had been Best of Breed at a number of Championship shows in his heyday, had died four months after his master.

The footpath and the stiles were well used by day. Never by night. It was a lonely place, isolated within the boundaries of the small town that had grown from the old village.

Beyond the last field was her own house, part of a busy street. She could see the glittering lamps strung along the pavements. Light glowed, colouring the sky. The motorway, at the far edge of the third field, was bright with swooping headlights that flared upwards and vanished over the brow of the little hill.

Beyond that were the foothills that led into Wales, giving

an ever-changing view as sunlight and shadow dappled their flanks and gilded the trees that clothed them.

'. . . green days in forests and blue days at sea.'

Tom had loved poetry. She closed her eyes, and held the puppy so close that he squeaked and Tara looked at her reproachfully. She set him down, watching him snuggle in among his litter-mates, listening to the soft, contented puppy murmurs. If only life were so simple.

Brier closed the door gently behind her. She walked along the line, greeting well-known heads.

Hero and Marlo; Dane and Gretal; Kari and Sancho—all growing up to be brood bitches or stud dogs, with high hopes for a prizewinning future. They greeted her with rumbustious pleasure, whining and whirling, delighted to be noticed. There, among the dogs, she felt the day's pressures begin to ease. They were such happy animals. People who didn't own dogs would never understand, she thought, glorying as she looked at the mobile ears and bright eyes, alight with life.

'Oh, Kim, Kim,' she thought. 'What am I going to do without you.'

Last she came to Roi. The king of the kennels. Now what was he doing out here, instead of in the house with the two pet bitches, now retired from breeding? Why had her mother banished her darling? He was restless, pacing, his eyes worried.

He put his paws against Brier's shoulders as she opened the kennel door, and stared at her as if trying to tell her urgent news. He whined and pawed at her. He thrust his head into the hollow under her chin, whimpering forlornly.

'I wish I could understand you,' she told him. 'Is there a bitch here for you? Is that what's wrong?'

She looked at the wise head, the prick ears, the thoughtful brown eyes. He was magnificent and she broke the seventh commandment every time she looked at him, coveting him more and more. If only he could have been hers. Well, I didn't have eight thousand pounds to spend, she told herself, and laughed ruefully. That was another bonus from the lost land.

There was no way her mother could ever afford to give the dog away. Not this one. He was a brilliant animal, far more intelligent even than Kim, who had been the best of a bunch of six. This dog was one in a million.

Roi licked her face and his splendid tail waved thoughtfully.

He was one of the best dogs to come out of Germany in the last few years and his pups would make history. He was sensible and kind, yet could guard if need be. He was an ambassador for all German Shepherds, everything the breed should be and so often was not, because of cowboy breeders and eager buyers who never asked the right questions.

Most didn't even know there were questions to be asked. They fell for a tiny pup and lived to regret it a year later. The Breed rescue kennels had never been so busy.

'Roi, I don't know what's wrong, son, and I can't do much about it,' she told him, and shut the door and watched his head droop with misery. He lay with his nose on his paws, staring at her, as if reproaching her for her perfidy. She too had left him on his own instead of taking him into the warm kitchen, with company and laughter.

She closed the door and looked in the isolation block where, sure enough, a young bitch lay, nose to tail, forlorn and lonely. So that was what was wrong with Roi. His restlessness would infect the others.

She walked in through the kitchen door and the heat hit her after the frosty cold outside. The kitchen was the heart of her mother's house, a big room where almost every activity took place. These two bitches greeting her fervently might have been the dogs from her childhood.

Each had had three litters and earned her place in the home. Helena never put down or sold her retired stock, and never overworked them. Tansy, the Burmese cat, was in the corner, in her box, almost invisible. Bright eyes surveyed Brier across the room, decided she was familiar and no threat, and closed again.

Brier stroked the two eager bodies, wishing again that Kim were still hers. They settled on the rug after a few moments, trained to be sensible and not to overwhelm callers with their attentions.

Helena Grant pushed aside the pedigree form she was filling in in italic script.

'I hope your buyers realise your forms are heirlooms,' Brier said. 'You should see the scrawls most people produce.'

'Maybe they aren't as proud of their pups as I am of mine.'

There was a sudden outcry from the yard.

'What *is* the matter with those dogs tonight?'

'Roi, I should think, with a bitch waiting for him.'

'Bitch? I wish there were.'

'There's a young bitch in the isolation block.'

'She's my new acquisition. She isn't in season. Just come out of quarantine, but I didn't want her with the other dogs till she was settled in and got to know me.'

Brier suddenly remembered the point of her visit and reached into her pocket and took out the two parcels.

'Happy birthday. What did the children give you? Kate helped them choose and both told me I wasn't to know because I can't keep secrets.'

Helena Grant smiled and looked thoughtfully at the beribboned packet. She began to untie the bow.

'Ben gave me one of those quick-release gundog leads, which will be immensely useful. Gulley got it for him. Dana painted me a card with a horse on it.'

Brier looked at the mantelshelf, where her daughter's somewhat garish animal stared out at her from scarlet cardboard.

'Not bad for a seven-year-old,' her grandmother said.

She opened the little box, and took out its contents.

'A paperweight. It's Roi! Where did you get that photograph?'

'Ben stole it one afternoon when he came to tea. Marvellous way for a policewoman to bring up her son, isn't it? Mother, if I didn't know you better I'd say you were crying. It's not such a wonderful present.'

'It is. It's just that all my hopes are being dashed.'

'Aren't you getting any bitches for Roi? What's gone wrong? He looks wonderful.'

'That makes it worse.' Helena stood up and went to the window. The dogs had quieted, but Roi occasionally released a mournful wail. 'I suppose there isn't anyone around?'

'I'll look, if you like.'

Brier took a torch and went to the wicket gate. It had turned very cold in the last hour. The fields lay still and silent under a ghostly moon that was wrapped in a veil of soft cloud. Mist shimmered above the grass, which was silvery and crisp and crackled under her feet.

She shivered, and went indoors to warm her hands at the fire.

'Not a soul about. What's up?'

'You remember Roi was ill some months ago? He had a bitch brought to him, and then he had an infection Paul couldn't identify?' Paul Matthews was also the police vet. Brier knew him well.

She helped herself to a slice of chocolate cake. This was going to take longer than she had expected and lunch was a very long time ago.

'I need carbohydrate to make me able to face the family,' she explained to her mother's raised eyebrows. 'I thought you insisted all bitches were swabbed before they came to your stud dogs.'

'I do. This bitch belongs to someone I know. A rival.' Helena walked over to the freezer and opened the door.

'Do you mind a frozen meal? I've been up to my eyes all day.'

She unwrapped two packets of ready-made chicken dinners on a plate and put them into the oven.

'She showed me the vet's letter which said the bitch was clear. I don't think it applied to the bitch who came. I think she was a sister. I also think she was known to be infected. It was done either out of sheer wantonness or with the desire to sterilise Roi.'

Brier listened, still capable of being surprised at human wickedness despite all she saw in her own work. The pups would be worth £500 each if Roi was their father, and although the bitch was a carrier, the pups would survive. Roi would no longer be a threat, taking away business from other stud dog owners.

'So?' she said, as her mother sat staring forlornly at nothing, apparently forgetting she was not alone.

Helena picked up the Burmese kitten that was patting gently at her leg.

'He's had three bitches since then. Not a puppy in sight. I've had to return all the stud fees and now of course everyone's talking. You know the dog world as well as I do. Paul thinks he was sterilised by the bug. He's due to ring tonight and tell me the result of the tests.'

'Mother! You'll lose all your investment.'

'Not quite all. He's well insured and I get half his value back if he is sterile now. But what do I do with him if he is? My lovely lad. Who would want him? I doubt if I can keep him; he's only three years old and would be a passenger for the next twelve years. I haven't time to train him for competition.'

She looked at her daughter, her expression rueful.

'I pinned so many hopes on that dog. I hoped he'd be Best of Breed next year at Cruft's. There'd be no problem in qualifying him. He's already had one BOB at a Championship show, and has one certificate.'

'You could go on showing him. He has progeny.'

'Flaunt his inability to sire puppies? What do I say when people ask for him at stud? I couldn't do it.'

Outside in the chilly night an owl hooted, long and low. Roi added his mournful howl.

There was a glimmer of an idea in Brier's mind, but now was not the time to broach it.

'When's the vet ringing? Did he say a time?'

Helena glanced at the clock. Firelight flickered on the painted flowers around the dial.

'He said he'd ring about eight.'

'Can I bring Roi in? It seems a shame to ban him from the house. Can't you bear to look at him?'

'The sight of him makes me cry. I was upsetting the dog more by having him here than keeping him outside. He couldn't understand my feelings. How could he? So silly to feel it so much. I shouldn't have had such high hopes.'

She was suddenly silent, the only sound in the room the throbbing purr of the kitten now cuddled in her lap. Both women were thinking of all that had happened to change their lives over the past three years. Neither could put her thoughts into words, but both knew, without saying, what lay between them. Helena felt they needed to talk. Talk about anything.

'It's not the money. Roi's temperament's super, and now he can't pass it on. He's only sired three litters.'

'Keep one of his sons. One of Tara's pups.'

'They aren't Roi's pups. She was his first failure, but I refused to accept the evidence. By the time her next season came round I knew something had to be wrong, as there had been other bitches who missed.' She stared into the fire, as if there were answers there to her problems. 'So I used another dog. The timing was wrong. I couldn't afford the gap. I don't usually breed winter puppies. I had expected her to whelp early last June. But nothing happened.'

Brier could think of nothing to say. It was a major disaster, and there was no way of easing her mother's unhappiness.

Helena began to open Kate's gift and they both looked at it. A little bronze German Shepherd to add to her other models. A note on the card said, 'It was so like Roi that I felt it had to be for you.'

'I don't think I can bear it,' Helena said. 'I know what Paul's going to say. It's no use kidding myself.'

Brier stood up, and her glance fell on a tissue-wrapped object on the table, the gold glinting through the paper.

'That looks like a nice birthday present. Or have you taken to buying jewellery?'

'That is one of the biggest insults I've ever had in my life.' Two bright spots of red burned angrily on Helena's cheeks. 'It makes my blood boil . . . Brier, it's not funny.'

'It's so long since I heard you say that,' her daughter said, as she undid the tissue to reveal a gold bracelet made up of tiny links of flower-etched panels. 'Your blood was always either boiling or your marrow freezing. I used to ask Dad which when I came home from school.'

She laughed, remembering.

'Thumbs up meant boiling blood and thumbs down meant freezing marrow.'

'You were a pair. It was so long ago,' Helena said. 'I was thinking the other day about that time we all went boating on Windermere. Your father warned you I don't know how many times to be careful, and he was the one that fell in!'

Brier laughed.

'Do you remember that awful holiday cottage in Devon when I was about eight? It was jerry-built and everything fell off or fell down. There was some problem with the hot water tank and Dad went up into the roof, put his foot between two rafters and came through the ceiling. He fell onto the bed, which was very lucky or he'd have hurt himself badly. It did look funny to me. People didn't usually come into rooms that way and I suppose it tickled a small girl's fancy. I laughed and he was angry.'

She could see him now, sitting up indignantly on the bed, the gaping hole above him, saying, 'It's not funny, Brier.'

'It was very difficult explaining and getting it repaired,' her mother said.

Brier picked up the bracelet and examined it.

'It must be worth a mint. Where did you get it?'

'Read that.'

Helena handed her an embossed sheet of heavy notepaper, bearing the name of a distant breeding kennels.

Brier began to read.

Dear Mrs Grant,

I have admired you for so long and do so respect your totally honest judging. I have never been lucky enough to be able to show under you, but in three weeks' time my little bitch will be entered. I know you will love her. I enclose a token of my esteem which I hope you will accept as I know you have a birthday soon.

The signature was unfamiliar—a newcomer since Brier had left home. Once she had known the name of every well-known German Shepherd breeder.

'Who is she?'

'Someone I don't want to know. Have you ever seen anything more blatant?'

'Not really. What are you going to do?'

'You're returning it by registered post. As a witness to the fact that it wasn't kept. It's not the bribe that got me, but the thought that anyone could believe I'm bribable.'

'Maybe she's just an innocent? After all it is your seventieth birthday.'

'I very much hope she doesn't know that! I keep my age a strict secret and I hope you do too. It's useful having had you late in life, as I can shed ten years and still be believed. I couldn't if you'd been born when I was twenty.'

'I'd be nearly fifty then.' Brier looked at the thought and didn't like it at all. 'There go the dogs again. Something must be up.'

'One thing,' Helena said, and grinned at her daughter, her expression mischievous. 'She's made a mistake and it's wasted effort. She's showing a bitch and she hasn't read the schedule properly. I don't have a problem as I'm judging dogs. There's a man judging bitches. Perhaps I ought to send the bracelet to him with her letter.'

'Mother, you're impossible.' Brier laughed, unable to help herself. 'I'll give Roi a run. It might cure his restlessness. Maybe he just doesn't like being banished from the house.'

'Leave it for a minute. He's punishing me for making him stay outside. I've talked about me and you look as if you've just gone three rounds with a heavyweight champion and lost. What's up? It's nearly a month since I've seen you and your phone calls are hardly informative. "How are you, Mother? Good. We're OK. Byee."' Her voice mocked her daughter's softer intonation. 'No one would think you only lived a couple of miles away. Ten minutes across the fields. I do see Birdie and the children, but they aren't very informative either. Dana's paddies often occupy the time.'

'She's like Tom. Moody. I understand Ben.'

'Ben's like us. Can't expect every child to be the same. Come on. Tell mother. What's wrong that's more wrong than usual?'

Brier grinned. Her mother had an odd way of putting things. Age had softened some of her feelings, but she could still produce a tumultuous rage when life hit her hard.

'Everything. I'd have come before but it's a tough course, and there's so little spare time. Ben's had a fluey cold and Dana is being her usual impossible self.'

Helena waited, knowing that there was more to come.

'I've lost Kim. His owners wanted him back. Josh reckons we were conned. They now have a dog that's been trained for three weeks for free. I'm the sucker. Ben's distraught and won't show it and Dana threw a tantrum.'

Quite suddenly her misery overcame her. Helena, listening, knew whose genes were really responsible for Dana's temperament. It had been a long time since Brier lost control. She said nothing. There was nothing she could say.

'It would have to happen today of all days. If I don't get another dog I won't carry on. I'm sick of the job. Crooks come creeping out of every hole and cranny, and all the magistrates and judges do is feel sorry for them. Never for their victims.'

Helena picked up two mugs and took them to the sink to wash them. She clattered them against the tap.

'It's not as bad as you think. There are still good people. Like Alice Gulley. She was at the last show I went to and had just won a first with her latest bitch puppy. It's a lovely little thing. Alice and I had lunch together. She always cheers me up.'

'Alice is a tonic for all of us,' Brier said. 'She can turn any occasion into a party and makes us all laugh.'

The little grandmother clock sang its busy racing tick. The black cat in the corner lifted her head from her kittens, and Brier, intrigued, went over to look.

She was startled to see, instead of pedigree Burmese, five little ginger and black mottled babies.

'Mother! What on earth happened here?'

'Somebody's clever ginger tom got his oar in before I took her to the Burmese stud cat. Pretty, aren't they, and a total loss. I can't ask more than a fiver for each and those kits would have been worth £200, but for his nibs. That's why I bought this one. But these little mongrels are very sweet. I've a queue of people waiting for them.'

She had picked up the little Burmese kitten from the

floor. He was a newcomer to Brier, who hadn't seen him before.

'He looks good.'

Helena stroked the small head.

'He'll be grown soon and sire the next lot of kittens. I won't let my lady out.'

'Did you let her out?'

'Actually, no. I left the window ajar and clever clogs managed to wriggle through, lifting it enough to make a gap. I found him in the pantry and didn't realise till the kits were born that he'd made a call to Tansy on his way there. I'd cooked fish in aspic and left it to cool. I didn't have that, either.'

Brier laughed ruefully.

'The Villain in the Pantry. He had his way with the innocent maiden.'

'Some innocent,' Helena said. 'She's more like a nymphomaniac teenager. She has a call like a banshee. It goes right through you. Any cat with half an ounce of go in him could hear it miles away. There were about ten queuing outside, but he was the only one that actually did make it. The window was locked after that.' She yawned. 'You'd think I'd know by now.'

Brier sank into the old armchair that had been her father's. She heard him laughing, saying, 'Never bet on certainties. There are no certainties.'

'We need Dad to keep us both on the ground,' she said.

Helena looked at her daughter, noting the signs of stress, the dark shadows under tired eyes, the weariness in every movement.

'How are the men taking a woman on the team?'

'You're as bad as Kate. Knowing things without being told. Are you both taking up witchcraft?'

'No. Just long experience of people. Having trouble with the men? There's never been a woman dog handler here before. Also you know more than they do, having been born in a kennel . . . well, almost. And you very nearly got to Cruft's when you were twenty. I bet none of them have trained a dog before.'

'They don't know that . . . I never told them.'

'It's surprising what people do know. But you surely expected problems there?'

'It's not that. I guess I just miss having another woman to gossip with. They all treated me as if I were made of eggs today. A woman would have jollied me along and talked nonsense. They were being kind, and that was worse than if they'd been insensitive. They all knew Tom.'

She stared into the flames that Helena had just poked to life.

'I'm a selfish bitch, aren't I?'

Her mother walked over to her and hugged her briefly.

'No one can ever help,' she said. 'We have to go through it and come out on the other side. It does get easier, I promise.'

The kitten, having wearied himself by a private game with a rolled-up paper ball, jumped onto Brier's lap and settled himself sleepily.

Helena poured hot water into instant coffee. The brown mugs were decorated with German Shepherd heads. She cut an enormous slice of chocolate cake.

'Sin with me. I need to lose at least a stone and I get sick of trying.'

'I'll lose weight with sheer frustration,' Brier said. 'And I don't mean what other people mean by that, either. They keep on about my name. I know it's only teasing, and well meant, but they overdo it. Derek calls me Rosie. Pete says I'm thorny and prickly. If I lose my temper they call me Wild Rose. I wish Grandfather Brier had been called something different. You wouldn't have named me Wellington, would you, if that had been his surname?'

Helena took a large bite of chocolate cake, and waited before answering. Then she grinned.

'A girl called Wellie? I doubt it. I'd have thought you'd be used to it by now. Thirty-five years is a long time to have a name. I drew the line at Arthurina. He did so want a boy to carry on the family name.'

'Poor Grandfather. He was impossible, wasn't he? I never dared to disobey him. But why Brier Ruth? They see Brier R and call me Briar Rose and if there's one thing that gets my goat . . .'

'Don't let it. Ruth was his mother's name. I thought I told you. I had to make it up to him for producing a mere girl.' She sighed. 'You were lucky. You didn't grow up with him. I did. He needed sons and never had them and had little time for women. His generation never did. I think I'd still be terrified of him if he were alive today. He was very strict and had no sense of humour at all. Her own sense of humour was all that kept your grandmother going, I suspect. You can always change your name by deed poll to Amaryllis or Davida, or Athene.'

'OK, mother. I get it. Other people have daft names too. No, it's not the men, and I'm not being fair to them. They aren't so bad, really. I'm upset tonight because of losing two dogs in four weeks, and unless they find me another, I'm out, after just getting in.'

'To lose one may be regarded as a misfortune; to lose both . . .'

'I don't think I'm in the mood for quotations.'

'I'm sorry,' Helena said, 'but from what Ben told me Sabre wasn't a particularly nice dog.'

'Sabre? He wasn't and I wasn't too upset when they found his hips were bad. There was no way he could work. Gulley took him and is training him to make him more biddable and has found him a good pet home. He'll be all right.'

She lifted the kitten and stroked his nose. He put out a small paw and patted her cheek thoughtfully, and then wriggled free and jumped to the floor, to inspect the black queen and her kittens. Tansy floored him with a firm paw and washed his protesting face.

'That'll teach you,' Helena said, laughing at the kitten's struggles.

Roi was howling, a long, mournful sound that was sheer misery.

'I can't stand that any longer. I'm going to let him out.' Brier jumped up, suddenly impatient.

The icy wind slammed against her as soon as she stepped outside. As she opened the kennel door, Roi flew past her without any greeting, and stood at the wicket gate, barking. He pawed at it, frantic.

'There *is* something wrong.'

Brier opened the gate and the dog raced out, along the stacked line of drainpipes to the far end, against the corner of the yard fencing. That corner was close to the dog's kennel.

She listened in astonishment as his usual deep bay gave way to a very odd puppy yapping, the most extraordinary sound that she had ever heard from a dog in her life.

She raced towards him.

What on earth had he found?

Three

Roi knew the scent on the wind. Simon was there, Simon who played with him, who visited him, who understood him. There was a rapport between the dog and the child that no adult would ever recognise.

The dog couldn't reach him. The boy was trapped somewhere, and though Roi could scent him, he could not get near.

Simon longed for the dog for his own. His loneliness was assuaged by the warm tongue, and the hard body that let him cuddle and hug, and lie with his head against Roi's shoulder, feeling ease creep into him and tension relax. The dog was his chief pleasure, and his visits to him were memorable to both of them. Roi sensed the adoration and responded to it.

Simon Dennis was in the same class as Ben Morrey and he had been as excited as her own children when he discovered Brier was to be a police dog handler. He visited Ben as often as he could, and Birdie invited him to tea. He also visited the kennels whenever he was able, sometimes with Ben and Dana and sometimes on his own.

'He never seems to want to go to his own home,' Birdie commented to Helena one afternoon when she came to collect the children after a visit. That worried Helena, too, but the child never talked about his own affairs and changed the subject if she made tentative enquiries.

He was a small mystery, drifting in and out of the place, never taking his welcome for granted, always asking if he might come, with that desperate expression on his face, as if afraid the request might be refused.

Helena enjoyed his company and laughed gently to herself at his childish conversation. She could trust him to do exactly as he was told, and never to let out any dog unless she said he might.

He was, she had to confess, but only to herself, more reliable than her own grandchildren where the dogs were concerned. He was a solemn child, worried about doing wrong, and always seemed over-anxious. He checked and double-checked every request she made.

She had found that irritating at first, but then realised he had some deep inner need to be absolutely sure before he did anything she asked, lest he make a mistake.

Roi knew the child better than he knew Dana and Ben, and was frantic, dancing on the hard ground, racing to Brier and back again to the stacked pipes, his whole body compelled by the need to attract her attention. Simon was near. Simon needed to be found, to be helped. For some reason Simon was not moving, was making no attempt to come towards the dog, and Roi could not understand it.

Urgency possessed him, his senses telling him hard facts that people could never comprehend.

He had been trying desperately all evening to get the stupid humans to realise that there was something very wrong, but nobody had understood. Now, at last, they were taking notice of him and he was determined that, this time, he would not be ignored.

There was an alien scent in the air, Simon's own scent but added to it the smell of fear, which Roi had never met before. It alerted every instinct in his body. He wanted to find Simon and soothe away the feelings that dominated the child. He could hear soft, forlorn, almost inaudible sobs, and the pain was echoed in his own mind, driving him to impatient frenzy.

Brier, triggered by the dog's anxiety, ran after him and then slowed. A slip on the icy ground, a broken leg, would not help anyone now. What had Roi found? An abandoned puppy or kitten? A dead body? Please God, no.

The moon was teasing the clouds again, lighting the ground, making it easier for her to walk. Moles had patterned the field with their hillocks, which threatened her at almost every step. The grey expanse of winter grass glittered under the night sky and she shivered, worrying lest tragedy waited for her.

Her personal radio was in the kitchen. Why hadn't she picked it up?

Roi's yapping was insistent but muted, an astonishing deviation from the deep bay that warned intruders when he was guarding the kennels, a duty he took upon himself as his own. The younger dogs rarely joined in. Nobody challenged him, he was the King of the pack. Oddly, he in his turn submitted to the cats.

The torch's round glow danced over the ground. The dog, turning his head to make sure that Brier was following, caught the glare in his eyes and shifted out of reach of the light. The beam hit dark caves that revealed the entrances to the drainpipes that lay waiting for workmen to lay them. They were stacked in such a way that they formed a maze, and Brier had difficulty as she shone her torch into each opening, clambering over them, feeling the bitterly cold surface stinging her hands.

Roi was in front of one of them, his yapping muted now to a whimper, as if he were saying, 'Here, here, here. Hurry, hurry, hurry.' Brier shifted the pipe that lay at right-angles to it and almost blocked it. It was unwieldy and she was slow. The dog pulled at her arm, as if trying to make her move faster, trying to drag her with him towards his goal.

Getting fanciful, Brier scolded herself.

She shone the torch into the pipe, holding Roi, lest he terrify whatever was inside. The boy drew himself back in terror, scrambling frantically away from the entrance. He covered his face with his hands, as if that would hide him from view. Brier felt a sick fear. In that brief instant she recognised him. What on earth was he doing out here?

'Roi, hush. Sit. It's Simon. Simon, love, come out. It's all right; it's Roi and Ben's mum.'

The dog knew it was Simon. He obeyed her, aware that now humans could take over. He had done his duty. He sat, his head alert, his ears pricked, listening, moving gently backwards and forwards, puzzled by the strange sounds that the child was making.

'Simon!' He hadn't moved. Her voice was soft, coaxing, as she stifled anxiety. Was the boy hurt? 'It's me, Ben's mum. Come out, love. You'll freeze to death. Do come out.'

She was babbling at him, desperate to quell the panic she had seen in his eyes.

'Has he gone?'

Has who gone? What on earth had inspired such terror?

'There's no one here but us.' She must persuade him to move. He seemed paralysed. 'Come on out and I'll take you to Ben's gran and get you warm. Quickly, there's a good lad. I'm cold and you must be frozen.'

He crawled towards her and was suddenly clinging to her, holding on with a ferocity that hurt, sobbing in great gasps that were quickly out of control. Roi leaped at him, his tail waving wildly. The child was ice-cold, his hands blue, his face pinched. Roi, disturbed by the crying, licked at face and hands.

Brier whipped off her jersey and covered him. Half-carrying him, half-dragging him, she hurried towards the open gate. Roi, by her side, close to them, was determined to guard them from any kind of danger. Once he growled deep in his throat and pelted over the field towards the stile, as if he had scented someone there. Brier called him and he left the track and returned as she went through the gate.

Danger! Every instinct was alert. She listened for following feet, listened for breathing near to her, but there was nothing. Roi, once inside the yard, was intent on gaining the warmth of the house. He was not going back in his kennel.

What had led the child to seek shelter in such a place, and why had he come out at all on so bitter a night without a coat?

Helena, standing at the open kitchen door, took one look and raced inside, poking the fire to a blaze, flying upstairs for a duvet, drawing the child away from Brier's arms and into the big armchair. She wrapped the cover round him and held his hands, chafing them, murmuring to him as she would to a distressed puppy.

Brier eased herself into the chair and held the boy against her, feeling the small body throb with racking sobs. Simon clung to her as if he would never let go. Usually he was aloof, disliking contact, a small, unresponsive child who spoke to her politely. Not even Helena had been able to break through that reserve. Only Roi's presence made him relax.

'He said he'd find me, wherever I was.' The words were barely distinguishable.

'Who, love?'

She needed back-up if some man was involved, but for the moment the child must have peace to warm himself, and to still the appalling hysterical sobbing. How long had he been there? Was there danger of hypothermia? Ought she to ring for an ambulance? Ought she to ring a doctor? Almost anything just now was likely to add to his trauma.

'A warm bath,' Helena said. 'That's the treatment for exposure, isn't it?'

'You are pretty dirty, love.' It was an understatement. He was the opposite of her own son. This child was blond with a pixy face and eyes that often showed his unhappiness. She wanted, when she met him, to get close to him and chase the misery away, but he resisted every attempt. She wondered if he talked to Ben, but suspected he confided in no one.

She looked at him and smoothed the lank hair, longing to wash it clean. She wondered how to tackle him. He was a small, compact child, thin, tense, and as uneasy as a startled cat, every muscle primed as if ready to run if need be. He always looked as if he needed a wash. The fair, badly-cut mane of hair was greasy. Eyes the colour of a cloud-shaded sea stared at her, red-rimmed. Dirty streaks ran down his face where he had rubbed it.

Brier sighed. She was desperate to find out what had happened to terrify him so badly, but she knew she could not rush him. He would talk when he was ready.

Slowly the sobs subsided.

Roi, anxious and concerned, had followed them in. He glanced at Helena as if expecting to be told to return to his kennel, but she had eyes only for Simon. The dog thrust his nose under the child's armpit and stood there, as if sure his mere presence would bring comfort. The small hands reached out and buried themselves in the thick fur. The dog had a denser coat than most of his breed, though it was by no means long.

Helena began to talk. Words helped, even when they meant little. A gentle human voice always reassured her grandchildren and it reassured the dogs. It must surely comfort this child. She spoke to Ben and Dana as she spoke to her animals: softly, confidently, firmly. She had only just realised that, to her, child and dog had the same reactions to life. Simon was a terrified pup and it was up to her to allay that terror.

She shifted her papers off the table and walked over to the stove.

'I've marrowbone broth. Always make it for the dogs. It ought to make a good basis for a cup soup. There's some packets of it in the cupboard.' Helena ran her hands through her thick hair and looked at her daughter, frowning. 'OK to warm him that way?'

'What time did you leave home, Simon?' At least then she would know how long he had been out in the cold.

'Half-past six.' His voice was barely audible. The shivering had stopped and a little colour was returning to his face. The dark eyes were shadowed. His hands were still icy and he clung to Brier as if she and she alone could hold off his fears.

It was now just after half-past seven. He had been out in the freezing cold for an hour which must have seemed like eternity. Lucky she had decided to let Roi out. Quite suddenly both she and Helena realised what the dog had done.

'Roi was telling us,' Helena said. 'Why on earth were we so dumb?'

Because we can't talk dog language and don't learn it well enough, Brier thought. No use saying so. Her mother knew as well as she that they often let their animals down through lack of understanding.

'Bath.' Warm water would help to bring back his circulation. Brier lifted him out of the chair, and he took her hand, holding on tightly.

'Can Roi come too?' The dog seemed to give him a feeling of security. Something this mite lacked, Brier thought, as they walked upstairs, the German Shepherd following, obedient to her flicked finger.

Simon clung to her as if he would never let go. Brier thought of the mother who had died, died at her own hand, unable to fight the rival who had taken possession of her husband. She had known Jenny Dennis slightly. They met on parents' evenings at school. A quiet, shy woman, with little appreciation of her own worth, and a constant need to apologise even when she was innocent of blame. A victim, not a survivor.

The second marriage had been indecently soon.

Kate knew all the gossip. Brier only half-listened but this came back to her as she walked upstairs, still wondering what she ought to do. She needed to know much more before alerting officialdom. Once started, it went on remorselessly, and changed many lives.

'Feeling better?' she asked, anxious to dispel the expression in the child's eyes. His teeth were chattering.

'Come on, let's get you in that bath and Grandee will find you something to wear.' She forgot she was not speaking to her own child. She laughed, trying to lighten the atmosphere. 'It'll swamp you, as she's a large lady, but at least it will be warm.' Swamping was maybe an unfortunate word in the present context, Brier thought, momentarily aware of her own stultifying weariness. Somehow she must dredge up enough energy to continue.

The room had not altered since she was a small girl. She could still remember having to be lifted and dumped into the big iron bath. Her father slid her down the slope into the water with a great splash, flooding the floor with water, so that Helena came upstairs, grumbling, laughingly, at the mess they made. Over thirty years ago and the memory had been lost till now. Seal time, he had called it. Her mother intended to modernise it soon.

As she intended to modernise the kitchen. One day. She had announced both intentions over two years ago, when the land was sold. Somehow it had been too much trouble and Helena was always so busy. And there was always some marvellous dog much more worthy of the money spent than mere household goods.

Brier turned on the taps, and sprinkled her mother's bubble bath lavishly into the water. Simon watched the growing froth with amazement.

'Never had a foam bath before?' Brier asked. 'It's fun.' It might distract him.

The child shook his head, and watched as the bubbles rose to the rim of the bath.

'Just like a film star,' she said.

She helped him strip off his clothes, and stifled a gasp as she saw the weals on his back. Scarlet marks and purple bruises across the soft skin, some healed, some recent. Some surely inflicted today. Dear God, what kind of people were these? Anger overwhelmed her, shaking her, so that she wanted to find his parents and make sure they were punished for harming him.

It was made worse because this wasn't just any child. It was a child she already knew well.

'A quaint little soul,' Helena had said once. 'Too grown up. He seems to know things I don't.'

The dark blue eyes were watching her now, as if assessing her, wondering if he ought to trust her. He lay back in the water, and gasped as it stung his injuries.

'All right?' Brier asked, although she knew he was far from all right.

He nodded, unaware of her concern, and slid thankfully down in the warm water. Brier took soap and sponge and bathed the dirty knees, which were grazed and bruised. She dared not touch his back, and hoped the water was soothing the pain.

She had to ask.

'Simon, does your father beat you?'

'Yes. When he gets drunk. Only now he's nearly always drunk. He lost his job. He'd been drinking all day today. I keep doing everything wrong. Only I get frightened and when I'm frightened I do it more wrong. He gets so angry.' He spoke as if he thought he deserved to be punished. 'He chased me. I hid in the pipe so he couldn't reach me. He couldn't get in. I didn't want to eat my supper in the greenhouse. It was cold. I tried to stay indoors.'

The picture the child presented became more and more appalling.

'Does he use a cane?'

'A whippy belt. What do you beat Ben and Dana with?'

Brier glimpsed a terrifying world which she had not met so close to home. Too shocked to reply, she had no idea what she should do and called down the stairs to Helena to bring up the big bath towel that was warming by the fire. She needed a witness.

'Out,' she said, 'and I'll give you my favourite treat when I was a little girl. A lovely warm towel to dry you with.'

Roi, watching, lying against the wall, beat his tail as if the words had been directed at him, and Simon smiled for the first time, the darkness lifting from his face.

'Soup's ready,' Helena said, as she opened the door. She saw the child's back and stifled an exclamation. Brier put her finger to her lips.

'Soup would be a good idea.' Brier dried the child, patting gently at his back, and soothed the welts with calendula cream. He was so bony under her hands, his small body reminding her of a half-starved kitten. He was surely underfed as well. She dressed him in a purple and green velour tracksuit that Helena had brought upstairs. It was far too large and the colours shouted, but it was warm. She fastened the sleeves and legs with pieces of string and grinned at him.

'You look like an elf,' she said, anxious to distract him. She rubbed the wet hair dry. It needed cutting and was a shapeless mop, but at least it was now clean. He looked up at her from underneath the tousled mane, reminding her of an Old English Sheepdog puppy.

His own clothes were far too dirty to put on again. She led him downstairs. He accepted her hand in his meekly, too exhausted to protest at being treated like a very small child.

He watched as Helena spooned broth from the pan into a mug and added the contents of a packet.

'The vet rang while you were out.' Helena was watching Simon as he sipped.

'And?' Was the wretched man around still or had he

gone? Roi would have alerted her if there had been anyone else about. The needs of the child and the needs of her duty were conflicting. If she reported those beatings he would be taken away and put into care, and that might be worse than ever. If she didn't . . .

Maybe Derek Mott, one of her colleagues, was right and mothers ought not to be in the police. He was certain that anything that harmed a child made women so angry that they became emotional and couldn't do the job properly. But then the men were angry, too. She had a sudden memory of Derek himself with tears on his cheeks as he lifted a dead baby out of a car after a crash on the motorway. Derek tried to be the tough guy, cynical, with no feelings, but he didn't fool anyone.

He had glared at her and turned his back. Maybe he had never forgiven her for seeing that moment of humanity.

'Brier, you're not listening.'

Brier, suddenly aware of the enormity of her lack of attention, looked at her mother.

'I'm sorry. I really am. What did the vet say?' She tried to put her concern for Simon aside, and the idea that had come to her earlier flooded back. She did not want Roi to be sterile, but if he was . . . She needed a dog. Her mother had a dog useless for the purpose for which she had bought him.

A whole way of life depended on the answer.

Four

Simon, as if aware that something momentous was about to be said, stared at both of them, and then gripped the dog as if afraid that his life was threatened.

Helena walked over to the stove and took the kettle and poured water into two mugs containing instant coffee. She avoided her daughter's eyes.

'What do you want to drink, Simon?' she asked.

'Orange juice. Please.'

She busied herself pouring it out, as if unable to say what was in her mind.

'Bad news?' Brier asked.

'Yes. He's completely sterile. My lovely boy.' Helena's voice was desolate. So many hopes, so many plans, all of them destroyed. Brier needed to comfort her, but could find no words that would help.

Roi waved his tail, knowing they were talking about him. Simon whistled to the dog softly. Roi put his paws on the boy's knee, and accepted the clutch that held on to him as if he provided safety in a world that had little to offer.

'Is Roi ill? Is he going to die?'

He buried his face in the dog's fur. Roi, patient, sat quietly, leaning against the chair. The small voice was muffled.

'Roi found me. My dad chased me. He said things. He said he hated me and never wanted me and he had to marry my mother because I was coming. He hated her too. She trapped him.'

The words were spilling out.

'He said I'm wicked and a thief and I spoiled his whole

life and when he caught me he'd give me a beating I'd remember for ever. Only my back hurts so much. I don't want to go home.'

Some home, Brier thought, and caught her mother's eyes. Helena had forgotten her own misery, and was horrified by the recital.

'I was running away. Only I haven't any money and I didn't know where to go and I banged on the door here, only nobody heard me. The dogs barked and you said be quiet to them, and they were. Then he nearly caught me and I knew he'd beat me again when he did. I hid. I wasn't ever going to come out. Don't make me go back. I don't want to go back. Ever.'

Brier looked at Helena, who was standing as if unable to concentrate on anything at all, not believing a word she was hearing.

'Mother, I think Simon could do with something to eat. I bet he was hoping to share our supper, weren't you?' The child needed reassurance in so many directions.

'She told me to get out. I have to eat outside in the greenhouse always, even when it's cold. She never wants me. I get hungry. She doesn't make meals when my dad's away. She goes out for them.'

He caught his breath, stifling a sob. The two women stood silent, helpless, listening.

'Sometimes she leaves money lying on the table, when there isn't any bread, and I go and buy fish and chips . . . and then my dad beats me for stealing. I wanted to see Ben . . . Birdie makes me sandwiches. Only I didn't know if my dad was still there, waiting for me. I thought he wouldn't see me in the dark if I came across the fields. There are street lights in Ben's road.'

And I'm never home and don't even know what goes on, Brier thought. She took the boy's hand again, hoping human contact would help him. Tears were very near again.

'Roi found me. I knew he'd find me. He kept crying out

to me. I wish he'd got my dad and bitten him, so he knows what it's like to be hurt.'

The sobs were less, but Simon had hiccups. The younger bitch watched him, inquisitive, her head on one side, listening to the strange sounds. Roi licked his face, as if wishing to comfort him.

The boy stroked Roi's head, and the long, handsome tail moved slowly from side to side. The dog stayed leaning against the chair, as if aware that his presence was helping Simon return to everyday life after his appalling experience.

I wish I knew what to do, Brier thought. Why is nothing ever straightforward?

The kitchen was a haven of warmth. Helena took the two chicken dinners from the oven and divided them among three plates. She unearthed new-baked sausage rolls from a tin, knowing that Simon was as greedy for them as Ben. She brought the tin of shapes.

'I know you like dog biscuits,' she said. 'You always eat dozens when you come to help me with Ben.'

What else don't I know? Brier wondered, as the child grinned suddenly, and took one of the shapes. It needed imagination to see it as a dog, maybe a corgi. She took one herself. Helena began to cut sandwiches.

The dogs sat, heads eager, watching her busy hands.

'Mother, there are only three of us.'

'The child needs food. Look at him. Those chicken dinners are little enough for one and we've two between three of us. Simon's as thin as a sparrow. Food always makes things seem less frightening.'

Maybe it does, Brier thought, with a small, secret smile. Her mother, like Alice Gulley and Kate, produced cakes and tea as a cure for everything from a cold in the head to a death in the family.

Helena's voice was soft. Simon lay back in the big chair, his eyes closed, but the small hands were clenched into tight fists and occasional sobs still racked him.

'Eat, Simon,' Helena said.

He opened his eyes and looked at Roi.

'He'd make a good police dog. He knew I was there, and he found me.'

Police dog! The words hovered in the air and Brier held her breath, hardly daring to hope. She raised her eyes and looked at her mother.

Helena was staring at her daughter, electrified.

'That could be the answer! Why didn't I think of it? Would they let you? It would make sense, and I wouldn't feel it was such a waste. I'd love you to have him. To make something of him. It would make me so much happier to know he was of use.' There was hope in her voice.

Brier felt a great leap of elation. She had thought she might ask if she could have the dog. Not tonight, but maybe a day or so later when her mother had had time to adjust to the situation. She had expected the idea to be rejected.

She could take Roi home with her. The empty bed would be occupied, the water bowl was there for him to drink. There would be an eager dog to greet her in the morning, to take outside and train, and Josh would be over the moon. She must ring him as soon as she got in, and make sure he or Gulley didn't collect any other dog.

She would have the dog of her dreams. Life had point again and with that realisation came a sudden surge of energy.

'Don't see why not. I need a dog by tomorrow, and I'm not going to find another, am I? If I don't have a dog I'll have to leave the course, and then I'll be back where I was before, and I don't want that. I'm desperate, ready to steal a dog. I need a good one. Only nine weeks and a few days left and the other five dogs are well into the work.'

She picked up her knife and fork. Simon was eating as if he had not had a meal for weeks. Her own lunch was hours ago and she was very hungry. She watched with satisfaction as the child bit into his food and then took a second bite, hunger making itself known and abolishing fear.

'Why is Roi spelt like that and not R-O-Y?' It was written on the little plaque over the kennels. Simon was visibly relaxing. 'I keep forgetting to ask.'

'It's spelt like the King of France, not the English name. Silly, really. He ought to be called König, because he came from Germany and that's German for King.'

The child had finished his chicken. He helped himself to a sandwich.

'Can I give him a whole sandwich? 'Cos he found me?'

'I don't see why not,' Helena said. 'He was extra clever because he hasn't been taught to find little boys.'

Simon almost smiled as he held out the food. Roi took it with soft lips, thistledown gentle. The two bitches, jealous, came and sat beside the chair, asking for their share.

'Just one taste each,' Helena said, making an exception to her rule that nobody ever fed dogs from their own plates in her home. She grinned suddenly at Simon.

'Roi's shown that he'd make a good police dog and I'm giving him to Brier. Her dog had to go back to his owners today so she hasn't a dog at all,' she said. 'Don't you think that's a good idea? It was your idea. I wouldn't have thought of it by myself.'

'He's clever. He'll be the best,' Simon said, his voice suddenly enthusiastic. He hugged the dog again. Roi licked his face. 'Can I come and see him? Often?'

'Whenever he's off duty,' Brier promised. If it hadn't been for the child she might never have achieved her desire.

She was unable to believe that her craving had been satisfied so easily. Her lovely Roi, the dog she had coveted, and she had not even had to suggest it herself. They would have to have safeguards. Roi was to be hers, and if he failed his tests at the end of the course was to come home and live with her, not be given to anyone else.

He wouldn't fail his tests. Her mother had already begun

to train him and he knew as much as Brier's first two dogs; more than Sabre, who knew nothing, poor fellow.

Her thoughts were interrupted by a frenzied barking followed by a rap on the door. Roi and the two bitches added their warning to that of the outside dogs.

'Who's there?' Helena called, her mouth full of a hastily bitten sandwich.

'John Grace.' They both knew the CID man. His fourth daughter was in the same form as Dana and his second son was in Simon's form. Gracie might be able to help them. He was used to children, though the feminine nickname didn't suit him at all. Also Simon knew him, as he sometimes played with . . . what was the boy's name? Adrian.

Helena opened the door.

'Where have you come from?'

The visitor grinned.

'Out of the everywhere into here. I brought you a birthday present, or do you want me to go away again?'

The big man walked in, dwarfing all of them. A shock of dark hair and bright brown eyes that laughed at the world, long legs that covered more ground than anyone Brier knew, and large hands that could be surprisingly gentle. He unzipped his bulky padded blue anorak.

He looked at the child, at the odd clothes, at the signs of tears, and quirked one eyebrow at Brier, sensing trouble.

He loved conjuring and those hands were deft. He grinned at Simon, leaned over him, and produced a fifty pence piece from under the boy's hair.

'Funny place to keep your pocket money,' he said, pressing the coin into the child's hands and closing the small fingers over it.

His presence filled the room. The dogs raced to him, smelling him carefully, identifying the spaniel bitch and the dachshund, the rabbit and the three cats. He passed their scrutiny and was accepted as the right kind of person. They settled on the rug again. The CID man lowered his bulk onto a small stool, reducing his size.

'I bet you didn't know that Mrs Grant had a birthday today?'

Simon shook his head.

'Let's sing "Happy Birthday", then.'

His powerful voice filled the kitchen and Simon's small reedy notes echoed it.

'I didn't think Brier would make it, so I came armed with a bottle of wine and a pack of smoked salmon for you to enjoy tomorrow and think of me when you eat it.'

'Why should she think of you?' Simon asked.

'Because I'm such a nice man.' He sensed that something here was very wrong. Had a nose for trouble, his friends said. His enemies called it something quite different.

'You didn't have an ulterior motive, I suppose?' Helena asked. 'Like wanting the dogs kennelled?'

'How could you think it of me?'

'Meg forgot to come over for dogfood today,' Helena said. 'I thought she'd come tomorrow.'

'She's got what Adrian calls the dreaded lurgy and the rest of us call flu. It's a three-day job, the doctor said. Yes, I do need the dogfood. But we did have the presents for you. Cross my heart.' He made an extravagant gesture.

Simon giggled, and Brier cast a grateful glance at the big man. He had been one of Tom's most valued friends, a welcome visitor at their house.

'Meg had them packed ready to bring.'

Helena kissed him on the cheek and brought the sack of dogfood from the back porch.

'Can you stay and help us celebrate? Just for a few minutes?'

'Just a few minutes. Meg's as comfortable as she can be and luckily it's the cold sort, not the tummy sort, so she's in bed with hot water bottles, a stack of tissues and hot drinks and aspirin. Pam's old enough to look after her.

Would you believe that daughter of mine will soon be seventeen?'

'A glass of wine?' Helena asked.

'Not when I'm driving.'

He noticed Simon's sudden dark-eyed glance, an enigmatic expression on the child's face. Roi sighed heavily and lay down beside the chair, his head against the boy's leg.

Brier wondered what on earth she was going to do. One thing was certain. He couldn't go home. But Social Services would not be working at this time of night and she didn't want him taken into a children's home. What alternative was there? Maybe John would know. Maybe he'd support her own half-formed idea.

'Like me to drive you home, son?' Gracie asked.

'I don't want to go back.' The words were a yell and again there was a stormy sobbing. Helena knelt beside him and held him tightly against her, murmuring softly. When the sobbing eased she looked at Brier.

'Show John Roi's last trophy. It was most unusual. You haven't seen it either, have you? It's in the den.'

Brier beckoned to John Grace to follow her into her father's old study where, among the trophies of a lifetime, she told him about the beatings.

'Dear heaven. Now what do we do?' Brier knew he was as confused as she. No parent would lightly consign a child into the care of authority.

'I thought he might come and stay with us tonight. He practically lives with us anyway. He's always coming round to see Ben or coming here to see Roi. His own home is obviously a very unhappy place. We'll have to contact the Social Services, but maybe we can persuade them to let me foster him. I can't abandon him to strangers.'

She'd never forgive herself if she didn't try.

'He'd be better among his friends and at his own school. Do you know anything about the family, other than his mother committed suicide?'

'Driven to it, I'd imagine.' John Grace looked at the trophies, and picked one of them up. It was a patterned wooden picture frame, inside which was a photo of Roi, head and shoulders, his mouth laughing, his eyes vivid with life. Underneath it said BOB. 'Best of Breed,' he said. 'A lovely trophy indeed.' He put it down again, reluctant to give voice to his thoughts.

'We've had the father in the cells several times. Drunk and disorderly. He's lost his job and his driving licence. He's a near-alcoholic. I didn't know about the beatings, but that's typical of that type of person.'

The windows were uncurtained. Helena rarely used this room. The big kitchen had always been the hub of their home. Brier looked at the framed photograph of her father, standing among his cattle. He had loved his Jersey herd, but that, like so much else, had gone under the hammer after he died.

'It was so stupid,' Brier said. 'The poor kid was out there for an hour, with Roi telling us something was wrong. So did the other dogs. I looked, but couldn't see anything. I never dreamed of anyone being hidden . . .' She was condemning herself for her misreading of the restlessness in the kennels.

'If we all had second sight there'd be far fewer crimes. We'd prevent them before they happened. Oh, damn it, what do we do about the kid? He can't live with you for ever.'

'Whether he does or not depends on the Social Service people. He'd be at risk all the time. Suppose the father turns from beating to thumping? He could kill him.' The problem was suddenly overwhelming. She'd have to visit the parents and was not looking forward to that at all.

'What about the parents? Do they have to agree? Are those marks on his back sufficient evidence?' John Grace stood up and looked out of the window at the darkness outside. Far away, a car climbed the hill, throwing its headlights against the sky. The searchlight beam soared, levelled and died away. The lamps that edged the motorway glittered against the dark.

'They're appalling. He's been hit repeatedly, on a number of occasions. He says with a whippy belt, and that's what it looks like. The buckle has caught him several times. It made us both feel sick. He wanted to know what I beat my children with.'

'Maybe the royal children think everyone lives in palaces,' John said. 'How can a child ever know how the rest of the world behaves? He only has his own small experience to draw on.'

He sighed.

'A doctor ought to see him. It's only your word . . . but a doctor might recommend we put him into care.'

'Not the one I have in mind.' Brier was surprising herself: she had never considered any sort of scheming before. Annette had children of her own and she and Brier had been at school together. They had bent a few rules then. Annette wouldn't mind bending another two or three now.

She couldn't let the child go back. *Don't get involved.* The words were bitten into her brain, but she *was* involved. Would she have felt differently if she hadn't known the child? She didn't know and at the moment was too tired to care, her body longing for bed and sleep. Both were a long way off.

She led the way back to the kitchen.

'Simon's tired and needs his bed,' Helena said.

'No.' He clung to Brier. 'Don't take me back.'

The decision was made. It was too late to alert anyone now. Well after nine o'clock. The time had flown.

'I'm not going to. You can come and sleep in our house in Ben's room. Tomorrow we must sort out all kinds of things. Maybe Mr Grace will go round and see your parents and tell them you are safe and get some clothes.'

It was unfair to saddle him with the job, but he was

better fitted than she to deal with what could be a violent drunk.

'Gracie, I'm sorry to land you. Would you? Please? I need to get this little fellow to bed, and to settle my dog . . .'

'I was going to offer,' John Grace said.

'Can my cat come? She won't feed it, and she never lets it come inside. I let it in when they've gone to bed so it can sleep on my bed in the warm. Roi won't hurt it, will he?'

She was taking the dog home. The full realisation hit her suddenly. She stood, a grin on her face, feeling as if she had just won the pools. Better than any million pounds. She had a dog. She had a dog. And what a dog. The words sang in her mind and she thought she would explode with happiness.

Both John and Helena were grinning.

'You need food for Roi. You have bowls and bed?'

Brier nodded, somewhat bemused. Roi had a different diet from that fed to the police dogs. She would have to change him slowly. She couldn't risk time off with a dog with a tummy upset. She went out to the car and put Roi into the back. He settled as if he had been there for all of his life. She held him for a moment before rejoining the others, afraid he would vanish, that this would prove to be a dream. But the dog was real.

'I won't tell him where the child is. Let him stew, if he cares at all,' the big man said softly. Brier went out into the hall. As Simon bent over to tie his shoelaces, the bottom of the sweatshirt slipped up and Gracie saw the weals for himself. 'Let him think the wheels are beginning to turn and he's for the high jump. I can tell him why,' he added, his voice savage.

Brier looked at him, the thought of the dog coming home with her buoying her spirits amid her concern for the child. She stood on tiptoe and kissed him on the cheek.

'Thanks, Gracie,' she said. 'I was dreading it.' She

opened the car door. Helena helped Simon into the passenger seat, fastening the seat belt. He turned to look at Roi, who jumped into the well behind the front seats and licked the child's hand.

The moon had vanished. The faint light showed stormy cloud. Brier, straining to see the road, afraid of icy patches, could not believe the change in her life.

So much had happened. She glanced at Simon. Exhaustion had taken over and he lay, white-faced, his eyes closed, his head leaning against the back of the passenger seat. He needed bed, and sleep, as soon as she could get him home. She needed sleep too. She'd be more able to think straight in the morning. Her thoughts raced on.

Four hours ago she had been without a dog, the only woman on the dog handler course, sure that this was the end of that particular career change. Now she had the dog she had longed for for months, and had also, in the course of the evening, at least temporarily, acquired another child and, possibly, a cat. And along with them a whole load of new problems.

Five

As she drove home, Brier was aware of the small, silent figure beside her. She was also ecstatically aware of the dog lying behind her, of every movement that he made. Worry about the child was masked by excitement over the thought that she had her own dog, the dog she had coveted, and that he would not be taken from her. She was sure Josh would agree to Helena's conditions which were, after all, those that applied to any dog given to them by a civilian.

If the dog didn't make the grade he was either given back to his original owners or, if they did not want him, found a good pet home. Many a dog taking part in civilian Working Trials had started life as a dog discarded by the police as being too gentle for his job, or unfit to work the long hours that were often demanded.

'Can I live with you always?' asked the small, forlorn voice at her side.

Brier had not thought beyond the immediate future. She didn't know how to answer. She didn't want to make a promise that might have to be broken, or raise hopes that had to be dashed.

Before she could reply, Roi barked. She glanced out of the window. A motorcyclist sprawled on the pavement, his bike beside him. As she looked, he sat up. She parked the car at the kerb and walked over to him.

'Trouble?' she asked.

'I skidded.'

'Not knocked over by a car?'

'No. It was ice. I didn't see it and though I was going

slowly, I went out of control. I think I've broken my leg.' His voice was breathy, revealing pain. The young man was well dressed, his leather clothing thick and padded, but that would not save him from injury if he fell awkwardly. His right leg was at an odd angle. He removed his helmet. The thick fair hair flopped over one eye and he brushed it away impatiently.

'Sorry. I'm being a nuisance. Can you get help? It will have to be an ambulance. I can't stand up.'

'No problem. I'm police. I'm off duty but my radio's in the car.'

As she approached, Simon rolled the window part way down.

'Look after Roi for me,' she said, seeing his anxious face. 'I'll have to stay until help arrives. I'm sorry, Simon.'

'I'm OK. Now.' He added the word with immense feeling.

He handed her the little personal radio which was on the shelf in front of him.

'You'll need this.'

He watched her, wanting approval, and she smiled at him as she spoke.

'They'll be with you in a couple of minutes,' a disembodied voice said a moment later. 'Ambulance on its way.'

There was little she could do to help. She knelt beside him, knowing she must not move him. He gave her a grateful smile. He was younger than she had thought, not yet twenty, she guessed.

'You'll soon be in a warm bed. I won't leave you till my colleagues arrive,' she promised. 'I wish I could make you more comfortable.'

'Just having someone here helps,' he said. 'I was scared no one would find me till I'd frozen stiff.'

The police car reached her first, and she handed over to them thankfully.

'I've a casualty of my own in the car,' she said. She knew the men by sight, as they knew her. Roi was sitting on the back seat, his expression regal, as he watched the little group.

'You'll be OK now,' she promised the motorcyclist. She drove off.

'Is he very badly hurt?' Simon asked.

'I think he's broken his leg. But they'll deal with it. I'm not on duty now. Let's get you home.'

She was sorry for the young man but grateful for the incident that had saved her having to answer Simon's question. She drove into the garage and leashed Roi. He had never been to her home before and she did not want to risk him running off and exploring in the dark. She took the child by the hand. The garage door always crashed as it shut. Before she could put her key in the front door it opened.

'Helena rang,' Birdie said, as they walked into the hall. 'There's a nice warm bed for you in Ben's room, Simon. Hot water bottle, and pyjamas getting cosy on the radiator. How does that sound? I told Ben you were coming. He's pleased. Fun to have a friend to stay, he said.'

'Can Roi sleep by my bed?'

'I don't think that would be a good idea.' Brier's head was beginning to ache. 'It's his first night here and he'll be feeling strange himself. We can leave your door open and the light on the landing. Mr Grace ought to be here soon with some of your own clothes. He's gone to tell your parents that you're safe.'

'They won't care,' Simon said.

Brier glanced at the clock. Nearly ten. It had been a very long evening.

'I made some hot Ovaltine for Simon,' said Kate. 'It will help you sleep. Are you hungry?'

Simon shook his head.

'He shared our meal,' Brier said. She closed the kitchen

door behind them and sat at the table, unclipping Roi's lead. The dog looked around him, curious. He began to inspect the place, sniffing the floor, examining the dog bed with enormous and detailed interest, knowing another dog had slept in it. He returned to look up at Brier as if asking why he was here.

She put her hand on his head, and he sighed and flopped against her, leaning against her leg.

Simon was almost asleep. Kate led him upstairs as soon as he had finished his drink. She came down ten minutes later, her face grim.

'I helped him undress,' she said. 'Luckily Ben is asleep.'

'I don't know what to do.'

'He doesn't go home. There are bruises as well as belt marks on him. His father's one of the cunning ones. Took care never to hit where it would be seen.'

Brier looked longingly at the clock.

'Can't go to bed till Gracie gets here. He's supposed to be bringing Simon's cat. As well as some clothes.'

'And where does the cat sleep? In the kitchen with Roi? That sounds like a recipe for disaster.'

'Mother told you about Roi?'

'I knew what was likely a week or two ago. I did wonder about you having the dog, but Helena was too upset and the time wasn't right. She invested more money than she ought in that dog.'

'You know my mother.'

There was a soft knock on the back door, and Kate opened it. John Grace stood there. Beside him was a large shabby holdall, a box which obviously contained a somewhat angry cat and a huge crate.

'I saw the parents,' he said. 'They didn't seem too concerned. So long as the boy was safe . . .' He shrugged. 'I'll tell you about it tomorrow. You're asleep on your feet. First things first. Let's settle these animals. Simon gone up to bed?'

Brier nodded, looking at the box and the crate. She was glad John was there to help. Her brain seemed to have ceased functioning.

'Helena has sent her indoor kennel for Roi. Thought it might help him settle tonight,' he said.

Roi came over to greet him, was rewarded with a pat and told to sit before he could leap up in delight. Gracie was a well-loved friend, who always took notice of the dog when he came to the kennels for food for his own dogs, or boarded them there.

'The kennel might be better for the cat,' Brier said. 'Only we don't have a cat litter box.'

'One in the car. Helena has several and thought you'd need one. You can't let him out until he's used to the place, or he'll probably run back to his old home. He's a scrawny, miserable-looking animal. Needs feeding up and a dose of flea spray.'

He brought in the parcels and helped Brier erect the crate, which was a large cage made of thick wire with a door that shut by means of two thick metal strands that slotted into retaining loops.

Kate put sardines onto a saucer and put the saucer inside the crate. She vanished and reappeared with a cardboard box, its inside base covered with an old, thick jersey.

'He'll settle better if he's fed and comfortable,' she said. 'Simon says his name's Ginger. Not very original.'

John Grace laughed as he lifted the cat from the box. Roi, his ears alert, his eyes bright, sat, every muscle ready to spring, and Brier took his collar and held him.

'More original than you'd think,' Gracie said, lifting out a black and white cat with bright green eyes. 'I suspect young Simon has a sense of humour all his own, if only he could relax and give vent to it.'

The crate was ample, big enough for Roi. There was room for him to stand, to turn round and to stretch out full length. The cat, shut in, sat, eyes glaring, and then, as Brier released the dog who came up to the bars, he stood, fluffing himself to immensity, and snarled and swore.

Roi, used to friendly cats, retreated and looked at Brier as if blaming her for this odd behaviour.

'I'll be off,' Gracie said, 'or none of us will get any sleep tonight.'

'I'll see you out of the front door.'

She turned the key and shot the bolts and deadlocks after he had gone and leaned against the wall, her eyes closed, wishing she could go straight up to bed. Roi needed to go out and he would have to be leashed, otherwise she might not be able to get him in.

Kim had always been entranced by the dark, and spent his time chasing shadows in the floodlit garden. Once he found a hedgehog and another time a frog. Come when he was called? For his first two weeks, not he.

As she opened the kitchen door, Roi came into the hall. He jumped at her, and when she told him to sit he backed off, play-bowed to her and barked.

'Quiet,' she said, but it was too late. She heard Ben's bed creak, the pad, pad of his bare feet across the carpet, and then he appeared on the landing, Simon and Dana following him.

'Roi!' Ben shouted. 'You've got Roi! Did Grandee lend him to us till you get a new dog?'

Roi, hearing his name, had bounded up the stairs.

'Go back to bed. All of you. Roi is here to stay. You can see him in the morning.'

It was too late. Ben ran forward. Roi had met an old friend. He leaped in delight at the child. They fell together. Kate and Brier stared in horror at the sprawled boy with the dog on top of him. Brier flew up the stairs and hauled the dog away, expecting to see her son terrified.

How could she have been so stupid? She should have remembered Roi would be excited if he heard a voice he knew.

Ben was laughing and wiping his face, which had been licked all over.

Simon was standing by the bedroom door, watching them.

'Roi likes me wrestling with him,' Ben said.

'Does Grandee let you?'

'Of course not. She doesn't know. She says I mustn't. But I like it and he never hurts me.'

'You never do it again, or I give Roi back to Grandee. And I mean it,' Brier said, seeing ahead of her complications that she had never envisaged.

This had to be stopped immediately. Over-excited dogs sometimes bit, triggered by the child's thoughtless action. Also, Roi weighed more than any of the children and might easily leap up and knock one of them over. Dana was very slight.

'Take Roi out, and then for heaven's sake get yourself to bed, or you'll never be able to go in tomorrow,' Birdie said. 'I'll read the riot act.' She shooed the two boys back to their beds, and Brier went down the stairs, feeling as if her legs belonged to somebody else.

The cat had retreated to his box. He glowered at them inimically through the bars of his cage.

Brier looked at the kennel in the garden. It was unheated, and it was a very cold night. Roi was used to central heating indoors or a heated kennel. She would have to risk an interrupted night. He might not settle at all in strange surroundings. She did not want him upstairs: that would start a bad habit. She took him to the big polythene bed. Kate had changed the blanket and she hoped the bed held no trace of the other dog.

'Bed,' she said. 'And see you stay there.'

Roi slept in a similar bed when Helena brought him indoors. He turned round several times, and settled at last, looking at her thoughtfully. She bent down and stroked his head.

'You're wonderful,' she told him. 'See you stay there all night and show me what a good dog you are.'

She met Kate as she was returning to her own room after brushing her teeth.

'Have you got the message through?' she asked.

'I think so. The problem, of course, is that this is a dog the children all know well. Ben and Dana were much more wary of Sabre and even of Kim. Simon didn't know either of them. Roi knows them much better than he knows you.'

'That alone is going to cause me problems,' Brier said. Nothing was going to be as easy as she had hoped.

She woke when the alarm clock pealed remorselessly at five-thirty. Time to get up and groom her dog, to walk her dog, to train her dog. Time before the children began to rampage. Dana always fussed over her clothes, never liking what was put out for her. Both Brier and Kate wished that schools still had uniform. It made life much simpler.

She wanted to be early at the Training Centre and to talk to Josh. She had forgotten to phone either him or Gulley. Supposing they had found her a dog?

She was bone weary and yawned as she dressed. She hoped she'd wake properly and feel alert before the workday began.

She switched on the kitchen light and stared.

Simon was curled in the crate, his eiderdown over him, the cat held tight in his arms. He woke and smiled at her sleepily.

'Ginger was lonely,' he said. He was suddenly wide awake. 'I'll get dressed and help you with Roi.'

He settled the cat gently in the box and greeted Roi, who was overcome with pleasure at being noticed. The dog seemed to move every inch of his body, waving his tail, pushing against the bars of the cage, moaning softly in delight.

Brier looked at the child. His colour was better and he

seemed to have bounced back from the trauma of the night before.

'How do you feel?' she asked.

'Happy,' Simon said with a grin that transformed his face. Brier had never seen him smile so wholeheartedly before.

He let himself out of the cage just as Birdie came down.

'No need for you to get up,' Brier said.

'You needn't think you're going off on a cold morning like this with no food inside you.'

Simon had dressed with speed in too-short jeans and a jersey that needed a wash. He dived into the bag that Helena had sent with the dog and brought out Roi's brush. He found the lead and fastened it on.

'I can't reach the top bolt,' he said, after undoing the bottom bolt and turning the key in the back door.

'And what do you think you're doing?' Brier asked.

'I'm taking him out to empty himself. He'll need to. And then I'll brush him for you,' Simon said. 'Then he'll lie quietly while you have your breakfast in peace.'

'Can you manage him?'

'Of course I can. Grandee let me hold him when we walked round the yard. She showed me what to do. I go there lots. She says I'm a big help and sometimes she pays me for helping, specially when I walk the little boarders. She says I'm an adopted grandson.'

Birdie undid the top bolt and switched on the lights that Brier had had rigged to floodlight the garden so that she could train before she went to work, while it was still dark. The house was detached and both her neighbours slept in front rooms, for which she was thankful as her hours were far from normal. She slipped into the hall and brought back one of her own anoraks and put it round the child.

Brier took the mug of coffee that had been made for her and went to the window, watching anxiously. Boy and dog might have performed the same actions a hundred times.

Roi walked quietly, sniffing the ground, while Simon waited.

The dog, on unfamiliar territory, was slow to perform. He looked as if he were analysing each grass blade.

'That child's a natural handler,' Brier said, astonishment in her voice.

'He's twice as much sense as Ben,' Kate said. 'He helped me explain the facts of dogs last night. He told Ben that if children and dogs wrestle together, the dog thinks the child is a puppy. Pups play by biting one another, in fun. They have thick fur. Children don't. The dog doesn't mean to hurt, but he does.'

'Simon could be an asset. He seems so much more mature than Ben.'

'He's had to be,' Kate said. 'It's the only way he could have survived. I'm glad you brought him home. Dana is resentful—a bit jealous—but she'll come round. She adores Roi. He'll be good for her.'

Roi greeted all the children with more pleasure than he had greeted her. He sat beside Simon, his head on the child's knee, and ignored Brier's call. She had to take him physically by the collar, leash him and command him forcefully to follow her.

She realised, in the two hours before she set off for work, that she had a problem on her hands. When Simon was there, Roi ignored her. He had formed a bond with the boy, and that might be totally detrimental to his training. She put him in the car, knowing that if he bonded to Simon he would be useless as a police dog.

She was aware of the dog lying behind her. She would have her van back today. Maybe if the dog was too fond of the boys she would break the associations by leaving him with Gulley every night, and calling in for him first thing.

That didn't seem fair either.

She had the dog of a lifetime, and more problems than she had ever dreamed of the evening before.

She drove into the yard and parked, and sat and looked at her new acquisition.

'Oh, Roi,' she said. 'Why does life have to be so complicated?'

The dog, finding his own world very simple, looked at her with shining brown eyes and wagged his tail, glad that she was taking notice of him.

Six

Josh sighed as he looked at the photograph on his desk. It had been taken nine years ago, just before their fourth wedding anniversary. Ellie looked back at him, laughing, as she had so often laughed when she was alive. Behind her the hills were heather clad. It had been a day to remember, warm sun, small clouds, a long walk in the morning, a pub lunch, and then home to celebrate his promotion to take charge of the whole police dog section.

Wine and flowers on the table, and Ellie's special chicken casserole.

It had been too short a marriage. Only five years. Ellie had not yet reached thirty. Cancer was no respecter of life. Another eight years since she died. Endless years.

She had been an ideal wife for a policeman. The daughter of a policeman, she was used to erratic hours and broken appointments. She busied herself with the youth club, delivered Meals-on-Wheels, and produced plays for the Drama Society. They had wanted children so badly, but they never came.

Increasing gynaecological problems revealed cancer, and she had not recovered from the operation. Four short days during which they held out little hope and on the fifth day she was dead. Too far advanced, they said.

She loved the dogs, and had brought her year-old Dobermann with her when they married. After her death Josh had taken him to the police kennels when he was at work and left him in Gulley's care.

Gulley could never resist any dog, and was delighted to have charge of Dyke. In no time at all the two were enraptured with one another. Ellie would have approved. The dog had died a couple of years ago.

Ellie had been fun, a lively companion with the gift of laughter. She had competed in civilian Working Trials with Dyke, and Josh missed the long evenings when he had discussed dog problems with her. She often came up with a training solution that he had overlooked.

He glanced at the clock. Just after 7 a.m. These early mornings were valuable, as he could get through so much deskwork before the phone began to ring. The dogs were his life now. Spark was an extension of his own personality, a dog who appeared to understand everything he was told and who worked with a verve and a will.

Lim's first owners had, after a few fraught weeks, christened him Limb of Satan. He was handed over to the police with relief when he was seven months old. He was a darting, energetic Springer Spaniel, who had saved more lives with his nose than anyone outside the police force realised.

Josh had soon channelled the dog's enormous energy. Training occupied the brain that had been lying idle, inventing new mischief all the time. Lim adored the teaching games, his small tail busy wagging in frenzy as he discovered yet one more hidden 'toy', and alerted Josh to its presence. The dog never knew that the toy was a substitute for the bombs that he was being taught to find.

To him it was a wonderful chance to show his adored master how well he could work. When he found the trophy, as the substitute was harmless, the swift throw of his favourite toy and the fast dash to bring it back were all the reward he asked.

The dogs were excitement, and Josh found consolation in watching each untrained and uncouth youngster mature into an animal that was a constant pleasure, as well as a major asset to every working dog handler. The dog was extra eyes and extra ears and, above all, he had teeth, and a ferocious growl and bark that could be turned on and off at will.

Any truly aggressive dog was discarded. Spark might be asked to find a criminal one day and a missing toddler the next, and had to know the difference. The right dogs were not easy to find. He and Gulley had phoned all round the country the evening before, but good dogs were rare. It would have to be Kim, who was the best of the six he now had in training. Josh could have spared Jacko or Spike without a qualm.

He could ring round all the breeders, but that would probably only produce pups that were too young, or dogs that had been discarded for reasons that rendered them unsuitable for police work, such as sheep killing.

He was impatient now—with himself, with the quirk of fate that had taken Brier's dog away from him, with the weather, which had been making training a misery. He was never impatient with the dogs. He gave them all the time they needed to produce results for him.

He glanced at the clock again. Two hours before the six came in for their training. They started the day by hosing the vans. No policeman could ever go on duty in a dirty vehicle.

He began to doodle on his notepad, drawing dogs' heads with alert, pricked ears. The sketches were poor but the activity helped thought. The fourth week of any course was difficult. Problems began to surface, enthusiasms waned and tempers prickled as those who had never owned dogs before learned that this dog training, which they had thought would be a lark, was by no means as easy as they had imagined.

They had had visions of being excused from many duties as they taught the dogs their skills. Dreams of walking down the street, a large and handsome German Shepherd pacing sedately at their sides, while the general public looked on and was impressed.

The old hands knew better as they struggled with dogs that had been donated because they were out of hand, or had chased cars and bicycles, or were harassing the children. Boys especially were apt to tease and taunt, and no dog could understand that. Only the most submissive would tolerate it.

Josh had instructed on some sticky courses in the last fifteen years, but this was one of the worst. He had never had such an unfortunate mix of personalities.

Gulley came into the room with his small dancing step. Age hadn't slowed him. He looked at Josh and raised his eyebrows.

'Black dog got you?' He put down the steaming cup of coffee. He hated the machine and always brewed his own in the little hut he called an office. He added a small cardboard box.

'Alice made you a pasty for lunch. Says you don't take enough care of yourself.'

Josh grinned. Alice seemed to have adopted him as an extra son.

'Remind me to buy her an enormous bunch of flowers,' he said. 'She spoils me but it's nice to be spoiled.' He opened the box and sniffed appreciatively. 'I've not heard of the black dog on your shoulder since my grandmother died. Bring your coffee in here. I need to talk. I went home last night and did some more thinking.'

Gulley was good at listening. Josh filled his pipe and looked at it thoughtfully. 'Give it up,' the doctor had said at his last medical. He sighed and tapped the tobacco back into the pouch. He sucked on the empty stem.

'Bad night?' Gulley asked. 'I heard there was a call-out.'

'A bomb. A whopper. It gets worse.' Josh stared out of the window, seeing, not the snowdrops in the garden of the police house opposite, but the cordoned-off street, the parked cars, the garage with its string of petrol pumps, far too near, and little Lim searching. 'The call-out came at seven. It was three hours before we found the thing. In a bin about twenty yards from the garage.'

'Stupid,' Gulley said. 'What do they hope to prove?'

'God knows. I was whacked when I got in. We didn't dare leave without a further search. I didn't finish till nearly two-thirty. I'd promised to ring Brier, but never managed it. Didn't see the point of phoning her this morning to say we'd had no luck. Let her sleep. She won't need to get up early, with no dog to exercise, train and feed.'

He took the pipe out of his mouth. It tasted foul. He pushed it to the back of the top drawer of his desk, vowing not to take it out again, knowing he'd break that vow. It had been part of his routine for so long.

'I'm getting past it. I was scared silly. They evacuated the houses around. Thought it was a hoax at first but it wasn't. Thought they'd never defuse it.' The memory of fear returned, and he shivered.

He sipped the coffee. Hot and black and sweet. Gulley knew his need.

'Two lines in the paper or on the news. Nobody talks about the dogs that have to hunt. The dreadful moments that stretch out into eternity, when you don't know if it's timed to go off before you find it; if you'll end up blown to Kingdom Come, or maimed for life.'

He paused while he drank some more coffee.

'It's worse, every time. To think we risk the dog's life, putting him in the front line. No medals for Lim, yet I wonder how many lives that little dog has saved over the last two years?'

'He enjoys his work. And he doesn't know the risks.' Gulley looked thoughtfully out of the window at the line of kennels. The little spaniel was sound asleep, exhausted. 'Have you had any sleep?'

'I walked the dogs a couple of miles before going to bed. Too wound up to sleep. Out on the moors in the dark, blowing away stark fear. What kind of men are we breeding?'

'God knows. There's more than that wrong. Tell Uncle.' He glanced at the photograph of Ellie, which Josh had moved from its usual place and set in front of him.

'Memories?'

He had come round, night after night, the week after Ellie died, and sat there, quietly reading, giving comfort by his presence. Alice had sent food, and some evenings had come with Gulley and sat knitting, saying nothing, but comforting by her presence.

'That too. But suppose the worst happened and I had to be invalided out? How did you feel? What would I do?'

'The kennel job saved my sanity,' Gulley said. 'I was brooding. No more police work, and Miracle had died. The last of my father's line of greyhounds. Alice couldn't do with me underfoot. She's always busy and I had never been around all day except at weekends and holidays, and those you plan for. We almost came to blows some days. I didn't fit into her life; and I didn't have a life of my own.' He looked out at the changing sky. A blue dawn was giving way to heavy cloud and a thin, bitter wind that needled the air. 'I need to be with dogs. That's what you'll need, too, when the time comes to retire. You'll find something, not to worry. You have to do something, not sit at home feeling useless.'

'I do worry. And this damned course isn't helping. How did I get me so many misfits?' He glanced at the clock. 'Make another coffee, Gulley. And if you've any food, wheel it in. I forgot about breakfast.'

He sat, doodling as he waited. He drew more dogs' heads, thinking of past dogs, of triumphs and disasters. The best dog he'd ever had had died at less than two years old, knifed by a maniac. Gulley had helped him recover from that. He'd been with the dog handlers now for over six years.

Their friendship went a long way back. Gulley's father

had been a friend of Josh's father. Long time ago. Old Gulley's racing greyhounds had been legends once. Josh, as a teenager, had haunted the kennels. Gulley had inherited the last three and run them as a hobby. Miracle had kept him happy when he had to retire, but depression had set in when the dog died. Alice had been worried about him, but there was nothing she could find that would fill the empty hours happily for her husband.

Josh, tired of a constant change of kennelman, as few liked the work, had suggested he took the job, hoping Gulley would not feel insulted. He had discussed it with Alice before he offered Gulley the post. She had been elated.

'He needs dogs,' she said. 'We have mine, but they aren't his and though he loves his Jack Russell, Bess isn't a greyhound. The police dogs will be a godsend. He loathes being retired. He feels so useless. Half the time he sits around staring at the television set, but if I ask him what he was looking at, he doesn't even know.'

It was a marvellous appointment. Josh had been able to forget the daily running of the kennels, knowing his charges would be cared for, that any slight ailment would be seen at once, that the buildings would be immaculate.

Gulley shared his hopes and would, if asked, listen to his fears. He came back now, his wiry hair crested, reminding Josh, as always, of a perky elderly cock with a draggled comb. The older man glanced at the pad. Josh had given up dogs' heads and drawn a wild rose. Gulley, looking at it, drew his own conclusions.

'Toast. Peanut butter is all I've got. Put that inside you.'

Gulley treated his little office as a home from home. Alice had provided him with a toaster and percolator, and he kept a store of bread, of rolls, of fillings, and of chocolate bars and potato crisps, for men who might come off duty starving, having had no time to eat. His wife baked cakes for all of them. Josh dreaded the day when Gulley would feel too old to cope.

'Tell Uncle,' Gulley repeated and gave his quick, lopsided grin. Josh suddenly wished he were a small boy again, free from worries.

'Brier. I can't give her up and she hasn't a dog. Nobody has a dog that would be half-way useful. I saw three at the Rescue Kennels on my way home. Mad as hatters and not even she could calm them down. Scared of shadows, scared of bangs. Imagine them on a picket line.'

'Our Wild Rose,' Gulley said. 'She's a brilliant handler. Can't lose her.'

'Wild Rose?'

'It's what the men call her behind her back. She can be pretty thorny if they step out of line and try to flirt with her.'

'Do they?'

'I'm telling no tales, but there's no need to worry. I overheard someone being told she was a police officer first, last and all the time. Her sex didn't enter into the equation and he'd better watch his manners, or she'd prove it.'

'Tom is a very hard act to follow,' Josh said, somewhat inappropriately. But Gulley knew what he meant and nodded.

'Not many men like Tom and it's not long enough for Brier to have got over him,' he said. 'She doesn't show much, but she took it very hard.'

'Kim was bringing her back to life,' Josh said. 'Damn those people. It's hard enough without something like that happening, and it would be her dog.'

He bit into the toast, feeling strength return as he ate. It had been daft to come in without breakfast. He had been sure that the bomb would go off and he would join Ellie that night; and he had discovered he did not want to die. He wished he were as innocent of knowledge as little Lim, who thought he was playing a wonderful game.

'I can't do without Brier.' How often had he repeated that to himself? 'I had to fight to get her. Never had a woman police dog handler here before; it wasn't the time to start. They said the men would resent her, and they do, oh they do.'

'She's the only real dog handler you have. Born to it,' Gulley said. 'Helena says she was nearly born in a kennel beside a whelping bitch.'

Josh grinned.

'That figures.'

He blacked in two prick ears on the pad before him.

'I know why Brier wants to be a dog handler. Why does Derek? That's something I don't understand.'

'His mother moved in when her husband died, as he lived alone. He was enjoying life enormously and I suspect he didn't know how to tell his mum to go and live by herself. She does cramp his style. The dog needs walks and he can go out without hurting her feelings. He can leave the dog here when he has a date and not explain to his mother, who seems to resent him having any life of his own, and I gather never does like his girlfriends.'

Josh laughed.

'I doubt if my mother would have approved of the girls Derek chooses. Too-short skirts and long blonde hair, if it isn't green or pink. Only interested in having a good time and dancing.'

'He won a ballroom dancing competition with one of them,' Gulley said, throwing an unexpected sidelight.

'His mind's more on girls than on his dog,' Josh said. 'I need a dog handler, not a Romeo.'

'He'll grow up and settle down,' said Gulley who was an incurable optimist.

'How does he get on with Brier?'

'Not too badly. He can be tactless, but she seems to accept that he doesn't intend to hurt. She's much too old for him. He likes them barely out of their teens.'

'He's pretty taciturn with me.' Josh spread peanut butter on a second piece of toast.

'He's young,' Gulley said. 'In awe of the Gaffer. Did you confide in your headmaster?'

Josh grinned. Hard to think of himself as an authority figure, but he supposed he was.

'What about Pete and Rob? They give reasons on their application forms, but I suspect they're never the true reasons.'

'Rob's family's growing up. His wife took a job a couple of years ago. Their old dog died. Can't start a pup when you're out all day. She's always had a dog. It's a way of ensuring there's a dog in the house that isn't her responsibility. She's out, the dog's with him. Simple as that.'

'And Pete?'

'Oddly, the same reason. New baby, wife always lived with dogs, and no time now. Again they can have a dog that he will care for. She can enjoy it and it's his responsibility.'

Josh laughed.

'I was looking for deep motives.'

'They're deeper than you think. Could be holding their marriages together. Alice and me . . . the dogs are our only common interest. Don't know where we'd be today if we hadn't had that to cement us together.' Gulley looked out of the window. The winter trees were stark against the heavy, forbidding clouds.

'Maybe you're right. Doesn't do to get too psychological. Eat that toast for me, or give it to the dogs.' Josh pushed his plate across. 'Not got the appetite I had once. I could have finished off four slices of toast without even thinking.'

The food had eased tension. He sighed, longing for his pipe. Gulley watched him, saying nothing.

'How come you know all this and I don't?'

'I have time to listen and people talk,' Gulley said. He grinned in his turn. 'I'm just the hired help. Not the boss.'

Josh was looking at his list. He had learned more in the

last half-hour than he had in a month. 'Then there's Gwyn,' he said.

'Gwyn's easy. Farmer's son, always with dogs and joined the Force with that one idea in mind.'

'He'll make it and he has a good dog.' Josh was sure of that.

'He makes them laugh. Our Welsh humorist. Lightens the atmosphere, and has the knack of saying something that will defuse a situation. Good man, Gwyn. I've a lot of time for him.' Gulley stood up, easing his left leg. Arthritis was plaguing him again, but he had no intention of letting Josh see the slightest sign of disability.

'Worth his weight, that one.' He glanced out of the window. Rising wind and sleet in the air. Not a good day. The dogs were always more excitable when it blew.

'Tony?' Josh had only one name left on the list. 'Now there's a puzzle for you.'

'Wife had three miscarriages, and then a still-born baby boy. They must want a child badly. The last was some years ago. I believe she's pregnant again. Baby due very soon, and they'll both be scared. Hit him hard. Brier has two healthy children. That narks him.'

So I must make allowances, Josh thought, and sighed. It didn't make it any easier.

'What about me?' he asked, a grin on his face.

'I wouldn't have given tuppence for you fifteen years ago. Impatient, impossible, demanding too much of everybody. Ellie was the best thing that ever happened to you.'

Josh glanced at the clock. It controlled their lives.

'I'd best be off. Your dogs need food,' Gulley said.

'Another three-quarters of an hour's peace.' Josh picked up his pen.

'I think you've lost that.' A car rolled into the yard, parking neatly.

'Brier. Oh, Lord. Come to see if I've a dog. What the hell do I tell her?'

'Nothing.' The two men watched from the window, astounded, as Roi jumped out after her. He bounded at her in joy, and then raced off across the compound. She whistled and he turned fast, and sped back to her.

'Look at that. Look at that. Where did she get him? What a dog!' Josh pulled Gulley into the corner so that they were hidden from outside, and watched, fascinated. Gulley drew in his breath as the dog leaped at the woman's face in excitement, and the two of them ran off to the compound.

The dog turned to face them. Both men knew him.

'It's Helena Grant's Roi,' Josh said. 'She wouldn't make that sacrifice, even for her daughter, would she? He's worth a fortune and his pups are in high demand.'

They watched Brier as she exercised the dog and then played a game with him, throwing a small toy that he caught and brought to her, every inch of his body eager with life.

'Oh boy,' Josh said. 'If only he's not just lent to her until we find something else.'

'Shall I call her?'

'Leave her. She'll come when she's ready. She may not have realised I'm here. I used her van as mine's in the garage. Engine's been playing up. Probably thinks we left hers out all night.'

Brier knew that Gulley was there. His little moped was in its usual place. She'd play with the dog until Josh arrived. Meanwhile she savoured the peace: no one here but herself and her dog. She was unaware of the watching eyes, thinking Gulley was working in the kennels.

'I don't believe it. Why would Helena give Roi to us?' Josh was suddenly envious. If Star had lived, he would have been a dog like this.

Gulley studied the breed reports and knew all the ringside gossip. Whenever he was free, he spent his time at the shows.

'There's been rumours about his potency. He was very

ill six months or so ago. Last three bitches brought to him didn't take.'

Brier was racing, the dog running beside her, jumping up at her arm. Her face was alive, her eyes shining.

Josh watched, unable to believe his eyes.

'Our ice lady is thawing,' he said. 'Did you ever see such a change overnight in anyone?'

'They'll be as jealous of the dog as they are of her,' Gulley said. 'But it might make them work. Not going to be beaten by a woman, not one of those. Though Gwyn might bow to the better handler, the rest won't.'

Josh had to go outside, had to see the dog, had to meet him, had to watch him close to; had to make sure that he wasn't mistaken. Roi was moving over the ground almost without touching it, speeding away from Brier, to lie down at a word spoken so softly neither man heard it.

As they came towards her she turned and raised her hand. Roi dropped at her feet, his ears moving as first one voice spoke and then another. Once Gulley coughed and the dog put his head on one side.

'How did you persuade Helena?' Josh asked. 'He is Roi, isn't he?'

'Yes, it's Roi. Only . . .'

'He comes with conditions?'

'Oh yes. He's mine, and if he fails I take him home as a pet.'

'And she has the right to keep him at stud?'

'That's why we have him. He got an infection. He's sterile.'

'It's an ill wind,' said Gulley, always one for clichés. 'I'd heard the rumour, but you know what goes on. Knock the good dogs, so that they don't get the bitches. Didn't know if it was true or not.'

'It's only too true, but we didn't know for certain until yesterday. Mother got the test result while I was there.'

'And handed him over, just like that? She could have

used him for Working Trials and gone to the top with him.'

'She can't face the travelling and the Trials venues are all so far away. It means three days away from home, and she can't leave the kennels. Anyway, it wasn't just like that. It's a long story, and I don't know where to begin it.'

'What matters is you've got a dog. And what a dog,' Gulley said.

Brier grinned at him, unable to hide her pleasure.

'You didn't find one, did you? Something came up, and I forgot to ring you both last night to tell you.'

'Josh had a call-out at seven. I had dog club and we didn't finish until very late.' Gulley pulled at his moustache. 'You'd not have reached either of us.'

Roi was watching them, as if weighing them all up, lying quietly at Brier's feet.

'Told you something would turn up.' Gulley grinned at Josh. 'Third time lucky and I saw two magpies today.'

His voice smacked of self-satisfaction. Josh's father had sworn once that Gulley kept two tame magpies to bring him luck all the time. Sam Thornton often went to watch Gulley's dogs race. When Miracle was racing . . . that greyhound was a legend. Josh could hear his father's enthusiastic voice, even though both man and dog had been dead for some years:

'A dream of a dog, fleet-footed, flying round the race track, leaving every other dog behind him.' Miracle had been reared on Gulley's magic formula, which was now incorporated into police dog feeds. Alice provided the secret ingredient as she provided them all with her cakes.

'All our problems are over,' Josh said, feeling worry slide away from him. This dog was going to make history. They'd never had one as good before. It showed with every movement, with his instant obedience, with his watching eyes that never left Brier's face when he was lying still.

'Not all,' Brier said. She went over to the dog and praised him before leashing him. She handed the lead to Gulley.

'He may as well get used to the routine quickly,' she said. 'Josh, I need to talk.'

'Trouble?' Josh asked, instantly concerned.

'Bad trouble.'

He remembered her as a leggy schoolgirl. She had grown into a handsome woman, with good features and a wonderful skin. Brown eyes looked at him from under flaring eyebrows that were tamed to neatness.

Josh led the way indoors. Gulley took Roi's lead and led him to the kennels.

'Need to get to know one another better,' he said. The dog looked back at Brier as she climbed the three steps and vanished from his sight.

She seated herself, the light falling onto the sleek cap of blue-black hair. She glanced at Ellie's photograph. Josh, she thought, remained as faithful to his wife's memory as she did to Tom's.

'My mother's been training him for Working Trials. He's started search and he can track . . . and he has what we need. I found that out last night. And that's what started the real problem.' Josh knew Helena well. He had been a regular visitor when her husband was alive. Not so often since, as somehow life had become much busier than it had been even four years ago.

The second hand on the clock was racing round the dial. The rest of the team would be here soon, though they had to groom their dogs and walk them before the lessons started.

'I went round to Willowbank last night. The dogs were restless, especially Roi, and they had been all evening.' Brier tried to put her thoughts in order, to keep her report brief.

'Finally I decided to take him into the field, and let him run for exercise. He always comes when he's called. He raced to a stack of drainpipes and made the weirdest yapping noise you ever heard.'

Josh knew that odd sound. Not all dogs made it, only the rare animal that had a natural instinct and was worth its weight in gold.

'There was a child hiding inside the pipes, a friend of my son's. He's a forlorn youngster, spends as much time at the kennels, or with Ben, as he can. He adores the dogs, especially Roi. I've found him at home more often than I'd realised, having tea with my children.'

Josh picked up his pen. He preferred to doodle while he listened. He drew a wild rose and hastily scribbled it out and replaced it with a dog's head.

'And?' Brier seemed to be finding her story hard to tell and he sensed there was more to it than he had already heard.

'There are complications. The child was dirty and very cold and my mother suggested a bath. Simon's mother committed suicide two years ago. His father married again. When he undressed . . . he's ten, like Ben . . . his back was a mass of weals.'

'Have you reported that?'

'It was too late by the time I discovered it; and I can't get anyone until after nine this morning, can I?'

'Who was responsible? Did the child say?'

'His father. Gracie came round for dogfood, and we told him. Apparently the man drinks. He lost his job because of that and has also lost his driving licence. He's spent several nights in the cells, drunk and disorderly. He uses a buckled belt. It's not just one beating. There are old scars and they are scars.'

Brier glanced out of the window, wishing she could forget. Dark clouds banked in a threatening sky. Sparse snowflakes danced on the air.

'What did you do?'

'Took him home. Gracie went to see his parents. The father was apparently paralytic and the stepmother couldn't pack his clothes fast enough.'

'You're getting involved.'

That was a major crime.

Brier shrugged, turning her hands outwards.

'How can I help it? This isn't just any child. It's a child I know very well. I knew his mother. She wasn't exactly a friend, but I think she regarded me as one. This woman hooked her husband and Jenny committed suicide. Gassed herself in her car. The woman on Legg's Common two years ago, remember? Simon is always at our house. Kate feeds him, and Ben plays with him.'

The men were arriving. One van after another rolled into the yard. A dog barked and someone shouted a greeting. Another man laughed.

'Wonder if they rustled up a dog for our Wild Rose,' an unidentifiable voice said loudly just outside the door.

'Hope so. She's had bad luck.' That was Gwyn. The footsteps moved away.

'Did you know they called you that?' Josh asked, looking at her suddenly flushed face.

'Yes, it's an obvious one, isn't it? Josh, what do I do about Simon? I can't just keep quiet.'

'Social Services must be informed,' Josh said. 'Take it from there. If he reported it at school the Social Services would step in and put him in a safe home.'

'I want to foster him,' Brier said. 'He has his friends here; his school; he knows our family and others near him. I can't bear to think of him being taken away and put with strangers. He's terrified of his father and starts screaming hysterically if anyone suggests he goes home.'

The mere memory of the child's terror upset her.

The voice from the doorway startled them.

'Some home. The woman's no housewife and never cooks a meal for the kid. He's often banished to the greenhouse which they've fitted up as some kind of playroom, if you can call adding a stool and a table and a few games a playroom. It's got no heat. His only friend is his cat, which

I dumped on Brier last night, just by way of adding to her troubles.'

Neither had noticed John Grace's entrance.

'Well?' Brier did not want to go without an answer. Josh was her boss now, and she needed advice. 'Do you think I could foster him?'

'It sounds reasonable, if you can convince the Social Services people. You know the child. It sounds as if the poor little devil has suffered enough. Would Birdie mind? She looks after the children mostly, doesn't she?'

'She suggested it. Simon has spent so much time there or with my mother that he regards himself almost as family.'

She sighed.

'Another child will mean more responsibility, but there's something about the kid . . . I can't let him go back, and I can't bear the thought of him going to strangers who might be no better than his own folk.'

'I'll get on to the Social Services,' Gracie said. 'I'd imagine Birdie can cope if they come to see her?' Brier grinned. Kate could be formidable when roused.

'I'll be there,' he went on, 'as I saw him last night. Those marks on his back speak for themselves. We may be able to swing it.'

'Do our best,' Josh said.

The yard outside was busy with men and dogs, with chattering voices, and a sudden, rapturous bark.

'Time to work,' he added.

Within minutes they were all engrossed. Brier was aware of the covert looks each man stole at her dog.

Seven

There was more uneasiness than ever when training began. The men seemed unable to concentrate, their eyes constantly on Brier and Roi.

Josh seldom felt envy, but he felt it now. They'd not had a dog like this before. Brier was gentling him, teasing him into action, calming him when he excited, and the dog watched her with an interest that would strengthen into devotion. Helena had taught him, but he sensed that he was in a different world now, and starting a new life pattern. His eager legs almost danced as Brier put him through his paces.

Brier had forgotten everything in her joy. She had dreamed of a dog like this. He was better even than her long ago champion who had died before she could take him into the big ring at Cruft's. Helena had taught her daughter and they had vied against one another, an amiable rivalry. She had thought that she would never again find a dog like Arno.

She had been wrong and was delighted to be wrong. Roi was a miracle on four legs. He had been bred for this, born to this and, up to now, denied his birthright. Helena had shown him, but her training had been minimal. There was never enough time with a kennel full of boarders and eleven dogs of her own.

He had been taught to heel, to come, to stay. He knew how to search. As yet he was not sure what the exercise meant and was uncertain, but that would improve with practice. He had begun to learn the sendaway from the handler, which he loved.

Josh couldn't take his eyes off them. This was the team

he had longed for and never had. They would make history; a legendary pair. There had been names in the past, men and dogs who were still remembered. That white German Shepherd from Stafford, so many years ago. None of these men would remember him, but Josh had watched so often. The man's name escaped him.

Year after year he had tried to see or hear the dog's commands. The two were a unit, the dog apparently needing no telling, the man's delight in him revealed in his expression whenever the animal performed well. And he had performed superlatively.

As this dog would one day. Brier had moved into a new dimension, forgetting everything as she worked. Roi's eyes never left her face. What do you want me to do now? This, or this, or maybe that? He seldom made a mistake, although as yet he was far from perfect. That would come. This was the early part of the training.

How would any of the dogs react when put under more pressure? The time was so short. No pet owner ever trained a dog in thirteen weeks. Most of these dogs had been bred as pets.

Roi gave him hope. If the men saw how he worked, maybe they'd be inspired to put in more time, to spend their leisure dog-training, to reward him for the effort he was putting into driving them to produce steady, worthwhile animals.

Gulley, who ought to have been cleaning the kennels, was mesmerised, standing at the edge of the field, drinking in the scene. Helena Grant had drilled her daughter and taught her well. Herself a perfectionist, she had no time for those who made mistakes. Brier had resented the training at the time; now she appreciated it.

There was little that Josh could do to improve her handling skills. She was fast, swift to correct, her timing immaculate. Her praise was heartfelt and the dog responded, settling to a rhythm when heeling.

Gulley caught Josh's eyes and the two men grinned, unable to hide their pleasure. Josh stood, savouring the moment. This was as much his home as his own house. Far away, on the horizon, was a tall block of flats that stood at the edge of the town, within a hundred yards of the Force's Centre.

The poplars that edged the training paddock shivered in a small breeze. Until now training had been in any park or area where the dogs were able to work without problems with passers-by. At last they had their own venue.

It was a fifteen-minute drive from the main building where he had worked for the last few years of his life in the Force. It was bordered by farmland, and although the kennels and garages and the one-storey prefabricated offices had been there for some years, the land beyond them was recently acquired.

The two police houses were new, as yet incomplete, the builders having moved out a few weeks ago. Now plasterers and electricians were busy. One of the two would be his, and far more convenient for him. He wondered which of the men would be allocated to the other.

He collected his wandering thoughts as he realised that there was trouble ahead, the trouble he had feared but had hoped would not come to pass. Tony chided his dog, his voice sharp and angry. Jacko cowered, aware he had disappointed his handler. Everything about the animal irritated Tony. His dark, angular face showed his annoyance.

Josh had picked out the most placid of the dogs for the man, knowing that two excitable creatures together spelled disaster. Tony wanted a livelier animal. He also expected far too much of Jacko and did not realise that all dogs, even the brightest, took a considerable time to learn any exercise.

Josh glanced at the other men's faces. Gwyn looked grim, and his eyes were angry. Brier was concentrating on a small spot on the ground. The other men looked uncomfortable, aware that Tony was out of order.

Brier moved across the field, her own dog distracted, stopping to sniff the grass. She spoke to Roi, and he looked up at her. She gave him a command to heel, but there was a strong scent on the ground and he was absorbed.

Tony's irritation was replaced by a small malicious smile, as if he had seen something to the dog's, or Brier's, discredit. Pete and Rob were both watching with interest, aware that the dog was unusually clever, but unaware that Roi had a quality they were unlikely to meet again in a lifetime. Gulley, for reasons of his own, had christened them Tweedledum and Tweedledee, although they did not in the least resemble the pair in *Alice*.

Rob was a rangy man, his thick red hair greying. Pete was slighter in build, lacking the maturity that age would bring. He looked five years younger than his twenty-six years, and was often underestimated. He, Derek and Tony were all in the same age group. How different men can be, mused Gulley, his bright eyes noting everything.

Gwyn, in his late thirties, a few years younger than Rob, was stocky, dark, curly-haired, with a frequent infectious grin. He stood watching Brier, intent, admiration in his expression. His own dog, recognising his handler had forgotten him, growled at Jacko, who had come too near. Gwyn responded at once, chiding Loki, moving to a safer distance. Reluctantly, he remembered that he too was supposed to be working.

Josh realised with certainty that here at least he had a man who knew dogs, understood them and appreciated that what was in front of them was no less than a miracle. Gwyn had trained sheepdogs in the past. This was very different but the approach to the animal was the same. Loki responded well to his handler's praise and gentleness.

Every movement of her dog told Brier something about him and the way he had been taught. He was lively and eager, a tribute to her mother's skill. It was so easy to overface a dog with too much training, and sour his temperament so that he worked sullenly, instead of with verve.

'Roi. Stay.'

She wanted to send him away from her, towards the fence. It wasn't an easy exercise to teach, but Helena had said that he knew it, although as yet not well. She went over to the far side of the enclosure, the dog watching her closely. She rubbed the ground with her hand, as if she had left something there, and then returned to him.

He was off before she commanded him, bounding at top speed. That would have to be rectified. He must learn not to move until he was told. As he reached his goal she called to him to lie down. He turned and threw himself onto the ground with a tremendous air of self-importance.

Josh swallowed. He felt as if he had been given the crown jewels. His own dog, Spark, was good but Roi was brilliant. Just to have him on his team . . . He had visions of his handlers becoming the best in the country.

Brier walked back to them. She seemed to be treading on air. She hadn't realised just how good Roi was. Helena had given her a prize beyond all price.

'Will he do?' she asked Gulley who was still watching, thoughtfully rubbing his aching leg. He ought to be off, but he couldn't resist the performance.

He laughed, a joyous burst of sheer pleasure.

'You'll need padlocks on your home and your van and every kennel you put him in,' he said. 'Have us all so green with envy that we won't be able to keep our hands off him. What a dog. I've only known one like him and that was my Miracle. He won every race he ever entered. Born for it.'

He walked away and picked up his broom. A small, intense man, wearing a brown overall. He had voiced Josh's own thoughts.

'We can continue without needing to wait for Roi to catch up,' he said. 'No problem with him not keeping up. We've been lucky.'

No harm in emphasising that the credit would reflect on them all, but he knew, as he watched, that there would be problems with Derek and with Tony. He looked along the line of dogs.

Spike was bouncing, refusing to sit, and Derek was angry with him. The dog was reacting fast, picking up tension. Tony's Jacko sat, stolid, needing to be jollied out of his gloom. He hadn't yet settled to discipline. Home had been far more exciting, as he had been able to do as he chose and nobody had ever told him 'no'.

Major and Storm were improving. Both sat quietly now. Pete and Rob had patience. Pete, before he joined the police force, had worked with young offenders. Rob had learned patience as his family grew up, Josh suspected.

Loki flipped his paw at Gwyn, who bent and put it on the ground.

'Behave, boyo, or I'll swap with Brier and you won't like that. Be jealous, won't you, if I have a better dog than you?'

Josh began to worry. Was Roi going to cause more problems than ever?

The rain that had been threatening all morning lashed out of a darkened sky.

'We'll break,' he said to Gulley. 'I don't want a war.'

'I'll get Alice's walnut cake.' Gulley's lopsided grin brightened his eyes. 'Nothing like a bit of stodge to calm them down.' Alice varied her offerings and part of the day's fun was to guess what Gulley had brought in the saddle bag on his moped. He treated the men as he treated his dogs, aware of them in a way that Josh envied.

Brier shut the kennel door on her dog and looked through it at him. His morning's work had tired him. Helena had never asked so much of him. He settled in the shelter behind the run, nose on paws.

Weariness swept over her. If only they would let her keep Simon. She couldn't bear the thought of a foster home, maybe miles away, the child unable to understand what was happening to him.

It was difficult to concentrate. Her mind seemed to be in overdrive. She was afraid to let Simon become too much part of the family; there was no guarantee that he could stay or that she could manage to keep him. Nor did she want too much distraction during the rest of the course. Her whole future depended on whether or not she passed the final tests. Dog training was demanding. An extra child meant extra responsibility. Easy for the men, with their wives to shoulder the daily burdens, but even with Kate to take care of most of the chores, she still had to think and plan.

She had already discovered, practising at home, that the children's mere presence was enough to make Roi difficult to handle; he pulled towards them, asking for petting, every time they came near him.

No point in worrying. She would have to take each day at a time. She had learned that during the past two years. The morning had excited her, but she knew that she had problems ahead

She walked into the office and was at once aware that all was far from well, and that her difficulties at work had intensified.

'What is he doing here, then?' Tony was asking Josh. 'Worth a fortune, that one, isn't he, now?' He did not like his own dog, finding him stubborn and unco-operative, and he knew the dog returned his feelings in full measure. His voice was angry.

Derek came into the room, glanced at Tony and then at Brier and raised one eyebrow. He started to speak, thought better not to, and moved to his seat.

Josh motioned Brier to a chair. She sat down and took a slice of Alice's walnut cake, biting into it as if it would solve all life's problems. It was made into a sandwich, filled thickly with cream and jam. Wickedly extravagant, and if she took slices this size she'd soon be too fat to work her dog. The cream cascaded into her mouth. Good old Gulley. He at least didn't resent the fact that she was a woman.

She felt as if everyone in the room was ganged against her, wishing she were not there, jealous of her ability and her background.

Josh glanced at her before he answered, aware that she knew there had been angry words before she came in.

'He's Brier's mother's stud dog. Sterilised by a bitch that came to him. Mrs Grant has very kindly given us the dog, but on condition that he remains Brier's, and if he fails at the end he becomes a family pet. If Brier leaves the team the dog goes with her.'

There was a small silence and then Gwyn spoke, emphasising his Welsh accent, trying to make amends, aware that Brier was sitting alone, as if outcast, sure no one had a friendly feeling towards her. They'd have been better with a second woman on the team, he thought. Someone for her to chat to.

'There's a shame, now. I know Mrs Grant had high hopes for pups from that dog. Improve the temperament and the working qualities, she said. What's bad for one is good for us. A dog like Roi working with us . . .'

He smiled at Brier. 'Third time lucky. It was rough losing Kim, but maybe it was as well. If you hadn't, this fellow wouldn't be yours, would he? Do us a power of good to have a dog like that on our team. Make every other Force jealous.'

He took a second slice of cake and handed round the plate. Gwyn had lightened the atmosphere and Josh was grateful.

The rain eased to a drizzle and they returned to work. There was a new element among them. Brier's dog was the catalyst. He was at a far higher standard than any of their dogs, and the men knew it, but needed to prove themselves.

They might not want a woman among them, but, since they had her, they were not going to let her beat them.

Even Derek, whose mind was mostly on the end of the day and the girl he was taking out, made an effort, and his dog obeyed, going down on command so fast that his handler responded with a grin of pleasure and praise that was, for him, fulsome. Derek felt it silly to talk to an animal, and up to now had made no effort, but his pleasure in the dog's reaction brought a spontaneous 'Good dog' that earned him a smile from Josh.

There was a vibrant feeling in the air, a sparkle, a smartness that had been lacking, as each man tried to make his dog behave as Roi did. Up to now, Brier had not shown that she was far beyond them in skill, but today they realised it. Josh, watching his men, knew that Derek and Tony resented her. Rob and Pete seemed to find it difficult to talk to a woman as if she were part of the team, but Gwyn had found someone to whom he could talk dog, and would talk dog. At least she had one ally in the group.

At last they broke for lunch, which Gulley provided. Today Alice had filled baps with grated cheese and horseradish and crisp lettuce leaves. There were cheese and onion pasties, the pastry flaking in their mouths, and little almond tartlets that tasted of lemon.

Gulley joined them, taking the empty seat beside Brier. He added a small income to his very low wage by taking orders from the team each day. It saved all of them the need to remember, and saved their women the daily thought for imaginative fillings, and the time to prepare them. It made Alice feel good, and her efforts were always appreciated in full.

'Heard you found a child last night hiding behind the kennels,' Gulley said to Brier. Heads turned in her direction.

'Who told you?'

'Gracie. He rang to have a word, but you were busy. He's calling back.' Gulley manned the office phone when everyone else was busy. 'Gather his father is well known to us and a violent man, putting his hands on the kid as well as on anyone else who gets in his way.'

It was not a new situation to any of them.

'Penny for them. Can't be thinking about that dog of yours, not with that expression,' Gwyn said, looking at Brier.

'I was wondering about the child, and whether I'd be allowed to keep him with me. I can't bear the thought of him going into a children's home.' She didn't want to confess her worries about Roi.

'You've got him?' Rob stared at her, suddenly all policeman. 'Is that wise?'

'He's a friend of my son's. He's been almost a daily visitor for two years, spending more time with us than at home. We had no idea he was being beaten and hit. The marks didn't show and he never said anything.'

'Poor little devil. Too many like him,' Pete said. 'How would he know different? Mary made some sausage rolls. She doesn't see why Alice should have to do everything on her own. Says we're imposing. Any takers?'

Gulley took the bag and handed them round. Hours in the open air made everyone hungry.

'Alice enjoys it,' he said. 'She ought to have had a dozen kids. When ours left home she felt a need to be occupied, and she always did adore cooking. Keeps me too well fed. Doctor told me off at my last visit. If she's kept busy feeding you lot, maybe she won't fatten me up too much.' He laughed as he spoke, and rubbed the hint of a paunch.

'I hope you reported it.' Rob was still looking at Brier. He hated any laxity.

'Not much chance of getting Social Services at nine o'clock at night, is there? Gracie turned up for dogfood, while I was with my mother. He promised to report it and let me know what they said.'

She felt the wave of sympathy sweep round the room. None of them could bear the thought of a child suffering needlessly.

'You want to keep him?' Rob asked.

'I thought of it. A foster home might not understand the danger. Might let the father visit him. I don't think that would be wise. I just hope they'll at least let him stay with us for the time being. Kate's wonderful with the children.'

The ringing telephone bell startled them all. Josh reached out to answer it. Derek went outside to get his dog out of the van and put in a few extra minutes' practice before the afternoon session.

'Gracie.' Josh put the receiver down. 'Simon can stay with you until the case conference.'

Which could be weeks away. It was one worry less.

The lowering clouds were blown away by a rising wind. A small breeze compared to the gales that they had been enduring. The sun shone. Time to teach the dogs to search, Josh said.

Roi knew about searching, for Helena had already begun to teach him. He watched as Josh put down a number of items on the grass—the handle of a knife, a small key wallet, a cartridge case.

One by one the dogs were taken to search for the various articles. Each picked up the trophies and brought them, one at a time, to his handler. None of them was perfect, but it would come.

Had Helena taught Roi to search well? She sent him out. Roi knew this game. He excelled at it. He pounced on the leather and tossed it in the air and caught it. He ran with it to Brier, and threw it at her feet, and barked, wanting it thrown for him to race after and fetch. She stared at him in dismay.

'Oh my lord,' Josh said. 'We're going to make him very

confused by breaking him of that habit. He's been playing, not searching. Surely Helena didn't teach him that?'

'Ben and Simon and Dana always played with him when they visited my mother. I imagine that's how that happened,' Brier said, unhappily aware that now she had far more work than she had expected on just this one small exercise. What about the others? How much damage had the children done? How could she chide them and prevent them from playing with him?

Gulley had been watching.

He picked up every item from the ground.

'Come over here, away from the other dogs, and let's have a look at this,' he said, well aware of Brier's disappointment. 'Don't scold him. We have to teach him another game, one that he enjoys just as much, and hopefully he will forget this one.'

He threw the piece of leather to Roi, who caught it. Gulley whistled to the dog, who ran to him, and before he could toss his trophy Gulley had his hand in front of his mouth and took hold of it before it dropped. Brier worked on, all afternoon.

Roi did his best, time after time, to perform his little throw, unable to understand what he was doing wrong. Would he ever learn?

The worry stayed with her over the weekend. On the Sunday afternoon Kate took the children to Willowbank Farm. Brier took the dog for a long walk. Simon wanted to come with her, but Kate persuaded him that Helena would be upset if he didn't join them all for tea. She had baked a cake especially for him.

The sky was blue, a faint springlike colour. She walked along the edge of the canal and turned off towards a large outcrop of rock known locally as the Lump. The grass was winter-weary, tufted and clumped, yellow, with occasional green patches. Furze bushes grew everywhere, several bearing the first traces of blossom. Love is not in season when the furze is not in bloom. Tom used to say that, Brier thought, suddenly missing him unbearably. There were couples everywhere and she was alone.

Roi was enjoying himself immensely. His excitement helped to change her mood. Everything enthralled him. He sniffed the ground, which told him of rabbit and pigeon, of rat and stoat and weasel and the spillage from a bottle that a wino had enjoyed two nights before. There was frost on the bushes and frost crisping the grass.

February had continued the relentless weather of the last week in January.

The hum of traffic sang from the other side of the Lump.

She climbed over it, Roi bounding beside her, and walked down the narrow path towards the common. A small group of people clustered below her, and for a moment she feared trouble. Three youths, two girls and an elderly woman. What in the world?

She whistled to Roi and leashed him, and hurried down the path.

'Is there a problem?' she asked.

The woman looked distraught.

'I came for a walk, and fell in the long grass. I tripped over a bramble shoot,' she said. 'I don't remember exactly where. When I got to my car I found my purse had dropped out of my pocket. All my keys are in it, as well as my money and credit cards. These people have very kindly been helping me to look, but we can't find it anywhere.'

Brier looked at the trampled ground. If she asked Roi to find he'd search, but would there be any chance at all of finding the purse? Also he'd bring it to her and toss it and undo all the good she and Gulley had, hopefully, done a few days ago.

She had to try.

'Stand quite still and let's see if my dog can find it,' she said. 'He's being trained to search and he loves looking for things I've hidden for him.' That at least was true, even if he didn't indicate them the way he should.

'Do you think he might?'

'Someone may already have found it, and either taken it or handed it in,' one of the youths said.

'I don't know that anyone would walk where I fell. It's somewhere over there.' She pointed to a thick patch of spiky furze bushes. 'I saw a sparrowhawk in the sky, chasing a smaller bird, and was watching them. I wasn't looking where I was going.'

There were scratches on her face and hands.

Brier unleashed the dog.

'Find it,' she said. 'Good boy, find it.'

Roi bounded off, running through the grass and heather. Brier walked behind him, casting him wider and wider. He hunted assiduously, his busy nose seeking news. He raced towards the Lump again, and Brier slowed him, sending him off in another direction.

'I'm sure I didn't walk over there,' the woman said, her face anxious.

Roi stopped and his head went down. He looked up at Brier and nosed deep into a thick clump of straw-like grass. He surfaced, and raced towards her. She put out her hand and took his find, exulting. He hadn't tossed it and he hadn't dropped it. She was holding a worn brown leather purse, the keys attached to a ribbon-like thong by a dog clip.

'You clever lad,' she said, overcome with joy. The lesson had been well and truly learned. She couldn't believe it. She walked over to the little group, smiling happily.

'Would this be what you were looking for?'

The woman gripped Brier's hand.

'I can't thank you enough. What a wonderful dog. May I stroke him? Would he let me?'

Another voice broke in.

'Is he a police dog? You're Ben's mum, aren't you? I've

seen you with him and Dana. My kid sister's in Ben's form. He's been making them all sick by talking about your dog and how wonderful he is.' The tall boy laughed at her. 'Maybe *she* can make them all sick when I tell her about this, and how I actually watched the dog working out where the purse was hidden.'

Roi revelled in the fussing. He knew he had done something splendid and his tail waved. When the little crowd had dispersed he danced round Brier, full of a sudden remembered puppy silliness, and barked at her, telling her he didn't want to go back on his lead, that he was a big dog now and could run where he chose.

He found the scent of rabbit and flew up the hill. His refusal to come back brought Brier down to earth. There was a chill in the air and it would soon be dark. It was some minutes before he condescended to return to her.

She leashed him, reminded forcibly that it was never wise to assume the dog would do exactly as told all the time; there was a long way to go before he was ready for the tests. She turned to go home, but he almost pulled her off her feet. He stiffened suddenly, and nosed at the base of a bush. His head emerged, holding a piece of plastic drainpipe about ten inches long and eight inches in diameter. He held it in his mouth, his eyes laughing at her, his muzzle completely hidden.

She tried to take it from him and he refused, hanging onto it, tugging at it. She looked at the tube. It would make a wonderful toy. If she used it perhaps he would become more attached to it than to the bright yellow chucky stick that Simon used to play with him. A game of her own that she would play when the children were not there, a game to bond him to her, without question.

They were at the edge of the common and nobody was about. The half-light was shading to dark, but it was still possible to see. She unleashed the dog and persuaded him to release the tube. She threw it and he raced after it, sending it spinning and rolling it with his nose, playing with it, skidding it. He picked it up and brought it to her, wanting the game again.

This wasn't a search. It was a retrieve and he had to learn to fetch as well. He already knew he must bring her his dumbbell. She began to think about the game, using it to improve her control over him, making him lie down and wait until she told him he could run, telling him to sit and bark before she threw it, holding both hands above her head as if arrested.

He had no idea this was training. This was a wonderful game. At last he was panting and tired, and she leashed him. He carried his trophy home, swaggering.

There was no one to see her absurd dog with his ridiculous find. He trotted blithely beside her, his eyes alight with fun. He looked up at her, seeking approval.

'You're clever,' she told him. 'You're wonderful. You'll never know how wonderful.'

They reached home and she hid the tube under the seat of her car. Tomorrow she would have her van back. Josh was fetching her. His own was being returned to the Training Centre, with a new clutch.

She went indoors. Ginger was crying plaintively for his supper. He arched his back at the dog, and swore, but Roi made no move towards him and he relaxed, though careful to keep his distance. Like Simon, he was underfed and would repay Birdie's care in a few weeks' time. Brier scratched the cat behind his ear and was rewarded with a raucous purr which made Roi put his head on one side. It reminded him of the cats at Willowbank Farm.

He settled himself quietly after his feed. He had worked hard and he was tired. He curled himself, nose to tail. Time to relax, which did not last long as Birdie and the children came back from Willowbank, Ben talking about Tara's puppies, Dana and Simon both wanting a ginger and black kitten.

The door bell rang.

Simon, anxious to please, ran to open it and returned with a beautifully wrapped parcel.

Inside it was a little trinket box, with a tapestry top depicting a dog's head.

Brier read the embossed card.

'I can't thank you enough for finding my purse for me. This is a small token of appreciation.'

'What does she mean?' Ben asked.

'She lost her purse on the common. Roi found it. She's saying thank you.'

Birdie was examining the box.

'That must be Miss Hunt. She makes these for the export market. They cost a fortune.'

That wasn't important, Brier thought, remembering that the dog had retrieved the purse, and put it in her hand without tossing it in the air or trying to play with it. He had found more than just the purse: he had found new hope for her. She would treasure the little box as a symbol of a new purpose in her life.

She went to bed feeling happy. Sleep came fast. She never closed her bedroom door, aware always that the children might need her in the night. Kate's room was at the far end of the landing. The house was large and sprawling, built at the end of the last century for a big family with servants. It had been cheap because of its age. The rest of the estate had sprung up around it.

The dog woke her. Roi was pulling at her bedclothes, nuzzling at her arm, trying to drag her out, knowing she was needed. Startled, she sat up, listening to the wild screams that rang through the dark house. She flashed the light switch, was out of bed, the dog beside her, still tugging at her wrist. Dragging on her dressing-gown, she raced out of her room. Dana was on the landing, her small body tense with terror. She ran to Brier, and buried her head in her mother's pyjama jacket.

'Stop him, stop him, send him away. Why does he do it?' Her wails mingled with Simon's hysterical yells and Ben's sobbing voice, attempting, desperately, to soothe.

Kate appeared, pulling on her own dressing-gown, an unexpected riot of colours, and put her arms round Dana.

'Come on, lovey, let's go downstairs and make drinks for everybody. We'll have a midnight feast. Mummy will help Simon.'

Bless you, Kate, Brier thought as she went into the boys' room. Ben knelt beside Simon's bed. The child was sitting up, lashing out, flailing at the air, and Ben ducked to avoid the frantic fists.

'Go away! Go away! leave me alone, Don't hit me, don't hit me, don't hit me!' The wide eyes were wild, seeing neither of them.

'He doesn't know who we are, Mummy. I tried to wake him. I don't know if he is awake . . . he won't stop.'

'Ben, love. Go down to Kate. Let me cope with him. It'll be all right, I promise.' I hope, she thought desperately. I don't know how to deal with this.

She had her arms round Simon, who was pushing her away, his small body surprisingly strong.

'Don't touch me. Don't touch me. Don't touch me.'

She was aware that Ben had left the room, casting an anxious glance behind him. The screams continued, so that she seemed to be sharing the child's nightmare. He resisted her arms around him. He seemed incapable of hearing her voice and behaved as if he were seeing visions, not the reality of the room with Ben's tumbled bed and the train set on the big table, and the model plane that Tom had made, suspended from the ceiling.

'Simon.'

Her voice didn't penetrate his senses. He had gone beyond reason.

'Make him go away. Make him go away. He's there, by the door.' Perhaps the shadow thrown by the wardrobe did look like an enormous man.

'Roi, on the bed.'

The dog looked at her. Beds were forbidden places.

'Good dog, on the bed.'

He jumped up, and lay down against the child, pushing his body hard against the small, tense figure, reaching up to lick the tears away from the contorted face. Slowly, the screams quietened, and gave way to noisy sobbing, and Simon hugged the dog as if he could bring back sanity. Brier, almost in tears herself, gathered the boy in her arms and murmured to him, as though he were still a tiny child. He gripped Roi's fur like a talisman that would prevent harm coming to him.

'There, there,' she whispered, over and over again. 'It's all right. You're safe. You're with Ben and Dana, and Roi's beside you. Roi won't let anyone come near you except us, and we'd never hurt you.'

'He was here, in the room, standing over me with the belt. He was shouting at me. I saw him,' Simon said, as his sobs subsided. She didn't need to be told who he thought had been there.

'You were dreaming, my love, it was a nightmare. It wasn't real. Look, let's go and check all the downstairs doors and windows. No one can get in, no one at all. Roi would have barked and he didn't bark, now, did he?'

Simon shook his head.

'Now, dressing-gown on and let's wash your face, and we'll go round the house and then we'll go into the kitchen. Kate's making a midnight feast. I bet you've never had one of those, have you?'

He stood patiently while she sponged him, clutching at her with one hand while the other clung to the dog.

'Can Roi sleep on my bed?'

'He can tonight.' It would do no real harm, she hoped.

It might prevent another nightmare. The child would be afraid to sleep lest it happen again.

'Look.' She checked the bolts on the front and back doors, and took him round all the windows, letting him see for himself that the house was secure. 'Not even the tiniest garden gnome could get in!'

He gave her a watery smile and followed her into the kitchen. It was bright and alive, the kettle coming to the boil, a plate of cakes on the table, and Kate jollying the other children, so that Ben was laughing and even Dana was smiling.

'Birdie and her sister used to creep down to the kitchen and make midnight feasts, when no one knew,' Ben said. 'They didn't have fridges then and the meat and milk went bad.' He spoke with awe as if Kate had lived long ago in the cave era.

'Don't you go getting ideas,' Brier said, but there was laughter in her voice.

'We lived in a big old house,' Kate said, making cocoa for the children and deciding on camomile tea for herself and Brier. 'My sister and I slept up in the attic in a tiny room right under the roof. There were back stairs and we crept down those, and into the big old kitchen. The meat and the milk and all the cake tins were kept in the cellar, which was very cold, so it was spooky to go down there for what we wanted.'

Simon was listening, relaxing, though there was still an occasional uncontrollable sob. He was as close to Brier as he could sit, with Roi leaning against him. He took one of the little rock buns when Kate passed him the plate and looked at it as if unable to decide what to do with it.

'It was scary too because we didn't have electric light. Nothing we could switch on. We had candles and weren't supposed to walk round the house with them, in case of fire. The draughts blew them out and we had to light them again.'

'You're making it up,' Ben said. 'You aren't that old.'

'No, but that house was when we were small. It was an old farmhouse right in the middle of nowhere, and it was too far for the electricity to be brought to us. And too expensive. We didn't have that until I was about fourteen years old. We had coal fires. Those were wonderful, with bright flames and fascinating shadows.'

'I don't like shadows,' Simon said. 'Things hide in them.'

'I don't like shadows either.' Dana for once was in agreement.

'There are friendly shadows,' Kate said briskly. 'Let me tell you the grace my grannie used to say when the oil lamps were lit. The grace for light. It's lovely. I still think of it every time I flick a switch. Those early years are never forgotten.'

Brier hoped that Simon wouldn't take the words personally. Kate, she knew, from her expression, wished them unsaid. Life was not going to be easy with this little addition to the family. There were so many unseen pitfalls. Just as well dogs can't interpret words, she thought with a wry smile.

Kate was giving the child time to relax, to forget his dreams if that were possible. No use sending him back to bed immediately. It might start all over again. They'd all be tired next morning, but there was no choice.

'It's a poem my grandmother used to read,' Kate said. 'By a lady called Moira O'Neill. I always felt she must have known our house, though the house she wrote about was a quare wee house, and ours was a quare big house.'

'What's "quare"?' Dana asked.

'Queer. It was written the way they talk in Ireland.'

Brier was watching the children's faces. Sleep would come easily now, she thought. They were all relaxed, listening, and Simon yawned. Kate's voice was soft, a beautiful voice that almost sang the words, triggering the dog to put his head on one side and then the other, intent, as if he longed to understand this human speech and make sense of it. Or perhaps there might be a command for him hidden among the unintelligible sentences. Simon watched the dog, adoration in his eyes.

'The poem tells of their little house by Brabla burn, with hares scooting and grouse in the heather, and no room for any of them to turn. Their home was so tiny and there were so many children.'

'How many?' Dana asked.

'I expect there'd be ten or more. They had big families in those days,' Kate said. 'When the youngest two had been put to bed, the rest of them sat wherever there was room and then, the poem says:

"Herself 'ud take the rush-dip an' light it for us all
An' '*God be thanked!*' she'd say—'*now, we have a light.*'"

When she'd said that the children would stop laughing and playing and pushing and sit quiet while their father took over from their mother. It goes on:

"Himself 'ud put his pipe down, an' say the good word more,
'*May the Lamb o' God lead us all to the Light o' Heaven.*'"

'It ends by saying that many things have had their day and the nine glens of Antrim can show you many a sight, "but not the quare wee house where we lived up Brabla way, nor a child in all the nine Glens that knows the Grace for Light".'

By now, not only Simon, but Ben and Dana were yawning. Simon got up from his chair and went over to Kate and kissed her. The unexpected action caused her to blink away tears.

'I'd like to know all the poem,' he said. 'It's lovely. If God hadn't made light, everywhere would be frightening all the time.'

There was a tiny bulb in a drawer in one of the chests,

left over from baby days. Brier remembered it and fastened it into the lamp by Simon's bed. It gave a dim, comforting glow, lighting up the room just enough to see, banishing terror, and showing the dog, curled up on the bed.

Simon smiled up at Brier sleepily as she kissed the boys goodnight.

'Sleep well,' she said.

His small clear voice followed her as she went back to her own room.

'I can think about Birdie's poem. It's lovely. I'd like to hear it all tomorrow. We know the grace for light, even if the children in the nine glens don't. "May the Lamb o' God lead us all to the Light o' Heaven." I'll think of that if I have bad dreams again.'

Sleep evaded Brier for a long time. She realised that a far greater task lay ahead than she had imagined.

Eight

Nine weeks to test day.

Gulley went back that night to an empty house, except for Bess, his six-year-old Jack Russell, the last member of a long line of such terriers. Alice's sister had just come out of hospital after an operation and she had gone to look after her for a few days. Up to him to make the sandwiches, he thought.

The note on the table told him to look in the deep freeze. Pies and pasties and packs of food made up for him and labelled with each day. His own food in a separate compartment. She must have been baking for weeks, he thought, with a stab of compunction. Did she feel she neglected him?

She had taken her three Tibetan Terriers with her. The house seemed unnaturally quiet and Bess was forlorn, missing her playmates.

So much of his life was still at work, in his little office, among the men, or outside with the dogs. He had never lost his hunger for the old days, when men envied him for his greyhounds, and he still visited old friends, savouring the yell and roar of the crowd. Miracle had died six years ago, at the age of seventeen, as well loved in his retirement as he had been when he was racing. No more greyhounds. The end of an era.

Gulley had been born among greyhounds, bred among them, his mother and grandmother as fanatical as their husbands. Even after he joined the police force, he had spent all his leisure among the hounds. His magic potion was his grandmother's recipe, prepared now by Alice. He missed the pups. He had spent so much time watching them, picking out the best, making sure that they knew the world well before they were eight weeks old.

He had never met another dog like Miracle until Brier brought Roi to him. The dog had much to learn and was yet uncouth, just coming out of the hooligan adolescent stage, which bedevilled every dog.

There was no mistaking his quality. Another fantastic dog in his lifetime. He would treasure every moment that Roi spent in the kennels. Gulley's judgement was invaluable. He had a sure instinct and could tell within moments whether a dog was sound or not, whether it was sensible or nervy, whether it would be an asset or a dog that had to be abandoned because of lack of courage.

He watched each dog, able to guess at its past, knowing how it responded to its handler. He watched the men, knowing them better than Josh knew them, seeing them off duty, hearing them when the boss wasn't present. They often forgot that Gulley had ears and eyes. He was background and few of the men realised how great was his expertise.

He heard the remarks they would never have made if they had realised he was listening. Legend had it that Gulley was deaf. It was useful, at times, to pretend. He learned more that way.

'There's a problem with our Wild Rose's dog that she's not telling us,' he said to Josh at one of their early morning sessions, towards the end of the fifth week. Roi had been part of the team for six working days. February was halfway through, but there was a chill in the air and snow was forecast. When the sun shone, spring seemed a moment away, but today was overcast and the wind blew from the north.

'How do you know?'

'Sixth sense. She's not enjoying him as she should. The euphoria's worn off too fast, and there's something wrong. Need to find out now or it could build up to bad problems.

When Roi chooses to work he's really something. But there's times when he switches off and plays the fool, much too puppy-like.'

'Goes for all of them,' Josh said. 'They're young dogs. Can't expect them to behave like adults all the time. They're coming.'

Too slowly, he thought, but didn't say it. Nobody had yet developed the enthusiasm he needed and even Brier was disappointing him.

He frowned.

'Brier's distracted. She's worried about Simon. I gather his father's been making waves. He'll lose the family allowance for one thing. Also they've delayed the case conference until after the tests. Do you think that's the problem? Boy not settling in with her own children and the father trying to get him back?'

Gulley looked out at the yard and compound. A small van had drawn up in front of the new houses. Spark was barking. Lim left his companion to guard. Gulley shrugged.

'I'm guessing. I just know that there isn't the rapport I expected between the two of them. I expected her to be so thrilled with him that she took fire. He's a marvellous dog and she's a brilliant handler, but she's missing on two cylinders. Think I should have a word? A Gulley special?'

'Leave it. It isn't a real problem yet. He's still streets ahead of the other dogs. Never wise to interfere too soon.'

They had developed a shorthand between them, each able to interpret the other's thoughts. Not for the first time, Josh wished that Gulley were thirty years younger and on his team.

'We need something to make them pull together,' he said. 'Do they take it out on Brier? All of them know that dog has something special in his make-up.'

'Can't protect her. She's been in the Force long enough to have come up against prejudice before. Still a lot of men who resent women in the job. Not to worry. Our Wild Rose has thorns and can use them.' Gulley had known Brier all her life and regarded her as a devoted uncle would regard a favourite niece.

Tony Spence drove his van into the yard and stopped, tyres squealing. He had had a difficult evening, the day before, as his wife, in the last weeks of her pregnancy, was terrified that they would lose this baby too. Nothing he said could comfort her. He was emotionally drained and overwrought.

Josh swallowed his second cup of coffee fast and regretted it, as his tongue burned.

Tony erupted into the room.

'Now what?' Josh said.

Tony exploded.

'I'm not happy with Jacko,' he said. 'I'd like to change. Take Roi on. He needs a man to handle him.'

Josh felt a sudden stir of anger.

'I'll be the judge of that,' he said. 'Roi came to us on condition that he belonged to Brier and leaves if she changes her mind about him. I told you that. If you can't cope with your dog maybe you should be considering leaving the team.'

Tony glared and left the room, walking out into the busy morning as, one by one, the vans parked and the dogs came out for grooming and exercise.

The day began badly and got worse as time went on. Everyone was irritable. The cold wind needled and there was sleet in the air. Tony was on edge and his movements were rough. Josh watched him, his mouth grim.

The dogs responded by behaving idiotically. Roi in particular reminded Josh of a stud dog trying to work with a bitch in a nearby kennel, but surely that couldn't be the reason for his behaviour. Though the scent could carry for miles on the wind.

Brier was heavy-eyed, blue shadows marring her cheeks. She looked as if she rarely slept at night. Derek was snappy after a disastrous evening with his girlfriend, Sue, which had ended in recriminations and tears on Sue's part. He wouldn't see her again. His thoughts drifted away from his dog, who promptly began to play up.

Brier kept mistiming her commands. Roi was becoming more attached to Simon instead of less, and at home had little time for Brier at all. Simon, bedevilled by nightmares, was interrupting everyone's sleep and the only way to calm him was to let Roi soothe him. The dog now slept on the landing.

Ben was bothered and Dana resentful, begging her mother to send Simon home. The screams in the night frightened her and it took all Brier's and Kate's energies to persuade her to go to school with the boys.

Watching Brier, Josh became more and more worried. He had expected so much from her and from Roi and felt betrayed. It was hard to hide his feelings.

Loki, Gwyn Williams' dog, upset by the atmosphere, decided that today he would clown and make everyone laugh. Instead of lying quietly, he rolled on his back and bicycled his legs in the air. Reprimanded, he sucked his front paw and looked at Gwyn, daring him to scold. Gwyn, starting a cold, was in no mood for laughter. He chided the dog and Loki cringed, unused to a sharp voice.

Gwyn stared at his dog, dismayed.

'Tells us something about his past,' Josh said, stopping the class. Everyone would be better for a rest, and perhaps the dogs, after being kennelled for an hour or so, would be pleased to work instead of fooling.

'He's been yelled at and maybe hit. We'll need to be careful not to trigger memories or we'll go nowhere.'

Rob Jacobs, his attention drifting, had not noticed that his dog, Storm, was curling a lip at Pete Harlow's Major. A moment later both dogs barked and lunged towards one another. Four weeks ago there would have been trouble, but both men were learning well and reacted fast.

Josh made a mental note of good marks for them.

'That's it.' He saw no point in continuing. That would do more harm than good.

Gulley was watching, a frown on his face. A sudden thought hit him. Fifth week regression. Every dog in the world behaved as if he had been taught nothing five weeks after starting any exercise. No one quite knew why, though some said it was when lessons went from short-term memory into long-term memory.

The brain was overloaded, and nature took a hand and switched it off. It happened with humans, too. A sudden lapse, an inability to remember how to turn the wheel to reverse when learning to drive, well-known lines forgotten by actors who thought themselves word perfect.

They saw it every time, and always forgot. Five dogs were now nearing the end of their fifth week, and their mood would rub off on Roi. Dogs were always sensitive to atmosphere: one handler or one dog, in a bad mood, could destroy the concentration of a whole class. Gulley did not know that Roi was disturbed by the atmosphere in his new home as well.

'Early break?' he asked.

Josh nodded.

'Fifth week. Remember?' Gulley asked, and a sudden light came into the sergeant's eyes. Daft. He always needed reminding. He'd tell them, and maybe they'd all feel better about their dogs.

A car streaked into the parking area in front of the offices.

'We have a visitor. An extra cup.' No one needed to tell them who drove like that.

John Grace uncoiled himself from behind the steering wheel. He always moved fast but today he seemed possessed by a demon.

'Well timed,' Josh said. 'Coffee's due.'

The dogs were kennelled during the breaks instead of being put in the vans. They had more space, and room to run. Spark and Lim spent most of their non-working time there. They were Gulley's joy as he groomed and fed and exercised them. Bess followed him around and slept in a bed in his office, her eyes watching him as he worked, her small body greeting him with ecstasy every time he returned to her after his trips outside.

'Bess is getting fat,' Rob said, as the little Jack Russell trotted after her master.

'Spoils her.' His unruly dog had made Pete surly.

Brier shut the door on Roi. She felt miserable, because she was glad to be able to walk away from him. The whole morning had been a struggle.

Derek was brooding over his lost girlfriend and absent-mindedly let Spike pass too close to Storm. He was the biggest of the dogs, a spectacular animal, almost all black, where the rest were black and gold. He was a dog that stood no nonsense from other animals and had already been upset by his encounter with Major.

Spike, tough and wily, had been allowed to run wild by his original owners and had learnt to stand up for himself. He was quick to react. His tendency to fight had to be watched and would have to be cured, or he would be useless.

Rob had started the day with a quarrel with his elder daughter who had come home at midnight, having promised to be home by ten. He was unable to switch off his fear that Penny would fall into bad company, and Storm's perversity caught him unawares. As the dog lunged and roared, Brier, who was close to him, jumped backwards, out of the way, slipping as she did so. Gulley gripped her arm and steadied her before moving fast, ready to intervene.

Josh, always alert, reacted swiftly. Both men tried to pull their dogs off one another, but Spike, seizing his opportunity, gripped Storm by the leg and held on. Storm, infuriated, snapped, but missed. He caught Rob's hand as his handler reached for his collar.

It was over in seconds. They had all learned a lesson, but at too high a cost. One man and one dog would be out of action for several days.

Gulley put Storm in his van, to take him to the vet. Pete took Rob off to the hospital after Josh had inspected the bite.

'Could have been a lot worse. A couple of stitches. You'll be sore for days. Next time, keep plenty of space between those two dogs. It's early days yet, and nobody taught either of them to behave before we got them.'

He watched his invalids drive off. The sullen sky added soft flakes of wet snow to the day's high wind and scudding cloud.

Gwyn finished preparing the coffee and brought in the tray.

'Have you news about Simon?' Brier asked, as Gracie came into the room. He had been watching the fracas, careful to keep out of the way.

'His father's being awkward. Came in demanding to see me. Wants the boy home. Says it's his right and that he's not responsible for the beatings. That we've made it all up, and even the doctor is in league with us.'

Everyone in the room stared at him, wondering at the anger in his voice. Gracie was a placid man, rarely showing his feelings. He did not mention that the man had accused John himself of being responsible for the beating and the bruises:

'Police brutality. What had the poor little beggar done? Caught him with his fingers in some lying shopkeeper's till?'

The accusations had raged on, turning to obscenity.

He paused to drink, looking thoughtfully at the German Shepherd head on the thick china mug. Gulley had spent months collecting them, and presented them two Christmasses ago. Each man had his own as each mug differed slightly. Gracie's was labelled 'Rob'.

John Grace had listened in disbelief, knowing the man was drunk and lashing out blindly because he felt the world had treated him badly.

'I'll be waiting for him at school and find out where you're hiding him,' he had said. 'This is his home and where he belongs and no one has any right to take him away from me. He's my son.'

Gracie was thankful that the man had no idea where the child was now living, or where he had spent his time before the night when he had run away.

'I'll get him and he'll pay.'

Gracie heard the words again in his memory and his voice sharpened as he relived the anger he had had to hide.

'You'll end in gaol if you touch the child again,' he'd said, but doubted if the warning was sufficient deterrent.

A family man, with a noisy house spilling over with children, dogs, cats, and various small animals, he could not understand a father like this.

'I hope there's some of Alice's goodies here,' he said, wanting to lighten the atmosphere. 'Only came for a taste of her walnut cake.'

Gulley hadn't put the tin out. Gwyn fetched it from the little office.

'Hope it's for us and not his dinner,' he said, revealing layers of tiny bakewell tarts. Josh, watching them, thought how like children they all were, descending on the cake tin like wasps round a honey pot. Gracie rescued the tin and passed it to Brier and then Josh, before it was completely empty.

'And?' Gwyn prompted the CID man, reverting to their earlier conversation.

'That's all about that. But we've more problems than we can deal with. We had every handler out last night. Not nearly enough dogs. We'd have had at least three more arrests if another dog had been available. We count on you lot. I know the difference a good dog can make. Six more of you; the dogs have senses we don't have.'

Gracie looked round at the tense faces. They needed encouragement today: nobody was happy. He had sensed the mood as he sat among them, and glanced at Brier, worrying. He knew about young Simon's nightmares, and he also knew that when the children were there the dog had little time for Brier at all.

Hopefully time would cure that, but time was not on her side and he was painfully aware that if she failed to pass at the end of the course and the dog was discarded, it would devastate her. Meg, his wife, calling round one evening, had found Brier almost in tears, exhausted by broken nights and worrying about the children as well as the dog.

He drank again and then grinned.

'Let me tell you a silly story. Only don't let on how silly it is, because it's convinced even the blokes who think dogs are no good that they can be something special.' He looked at Josh. 'Not holding you up?'

Josh looked at the falling snow that was beginning to lie on the ground.

'In this? I was going to talk to them anyway. If you've something to add that's useful . . .'

'I rang Tiger last night.'

Tiger Thomas was one of the older dog handlers, due soon to retire. He was a riproaring man with a flair for practical jokes that were never malicious. His name was a legend. In spite of his size and his ability to bellow he was remarkably gentle with his dog, which had twice been Police Dog of the Year.

Gracie's voice lightened and there was amusement in his eyes.

'You know what a steady dog Inky is.'

Inky was short for Inkermann, named in desperation by a breeder who had bred her ninth litter and used alphabet letters for each one. 'I' proved difficult. She had Iceberg and Indra and Ironside as names for some of the other pups.

Inky had been sold to an elderly woman who soon found her tiny adorable pup had matured into a hooligan who respected no one. Tiger had changed him into a very good dog indeed.

'Tiger was patrolling when he came to traffic lights. An elderly bloke sat there, quite well dressed, conventional-looking type. He was waiting for the green, riding a moped.'

Gwyn glanced at Josh, wondering what on earth this had to do with dog training.

'The lights changed, the rider put his foot down and the moped backfired. Gunshot! The one time a police dog can attack without a command, and Inky did. Leaped out and knocked the old boy to the ground.'

His hearers were fascinated. If it could happen to Tiger . . .

'Imagine it. Saturday afternoon. Everyone shopping and there's this police dog knocking an innocent man to the ground, standing over him, barking at the top of his voice. Tiger rushed to the man to help him up, praying hard that he wouldn't be sued.'

By now they were listening eagerly to every word. They might need to know how to deal with such a case in the future. No dog could tell the difference between a car backfire and a gunshot.

'Tiger was just about to apologise and explain when the man stood up, his face awed.

'"It's a fair cop, Guv," he said, "but it beats me how your dog knew."'

Gracie grinned.

'The moped rider had just done one of the local jewellers. His pockets were stuffed with rings and bracelets and other valuable trinkets. He went along as quiet as a boy being sent for by the Head, and Tiger and Inky and his catch arrived at the station just before the raid was reported.'

He looked round at them.

'No bets as to whether Tiger told them about the back-fire. He let everyone think the dog had a sixth sense that told him this was a villain. He and his dog are heroes . . . they'll have Inky telling fortunes next.'

He went off, feeling better himself. His story had done everyone good. By lunchtime the snow had stopped. The wind blew the clouds away and a faint sun warmed the air, thawing the ground.

That afternoon there was an urgency among the dog handlers that had not been there before. These dogs needed to be trained, and trained fast. Gracie's story had reminded them there was purpose in their job, had brought an atmosphere of lightness that had been lacking, had given them all a laugh.

* * *

The days sped by. Gulley reported that all of them were now out with the dogs in every spare moment, practising, commanding, turning from greenhorns into men with experience. March brought warmer days, driving rain and wind several times during the first two weeks.

Josh, watching them during the eighth week, worried about them now as people. Brier was losing weight and still not enjoying her dog as she should, though he could not fault Roi's progress or his handling. Nor could he understand what was wrong. Surely the extra child wasn't causing her too many problems. She was not there to deal with him on a daily basis. Or was he not sleeping at night, and needing comfort?

He didn't like to ask. If he was told he would listen, but he respected privacy.

Tony, resenting Brier's progress with her dog, teased her, with a certain amount of malice.

'Got the best dog of the lot of us, through your Ma. Not fair, that. Women aren't strong enough to handle these big dogs.'

'I can handle any dog. Anyway, who said life was fair?' Brier asked, stung by his constant needling. 'It wasn't fair that my husband should be gunned down on duty while a useless creature like you gets away untouched. He'd make ten of you. How many of you even remember him?'

'You asked for that,' Rob Jacobs said, as Brier walked away, her colour high. 'Leave her alone, or you'll have me to reckon with, and Gwyn and Pete too. She's had a raw deal, and deserves anything good out of life she can get. Tom was a great guy and she hasn't got over him by a long chalk. Probably never will.'

Tony, his own worries overwhelming him, was dismayed. Brier's sharp words had touched a nerve.

The conversation had taken place outside Gulley's office and he heard every word. Later that day he waylaid Tony himself.

'I heard you talking to Brier,' he said. 'I heard Rob. You'll have me to reckon with too, if there's any more of it. Leave her alone. What's wrong with you? Too macho to accept a woman can be a darn sight better handler than you? If that's so, it's time you thought again. I'd call it sexual discrimination and there's rules against that, if not laws.'

That hurt even more. He hadn't meant to be so ungenerous, but Sheila was frantic with worry and he couldn't console her. He longed to confide in Gulley or Josh but found it difficult to speak about his own personal fears.

Everyone seemed to have problems. Rob had more worries of his own. His daughter had a new boyfriend and his wife disapproved.

'Long green hair, leather jeans and one ear-ring,' she said. 'Chews gum and talks out of the side of his mouth. It may only be a silly act, but there's something about the boy I can't stand. Penny's besotted.'

No use saying anything. She'd only become more devoted. She was as prickly as a cactus and home life was anything but pleasant. The dog was a companion and a solace. It was a relief to be out with him and away from the bickering. He spent more of his leisure time training, and that upset his wife too. He looked forward to the children leaving home and peace descending again. Just the two of them and time to talk without frequent interruptions and teenage tantrums.

Derek thought about Penny. She was a pretty girl, but maybe a bit young for him, and he doubted if Rob would welcome him any more than he did the present young man in her life. She had wonderful legs.

The days went by. Good days, bad days, cold days, windy days. Wet days. They all began to listen obsessively to the weather forecasts as if listening might influence the climate. It never did.

Pete enlivened them with reports of his small son's progress. The baby smiled and then cut a tooth. A whole night's sleep was a triumph, to be reported with pleasure. Brier, thinking of her own broken nights, with the nightmares more frequent as Simon began to be afraid his father would succeed in getting him home again, felt a perverse envy.

A baby was easily soothed. Simon clung to her and would not let her go, and even when he had fallen asleep she lay awake, waiting for another burst of screaming. Ben and Dana had to be comforted too, as the screams frightened them. Even Birdie was showing signs of stress. Loss of sleep, combined with her desperate anxiety about the boy, was wearing Brier down.

The dogs were learning to search for hidden clues. Loki

was best at this, which pleased Gwyn, as Roi was the star most of the time. Roi was still apt to toss small objects, especially if they were metal. Brier was unaware that Dana, intrigued because the dog responded to her, carried an old-fashioned key in her pocket and hid it for the dog to bring to her, laughing when he tossed it, or dropped it and played with it.

Dana played the game daily, but only when Brier was out of sight. The dog revelled in it: Dana's game was much more fun. She knew it was wrong and made sure that the boys did not see her.

In the ninth week of the course Josh took them tracking. It was mid-March and there had been a number of warm days. There were catkins on the willows, celandines and the first primroses in the hedgerows, and the branches were misty with the soft green of swelling buds.

The distant hills were smoky blue and the sky echoed the colour. A local farmer had offered them the use of his fields. They would be cow-fouled, but the confusion of intriguing scents would provide good experience. What police dog could always track on clean ground?

Brier was the first to work. Josh walked to the brow of the hill, laying food on the trail for the dogs to find, as this was the first time they had trained on anything but a field where stock had never grazed. It was not a standard method but the Germans used it with great success when they prepared the dogs for their own competitions, to gain the title of *Schutzhund*, a qualification needed by all their breeding German Shepherds. Any that failed to pass, especially where temperament was concerned, were not allowed to breed.

Josh's motto was that if it works and isn't cruel, use it. There was no one way of training any dog. His team was learning at last that each required slightly different handling techniques.

Loki cringed at a shout. Jacko, reprimanded, produced

every trick he knew to try to put Tony in a better humour. He might have succeeded with one of the other men, but not with Tony who only grew more annoyed by his antics.

Storm needed a very sharp voice. Spike responded to signals better than to words, while Roi could be handled without words at all, watching every movement of Brier's body and matching his actions to hers. Major was the gentlest of all the dogs, and easily became anxious, though Pete was inspiring him with confidence. He might be the one that failed the test of courage, which would be a pity as he did everything else well.

Josh made notes nightly, and agonised. He couldn't afford to lose a single team member.

He thought about the dogs as he walked the first track. They must always be successful and today there would be many distractions. The old droppings were leather-hard, but would still hold scent.

There was the trace of birds and memory of unseen animals on any field, Josh thought, as he passed a bush and heard a rustle and a soft hiss, which he ignored.

Some small creature sheltering there. A hedgehog, maybe. It wouldn't come out while there were folk about. It would be safe enough. It was a good day, with very little wind. The promise of warmth to come had lightened everyone's mood and the men were joking and laughing, telling Brier that there was a bull hidden at the top of the field that she'd meet face to face.

Roi loved tracking and was dancing with impatience. The other dogs were as eager. The men grinned as they battled to quieten them and make them sit. It wasn't as bad as the practice chases when the waiting dogs screamed with excitement, impatient for their turn.

Brier had seen the line of the track up to the hill brow, but had no idea where it went after that. It was entirely up to her dog. She had to trust him. He was on his own.

He started well, his nose down, pulling on the line. Roi

was lost in his own world, and nothing else mattered. He recognised the trail on the ground where Josh had walked, but there were other scents to attract him and discard. A weasel had run across the path. There pheasants had grazed, flattening the grass, leaving their mementoes. He nosed a feather. Wrong smell. Back he went, knowing why he was there, knowing that there would be a reward for him when he reached his goal.

His body tensed, every muscle outlined. He sniffed deep into the grass, ignoring the food that was put for him. He recognised it, but that was not why he was hunting. He knew that at the end of this trail there would be his tube, the sight of which always made the men chuckle. It was a wonderful toy, an obsession, and the thought of it waiting and the game that would be his reward led him on.

Brier followed, excitement drowning her worries.

She had never had a dog that gave himself so totally to his work—just so long as the children were nowhere near. She didn't want to break that bond, but Roi had to learn to work with her, even if Simon were present. Of the three, he had the most rapport with the dog, but Dana ran him a close second. Roi adored playing with any of the children.

For the moment there were just the two of them, the empty field and the sun gilding the grass.

Dreams do come true, she thought. Her mother had trained him well. She had no need to guide him. He was master, leading her. Exultation lightened her step and she grinned at the sky, unable to hide her pleasure and glad there was no one to see.

She knew that Josh, following quietly some yards behind her, would be as delighted as she. She wished that Gulley were with them. He'd love to see this.

One day, this would be for real as they followed the trail of a crook. One day they would bring wrongdoers to justice. One day they would prove themselves.

Brier was determined that she and Roi would be top of

the list when they passed out at the end of the course. And pass out they would. Simon wouldn't be there to distract him by day: surely she could overcome that attachment to the child in the next few weeks.

Roi was working, his head down, his body intent, his tail moving very gently from side to side. All the men were watching now, knowing that this dog could make theirs look like amateurs. They wanted to learn. Roi moved confidently, smelling every blade of grass, knowing where the footsteps led.

Up the hill, one hundred yards, and then a sharp turn. The dog lost the scent, having overshot the bend, and came back towards Brier. She stopped, knowing Roi needed to work out the new direction. She paid out the long tracking line and glanced behind her at Josh.

She received a thumbs up sign.

He was away again, faster, his head down, pulling hard. All eyes were intent on the dog. They would have their turns soon.

Up to the bush. Again a soft hiss. Roi paused, curious, and sniffed the air. He turned off the track and put his nose into the long grass that masked its base.

The goose who had made her nest there had five goslings and they needed to be protected at all costs. An infuriated white demon, with stabbing beak and thrusting, outstretched wings, she drove out of cover, intent on attacking the dog.

Roi had never met a goose before and had never seen such a large or angry bird. He turned downhill, racing towards the gate, towards the safety of the lane, unaware that geese could fly. Brier, after one appalled look, followed him. If the goose caught them and attacked them they would both be in serious trouble.

An enraged gander was a better sentinel than any dog, and likely to do quite as much damage. Any mother with babies would defend them to the death.

Her breath catching in her throat, a stitch in her side, Brier sped downhill so fast she was sure she would fall. Behind her came the raging bird, wings extended, half-running, half-flying.

They would never reach safety in time.

Nine

A yell of laughter burst from the watching men; a moment later they realised it was far from funny. There was a hasty evacuation as they charged towards the lane. Gwyn, quicker than the rest, realised Brier was at risk and had the gate open and his van driven into the field, with his passenger door ajar, as she and Roi sped towards them. In at the open door, woman and dog spilling all over him as he slammed the door shut. Josh thought it the quickest piece of action he had ever seen.

Brier sat, with Roi lying on top of her, trying to get her breath. The enraged goose hit the van and backed off, shaking her head.

Brier untangled herself from the line, quivering, as Gwyn, laughing, accelerated through the gate. Two of the men slammed it shut, hoping the goose wouldn't fly at them.

She stood, neck outstretched, challenging them, and then stormed back up the hill to protect her nestlings.

Brier almost fell out of the van onto the verge.

'Nearly got goosed,' Tony said, with a broad grin. He roared with laughter at his own joke.

'Never know what's lurking,' Gwyn said. 'Never did like geese. My da used to keep them. Only thing is they're a bit stupid, see? Never occurred to her she could fly over that gate. Suppose she was wanting to get back to her babies.'

His Welsh lilt was more than usually pronounced in his excitement.

'You OK, then, Brier?'

'I had the fright of my life,' she said. 'What would she have done if she had caught me?'

'Doubt if she knew what she'd do either,' Gwyn said. 'Bitten, like. And thrashed you with her wings. Saw a heron do that once. I was fishing, see? And the babies were at the sea's edge glutting as the mackerel were shoaling and all the little fish coming in to safety.'

He grinned at the memory.

'The parents called them and they wouldn't come, so the big birds came and beat them with their beaks and wings. Really funny to see them, just like angry humans. The babies flew off after that, leaving behind a pile of dead fish they couldn't even eat.' He laughed. 'Reckon they had tummy ache next day.'

'Nothing like fishing,' Derek said unexpectedly. 'By yourself, though. Just yourself and the river talking, and the fish waiting to bite.' His thoughts went wistfully to a running river, the mayfly on the water, and the sudden kicking thrill as his rod dipped and he had a lusty trout on the line. He had not been fishing since his father died. He missed the old man.

Brier's mind was still on her dog. She frowned. 'Is this going to set Roi back? Sure there's a goose under every bush waiting to chase him?'

It could be a major problem. The dog might refuse to track at all next time.

'His tube,' she said suddenly, remembering his plaything. 'We never reached it.'

'I'll get it for you. I'll go in from the top of the field,' Josh said. 'No desire to be goosed myself.'

Every dog had his own toy. Spike treasured the arm of a rubber doll that he had found when running free on the common. Major walked around with an outsize cartridge case in his mouth. Loki had a stuffed felt tortoise, stolen from the child next door, who had hated it. Every dog needed a major incentive to learn to track; there had to be a reward. As yet, Jacko and Storm were only interested in finding sausages. Neither dog had ever been taught to play.

Roi played endlessly when they were at home, much of the time with Simon who threw the yellow stick for him to bring back, over and over again. It exercised the dog and it occupied the child, although Brier wondered if she ought to stop it. She hadn't the heart, but whenever she could find an extra moment she spent it in the compound with Roi on her own, throwing his tube for him, urging him to be as devoted to her as he was to Simon, trying to win his affection and his respect. The dog loved all the children, but by now it was obvious he and Simon had a special relationship.

If she were not careful he would be Simon's dog and she would have no dog again. Those tests were crucial. She began to wish they were much farther away. She would never achieve the rapport she needed in time, and that would show when it came to the critical stage. He would let her down; she would let Josh down and also the team, though she suspected the men would not be sorry if she did worse than any of them.

They sat on the low wall, eating sandwiches, to give Brier time to recover. The dogs lay by their feet, watching for dropped crumbs. Loki, faster than Gwyn, snatched half a sandwich from his handler's hand and was scolded, though with laughter.

'We'll give Roi a tiny fun track after lunch,' Josh said. 'Food at every step. Everyone save a bit of meat from your sandwiches. Make it exciting for him. A real treat. Only a few yards and then a really good game at the end of it. We'll use a different field.' He grinned at Brier. 'I'll inspect it first. I ought to have investigated that hiss, but I thought it was just a small animal.'

Brier continued to worry as she ate. That mishap could cost her her place at the end of the course. If only Roi recovered fast from his fear—and he had been afraid. Be daft not to be, she thought ruefully, remembering the size of the creature that flew at them.

'Had a funny thing happen to a friend once,' Rob said, hoping to distract her. He knew that everyone was weighing up the chances of their best dog being put out of the running when it came to the final day. Like Josh and Gwyn he thought that would be a shame, but guessed that both Tony and Derek were hoping to see Brier demoted. He took a large bite and chewed thoughtfully.

'Took part in civilian Working Trials. He was out with his dog tracking in the woods for practice when someone shot a squirrel in the tree as they approached.'

He grinned at them.

'You'll never guess what happened.'

Nobody could.

'It fell out of the tree on to the dog's head, bit him on the nose and dropped dead in front of him. Weeks before the dog would track anywhere within sight of trees.'

He realised as he finished the story that it hadn't been at all comforting.

Brier stifled the impulse to say, 'And thank you too for that bit of cheering news.' She wondered briefly if Rob had intended to upset her, knowing that if she were upset, Roi would work badly. She dismissed the thought. Tony, yes. Derek, perhaps. Rob, no.

The rest of the day was uneventful. Josh found a field without bushes or trees, and laid the little track for Roi to work. Finding a sizeable piece of meat almost as soon as he set off stimulated him, and he galloped the rest of the trail, becoming more and more excited by each new trophy. He grabbed his tube with fervour, then dropped it and bounced at Brier, taking her hand in his mouth to show his pleasure.

His body was all delight when she threw his toy. He raced off to bring it back to her and offered it to her to throw for him again.

'No problem there,' Josh said. 'Next time we'll find a field full of bushes and trees, and set a track for him there.'

'Going to inspect all of them for geese?' Tony asked.

'I'll bring Lim. He'll seek them out.' Josh wasn't serious. He was elated because Roi had shown no sign of worry. 'He isn't afraid of anything.'

It was a rare day, a day to remember with pleasure. All the dogs did well. Tracking was a game to them and one that they enjoyed. The new handlers were learning to play with their dogs. Even Derek had found a means of making the lessons fun for Spike without the dog becoming over-excited.

Josh, drinking coffee and eating lemon buns, thought over the past weeks. He had begun to relax each morning as he watched his team. Not a team yet, but sometimes they worked together, and the griping stopped. Derek was obviously trying, although Josh could see no bond as yet between him and Spike.

Gulley knew better. The bond was there, but only on their long walks together when work had ended. Training was difficult and Derek had not yet learned patience. Neither of them enjoyed the lessons. Derek was too ready to put the dog in kennels or leave him with Gulley because he had a date. He'd need to find more dedication from somewhere, Gulley thought, but he was not a man to tell tales.

Gwyn stretched his hand across and took two more buns. 'Alice provides enough for an army,' he said. His dog's toy fell out of his pocket as he reached out. Loki's green and yellow tortoise with its red hat always made them laugh.

'Proper daft, my dog, see,' Gwyn said as he picked it up.

Josh asked Gwyn to stay behind at the end of the day to lay a track for Spark and give him some practice. He let Lim out for a run. His two dogs travelled often in the same compartment. Lim was tiny compared to the big Shepherds.

The spaniel hurtled joyously up the lane, under a gate,

and tore round the field. Josh whistled and he returned at the same speed, his long ears flapping as he ran. He dropped down by the van.

'Show us how it's done, see,' Gwyn said when they returned from the field. 'Pity you didn't do it when everyone was here. Did that well, Spark, didn't he?'

'Time for a jar?' Josh asked as he negotiated the roundabout that led them into the town. He and Gwyn had shared a van. The dogs were in their separate compartments at the rear, Lim settled against Spark. He adored the bigger dog. They were all fed late in the evening.

He drew up outside the Swan.

'Why not?'

Although it was early the little pub was already busy. Light sparkled on bright tankards that hung on the shelf edges, and on the fox heads, one wearing a checked cap and another with a pipe in its mouth. The local team was playing at home that week and a large teddy bear dressed in football regalia sat on the window seat, eyeing the crowd out of beady black eyes.

Voices rose and fell, punctuated by laughter. The background music was soft, and did not drown conversation.

Josh paid for two half-pints of bitter and brought them to the little table where Gwyn was sitting eyeing the crowd, as if searching for villains.

'Never know who's here,' he said. He took a long sip and grinned. 'That's good. Dilys is going to Weight Watchers' tonight and I've to get my own meal. Don't know why she bothers. Just a bit plump and cuddly I tell her, but she wants to be slim and lovely.' He chuckled. 'Women! They always want something else.'

'Ellie always wanted to be five foot ten with long blue-black hair like a raven's wing,' Josh said, suddenly recalling one of their more absurd conversations. 'I'd once admired a woman like that and she never forgot. Always felt I was hankering after something I didn't have.'

Somebody turned up the volume of the music and they continued their conversation behind a blaring screen of pop music. Gwyn stood up and looked down at Josh.

'I want some pork cracklings. How about you?'

'Potato crisps. Smoky bacon flavour.'

Gwyn fetched them and came back opening the packet. He bit into the pork crackling.

'Dilys is keeping us on a low fat diet. Got cravings.'

As they settled down again Josh asked, 'Gwyn, what's bothering Brier?'

'I think she's worried about losing Simon. The case conference is due soon. Roi isn't as consistent as she'd like, but it can't be the dog causing problems. She's besotted with him.'

'How's that going? The father still being a nuisance?'

'He's been outside the school several times waiting to try and catch him. Gracie or one of the men has taken to picking the kids up in the car, to save Kate having to face him as she walks home with them. She's made a point of meeting them since Simon came to stay. Luckily he has no idea who Kate is, and it's normal enough for the police to be taking an interest through Gracie. He's banned from driving, has sold his car, so can't follow them home.'

He glanced at the clock on the bar.

'Better be going soon. I want to give Loki a long walk before bed. He's all go, that dog.'

'Too much tickle in his paws,' Josh said and was rewarded with a grin. It was one of his favourite remarks.

'He gets restless at night. Still chews his bedding. I came down a couple of days ago and found the floor apparently covered in something I didn't like the look of at all.'

'What was it?'

'Sausage strips of yellow foam rubber. I gave him my old dog's mattress under his blanket. Thought he'd grown out of his baby ways, but he hasn't.'

'Time for another?' Josh asked.

'I'll have a soft drink and drive you home,' Gwyn said. 'Then I have the van in the morning. I'll collect you.'

He fetched Josh another half-pint and asked for a St Clements for himself. While he waited Josh sat, his long legs stretched out, considering. Brier had endeared herself to him, and he realised she was becoming important. Maybe one day . . . she would probably never know that sometimes she figured in his dreams.

He drained his glass and they went out. That night Josh took Spark and Lim and walked them until his legs ached as well as theirs, and went home to lie awake and worry about his team, and wonder if he would ever weld them into a unit.

Ten

Four weeks to the tests.

Progress was there, if Josh looked back at his notes on the early days, but the standard fell far short of his needs. Think like a dog, he said, over and over, and half the time nobody remembered.

'Time to ram home the lesson in dog psychology,' he said to Gulley at the beginning of the tenth week. The weather, after a passionate spell of high winds, snow and sharp frosts, had relented. Spring had come at last and the town gardens were bright with daffodils and early tulips. Flowers glowed on every furze bush, splashing them with sunshine. The dogs were frisky.

Sunlight flooded the room, danced on the papers on Josh's desk, and gleamed on Gulley's iron-grey mop of hair. He tugged at his moustache.

'You sure?'

'I'm in no mood for games today.' Josh glanced at the clock. Another half-hour before the handlers arrived and he had made little progress.

'Out again?' Gulley asked, dumping a plate of toast in front of them both, and removing butter and marmalade from the tray. The butter was on a flowered dish labelled 'JAM'. Underneath the word was a coat of arms and a further message: 'A Present From Blackpool'. A long-ago handler had bought it for Gulley on his birthday.

It had been wrapped in a small box inside a number of other boxes, the largest being big enough to hold a puppy. The mere sight of it made Gulley grin. The men often played tricks on him, not all of them so harmless.

One day, a couple of years before, one of them had locked him in a kennel. He had not been pleased, as that day Josh had taken them off to search a deserted army camp. No one had found Gulley for five hours.

The coffee was black and strong and sweet and scalding. The marmalade was Alice's speciality with a hint of brandy in it. Josh always had several jars given to him each January, when Alice turned herself into a small factory and produced a hundred jars which she sold for the little dog rescue kennels that she helped whenever she could.

'A call-out,' Josh said, spreading butter and marmalade lavishly. 'Turned out to be rather silly. They didn't need me. Bomb squad got there first.' He grinned. 'Something fallen off the back of a lorry, quite literally. They blew it up, as it responded to metal detectors.'

'And?' Gulley sensed an unexpected ending to the story.

'It was a consignment of tobacco. All those little tins. I don't think that the sender or the recipient are going to be very pleased.'

He glanced at the clock.

'I don't know where time goes to. Start of another day. Wheel them in here first, will you, Gulley. I want a word. And then I'm going to see how much control they have over the dogs. Operation Freedom.'

'Nothing like living dangerously,' Gulley said, and went out with a small frown on his forehead. 'On your own head be it.'

A few minutes later Josh glanced at his assembled team. He was used to edginess, but every single one of this lot seemed to have problems. Tony appeared to be absent in mind although present in body, Pete was yawning and Rob looked grim. He had confided wearily in Josh the evening before. Penny was rarely in, and when she was she was unhelpful, insolent and played heavy metal records at full blast, making the neighbours complain. He and his wife found themselves hoping she was on the pill. They both hated the modern lack of self-control. She was too young for heavy emotional involvement, and her school work was suffering. She would not talk to either of them.

'All very well to say families should communicate,' Rob said, sighing. 'We want to. She doesn't. All we want is to try and understand her point of view and make her see that she could wreck her whole life by getting involved at seventeen. Might as well try and talk to the cat.'

He grinned unexpectedly.

'At least that likes being cuddled and purrs, and is grateful for food and shelter. The kids just take it for granted.'

Josh tried to remember his teens. He had a dim vision of feeling, desperately, that life was passing him by and everyone else had fun and he had none, and that even little incidents had immense importance. If only they knew, he thought. If only they had more patience and were willing to wait for the years ahead.

Brier looked unhappy. Derek was always hard to read, but was almost certainly thinking of some girl. Gwyn had not made any kind of joke for some days and the day before had appeared to be battling with Loki rather than training him. Once the dog had growled at him and that was another worry.

Time for a sort-out. Today should help to prove a major point.

'Right,' Josh said. 'Problem day. Dog psychology day. Sorting you all out day. Tony, what's Jacko's worst fault?'

Tony, startled, sat and thought.

'Gets out of hand in the chase. He smashes his paws into the man's back, instead of taking the sleeve. Does it five times out of ten. I haven't found a way of curing him yet.'

'Effective,' Derek said ruefully, stroking a bruised chin. 'He sent me flying yesterday. I hit my face on a stone. Not funny.'

'It's not likely to impress our judge,' Josh said, making

a note. 'Don't practise that until I've had a look at it. Brier, is Roi still tossing in the property search instead of indicating without touching?'

'I try and try,' Brier said. 'I get it right and he's perfect, and bingo, next day it's gone again. It seems to be something he just won't learn.'

'He did his best to retrieve the immovable object yesterday, didn't he?'

There were sudden grins. Gulley had hidden a bicycle in a clump of high grass and brambles. When Brier sent Roi in to find it they heard grunts and strange noises. The dog had actually managed to drag it several feet by its handlebars before becoming frustrated and giving up with a moaning whimper, instead of standing and barking as he should have done.

'Major?'

Pete yawned suddenly and massively, totally unable to control himself.

'Sorry. Junior has a cold and he wants us all to be miserable with him. Major's main problem is his bite. He won't take a firm hold. He loosens and then tries again and it's easy to get the sleeve away from him. He chomps instead of gripping.'

Gulley, at the back of the room, put his thumb up and winked. The session was proving more rewarding than he had expected. At least they were aware of their own dogs' problems, and beginning to think about them. That was a giant step forward.

'Storm isn't too keen on searching,' Rob said. 'Half-hearted. I can't find out how to turn him on.'

'He can search for his dinner for a few days.' Josh looked at Gulley, who nodded. 'That ought to gee him up. No find, no food. Works best when they're hungry. Once he's keen, we'll think about improving the way he works.'

'That might make Spike keener on the track, too,' Derek put in.

'Gwyn, what's your problem with Loki? He behaved very badly yesterday.'

'I was going to report. Didn't get a chance,' Gwyn said. 'He pinched some fish off the table two nights ago. I was called to the phone just as I brought the supper in. Forgot he could reach so high. A bone pierced the inside of his cheek. Lucky it stuck there and not farther down. I didn't find it for two days. Went to the vet. He was in pain. He's OK now.'

The news relieved Josh. He couldn't understand why Gwyn's dog should suddenly go sour on him.

'Good. So we know what to work on. Outside now, and we'll see just how much control you have over your dogs. Then we're off to the moors. I've sent someone up ahead. He's supposed to be an escaped prisoner, a hard fellow who knows about dogs. He's setting tracks all over the place. We'll see who finds him first.'

Gulley brought the dogs out one by one. A small wind had dried the early dew. Brier looked out beyond the compound at the willow trees, new leaf just showing. The far foothills were hazed in cloud. They might have been in the middle of the country, instead of a few fields away from the busy town. A man standing on a painted narrow boat, apparently moving on land, reminded her that the canal was only round the corner.

She glanced at Roi who was studying a strutting pigeon which was undeterred by the group of people and dogs. As she turned her head, she saw that every other dog was watching it too.

'Sit your dogs beside you and remove the leads.' Reluctantly, the dogs turned their eyes back to their handlers.

Free heeling. All the dogs were now good at that.

'Without any command at all, throw your dog's toy as far as you can, and let the dog go after it.'

'All at once?' Gwyn asked, with memories of Loki's dislike of Major.

'All at once. When the dogs have their trophies, call them in.'

Brier decided the course had been too much for Josh and that he had taken leave of his senses. She had found a smaller piece of tubing that she used for Roi when he was working. His own tube was much too big to put into a pocket.

Out went the toys. The dogs, startled by the lack of any command, hesitated and looked at their handlers.

'Off you go.'

Six large bodies hurtled out, Loki pouncing on his tortoise and running off with it, Roi with his tube in his mouth turning to look at Brier. Spike and Jacko were too close and for one moment Spence thought his dog was about to fight, but the need for his toy was greater, and he picked it up.

Josh watched, noting the gleaming coats, the brilliant eyes, the speeding paws. They were already beginning to shape, very different dogs from the brash youngsters that had started nine weeks ago. Maybe there was hope for them all yet.

Urgent voices called the dogs, and each ran to his handler.

Josh and Gulley grinned with delight.

'A few weeks ago, that would have meant disaster, and probably a free-for-all, with none of them returning to you,' Josh said. 'Well done.'

He glanced around.

'You all seem to have paired off and found a partner to work with in your free time,' he said. 'I want a different partner for everyone today. Need to know the other dogs and the way the others work. Any of you might be teamed together in future.'

'Right,' Gulley said, consulting the list that Josh had made out earlier. 'Rob and Gwyn. Derek and Pete. Brier and Tony. Share vans and follow us.'

'I'll drive. My van,' Tony said, as Gulley put Roi into the spare compartment. Brier glanced at him, expecting some sour comment, but he said nothing.

She climbed in. She'd have to make the best of what she felt was a very bad job. Why couldn't Josh have teamed her with Pete or Rob? Was he hell-bent on disaster?

'Jacko's behaving well,' she said, hoping to start the day on easy terms.

'I wish he'd answer to a different name. Sounds so damn silly.' Tony negotiated a blind bend and cursed under his breath as he found a tractor in front of him. 'I'll lose them at this rate.'

'Gulley will pull in and wait for us all to catch up.' She thought about the dog's name. It certainly wasn't very dignified. 'Hey, how about Jago? It's a sight better than Jacko and if you take a few days to draw out that A, it'll sound like Jaggo, and then you can get it to Jago. It's worth a try.'

'Thanks,' Tony said, overtaking the tractor.

The other vans had pulled into a layby. He waited for them to set off again. He seemed unusually subdued.

'Did Derek tell me your wife is expecting a baby? Or am I wrong?' Brier asked, casting around for uncontroversial topics of conversation.

There was a long silence, and Brier felt suddenly uneasy. What on earth had made her embark on such a topic?

'We lost four. Three miscarriages and one still-born. Little boy,' Tony said, changing down for a long hill. The closeness of the van invited confidences. 'Nothing wrong that anyone could see. He just never breathed. Sheila wanted to try again. I didn't want her to. Scared.'

Brier looked out at a vista of fields below them, patched with brown tinged with green where the hedges were coming into leaf. Beyond them, the road led on to the moor. Great clumps of gorse reflected the sunlight. The memories of last year's heather and bracken stretched back from the roadside.

'The baby's due the same week as the tests. Bad timing. Sheila's scared silly it'll happen again. So am I, though I try not to let on. The last one was fine till the actual birth. They've taken her into hospital as her blood pressure began to soar. Kept her in the day before yesterday after her ante-natal. Talking of doing a Caesar. I'm just praying it won't be on either test day. They like the father to hold the baby as the mother can't. I want to be there. Can't cry off the tests, can I?'

'If they do a Caesar, can't you choose the day?'

'We can. The baby may have other ideas. If Sheila goes into labour they'll do it straight away.'

'Your turn to be lucky,' Brier said, aware the comment was absurd, but unable to think of anything at all reassuring to say.

'I put you through it,' Tony said. 'I'm sorry. I guess I resented your two healthy kids. Didn't seem fair. I put Pete through it, too. He kept going on and on about his little son.'

'You should have told us,' Brier said.

'Didn't want pity.'

There was a sudden thumping behind them as one of the dogs scratched, his leg beating against the van's metal side.

'There's a difference,' Brier said. 'I've learned that in the last two years. There are those who are pitying. You get to know them. They don't know what it's like. Those who have suffered themselves do. I turned everyone away at first. Now I know who I can trust. They help, like Gracie and Meg and Josh and Gulley.'

'You still miss Tom?'

'All the time. When I go home and he's not there. At night, in the silent room; nobody else breathing. I see a man in uniform, a back that looks like Tom's. There's a sudden wild and idiotic hope. Then he turns round, and I can't tell you the disappointment and the realisation that never is for ever, and I'll not see him again.'

'I know,' Tony said. 'Come three in the morning I find myself wondering if Sheila will ever come home; if this time . . . We're afraid to hope.'

'No use thinking like that. For her sake. You need to put on an act when you see her, make sure she thinks you're certain it will all go well . . .'

Brier found her thoughts returning to the conversation over and over. She could see why Tony had lashed at her and felt a wave of compassion. They took the dogs out of the van and put on the harnesses.

'We'll be lucky if we don't break a leg tracking through that lot,' Tony said, as his dog led him over tussocks and humps and he tried to avoid snaking bramble shoots. 'He's going like an express train. What's got into him?'

Brier, negotiating her own hazards, had no time to answer. Roi was air scenting. She tried to force his head down, but he refused even to think of sniffing the grass. Maybe the man who laid the tracks had been wearing strong-smelling clothing; stinking of fish or meat, or something equally attractive to the dogs, leaving a great deal of wind scent.

In the distance Derek was struggling to follow Spike, who was equally determined, racing ahead of his handler, almost out of control. The big man was leaning back and even then his weight did little to slow his dog.

There was a strong wind blowing on their faces.

One thing, they were all going in the same direction, but surely the man couldn't have laid so many tracks? They were racing now, as fast as any of them could go, between high furze bushes that scratched at unprotected hands and faces, each dog charging as if he were drawn by a strong magnet.

Brier stumbled over a slab of outcrop rock and steadied

herself. Any semblance of control had vanished. It was more a riot than a track.

Roi plunged down a twisting path and dragged Brier over a small stream, the frothing water, ankle deep, filling her shoes. The high bushes gave way to barer terrain, and there in front of her was a large farmhouse: the 'fugitive' must have taken refuge there.

Fast across the barren ground towards the farm gate, and then into the yard. Roi sat and bayed, the sound echoed by every other dog.

Josh and Gulley appeared at the farm doorway, both of them grinning.

'Well, well,' said Josh. 'As good a lesson as anything I'd planned. You'll find six stables over there. Put the dogs in and come into the kitchen.'

The stables were small, clean and each had fresh straw. The dogs did not settle. They roamed, restless, and even when unharnessed tried to follow their handlers.

The farm kitchen reminded Brier of her mother's home. The big table was spread with food—pies and sandwiches, scones and currant cake, cheesecakes and quiches.

'Meet our quarry,' Josh said. He whistled and a young collie bitch came from under the table. She sealed across the floor towards him, every inch of her body wagging. Her black and white coat gleamed with health. She licked Josh's hand and leaned against him, surveying the people in the room with shining brown eyes.

'This is Holly. She was mated yesterday to one of the top trialling dogs in the county. She's in full season. Did any dog put his nose down?'

'Dear heaven,' Pete said. 'You knew what would happen.'

Josh, always hungry, helped himself to a huge slab of pork pie, and added pickled beetroot and several spoonfuls of rice salad to his plate.

'I hoped it would. Mind you, I always hope we might

get a young dog so devoted to duty he forgets about sex. It hasn't happened yet, though they do learn to behave better as they get more experience. They got the scent on the air and they followed their noses. Not a thing we could do about that if it happened. Just remember it.'

A slight woman with long fair hair came into the room, and the bitch ran to her. She fondled the soft ears.

'This is Jo Lester. She can usually oblige me with a bitch in season for my courses. Breeds some of the top collies in the country. Vies with Alice to see who can produce the best nosh.'

'This is my party,' Jo said, laughing at them. 'My thanks to you all for providing me with the highlight of my year.'

'Were there any tracks out there?' Derek asked.

Gulley grinned.

'There were actually six tracks. They didn't lead here. They led back towards the vans.'

A log fire blazed in the huge old hearth. A cat with four kittens was tucked into one of the big armchairs. Derek ate as if he had never seen food before, and everyone else was hungry.

'Mick Lester works in oil,' Josh said. 'He's a trouble-shooter. He was out in the Gulf capping oilwells after the war there. Jo not only breeds sheepdogs, but trains dogs for film, theatre and TV. Puts us to shame.'

'How?' asked Rob.

'Show them,' Josh said.

'I'll show them my protection racket,' Jo said, a grin on her face. 'I need it here. It's so isolated.'

She pressed a switch. A buzzer sounded and across the yard a door opened, apparently by itself. Four large bull mastiffs exploded from the building, barking raucously. They cruised around the yard, searching, and found nothing.

'Any volunteers to go out there?'

Gulley stood up.

'You're crazy,' Rob said.

'Just trusting.'

He opened the door and the dogs hurtled towards him, baying. Jo blew a whistle.

Four dogs skidded to a standstill, and stood, uncertain.

'Friends,' she said. 'I'll put Holly in another room.' She took the bitch out and then called the four dogs in. They came with wagging tails, and greeted each person in the room with pleasure.

'Montgomery, Rommel, Hannibal and Alexander,' Jo said. 'Otherwise known as Monty, Rom, Han and Alex.'

'I'm impressed,' Gwyn said. 'How in the world did you train them to do that?'

'If you work the dogs for TV, film, or theatre, it's all distant control,' Jo said. 'I might be hiding behind a camera, or flat on the floor behind a piece of scenery. I control the dogs. The actors don't unless it's just a walk-on part. It's always done with food rewards.'

She looked at them, laughing.

'I've worked with dogs since I was two years old. My dad was a circus performer. I've all the time in the world with Mick away so much. Come on, eat up. He won't be home till the week after next and I don't want to eat this every day till then.'

On the way home, Tony voiced the thoughts that were in everyone's head.

'We've one hell of a long way to go and there's far more to learn than I ever dreamed.'

'You think you know a heck of a lot and then suddenly you find you don't know anything,' Brier said.

They stopped at a garage for petrol. There were flowers in buckets outside the shop. Brier went in, and returned with a mass of daffodils and tulips.

'Take them to Sheila tonight,' she said, knowing that Tony would visit as soon as he was off duty. 'They're from all of us. I had a word while you were out of the room.

You don't mind, do you? I thought it better they should know. Then no one will put a foot in it.'

'Thanks,' Tony said, tucking the flowers carefully behind his seat.

They drew up in the yard at the training centre. Tony took his dog out of the van.

'I think I know what Josh intended us to learn today,' he said.

It marked another step in their education.

Eleven

Three weeks to the tests. Twenty-one days. Brier felt as if she were on a roller coaster, sometimes up and sometimes down, but more often down than up. There was far too much to learn, to cram in so short a time, especially with young dogs who had never known intensive training.

Simon was edgy, terrified that, when his case was considered, he would be sent away from Brier. His small, tense face with its wide, tragic eyes haunted her, even at work. He clung to her when she was at home, dogging her steps. Kate reported that several times his father had been near the school, but made no approach.

The nightmares returned if Roi was not near Simon. The dog gave him security. Nothing would happen if Roi were there. Roi would protect him. He wished the dog could go with him to and from school, but knew that was impossible. Brier left before he did and was home after him. The only comfort in the dark came from Roi. Much against her better judgement, Brier now let the dog sleep on the mat by Simon's bed. Her morning sessions at home had ended; Roi simply refused to behave sensibly when the child was watching, and she hadn't the heart to be stern with him and make him stay indoors. Easier to leave home early and train in the compound at the Centre.

Simon was often up before she was, waiting eagerly to walk the dog round the garden, to brush him, and to feed him. It did save her time.

She was unaware that, when her back was turned and the two boys were elsewhere, Dana encouraged Roi to toss his trophy as it looked so funny. None of them could understand why Roi was so stubborn and insisted, more than half the time, in playing with those small articles instead of bringing them straight to Brier's hand.

It was a major fault and could well mean that Roi would not qualify.

In the middle of that eleventh week Brier went to see her mother, taking Roi with her. He bounded into the kitchen as if he had never been away, greeted the two bitches, checked on the cats.

'Got homes for those kittens?' she asked, watching two of the little ginger and black mites chase one another round the room.

'Homes for all but one of them, but not till after Easter, which would have to be late this year. Easter holidays seem to be popular and they don't want to start with them until they come home.'

Helena poured water onto instant coffee, fetched the tin and produced a walnut and coffee cake.

'I'm not surprised you can't lose weight,' Brier said with a grin as her mother cut two enormous slices.

'I make it for the children. Simon seems to be settling in. How's Roi doing?'

'Fine, as long as the children aren't around. He seems to have a special corner in his heart for Simon, and if he's there, I lose the dog's attention altogether.'

'Not much time left,' Helena said, smiling as one of the kittens jumped to her knee, turned round three times and settled himself, purring loudly. 'It can be done. You'll have to do it by cunning, and make up for that later.'

'And you've an idea?'

'Yes. You won't get results in a hurry, though. It may take a week or two. Roi has a ruling passion. He adores liver cake and if you keep him slightly hungry, you'll find that he'll even forget Simon if you have some in your pocket. Don't let the children know, though.'

'Liver cake's a new one on me. What on earth is it?'

'I was introduced to it by one of the old-time handlers at a show last year. You take a pound of liver and liquidise it, add an egg and beat together. Add enough wholemeal flour to get a scone-like mixture and then spread it in a swiss roll tin. Cook at a hundred and eighty degrees for about twenty minutes; it needs to be brown all through. Then cut it into tiny squares. It's hard. Won't mess up pockets and you'll find Roi will concentrate on that reward. I taught him to search with liver cake titbits.'

'I must get Kate on to it.'

'I've a stock,' Helena said, producing a large bag of small brown morsels. Roi, instantly alert, ran to her and sat, watching, an eager expression on his face. 'Too cold for you, son.' She substituted small bone-shaped biscuits, offering them to all three dogs.

Brier glanced at the clock.

'I must fly. I promised to play Monopoly with the children before they go to bed. Do you know, I think Roi has been very good for Dana. She's becoming much more biddable.'

Helena watched her daughter dash out, the dog racing after. She still missed him.

Helena's suggestion about the liver cake had triggered off an idea. The next morning Brier called the children early.

'I've a new way of training Roi,' she said. 'You can help. He mustn't pay attention to anyone but me when he's working. I want you to stand by the kitchen door while I teach him, but not to make any move towards him. Can you all do that? He has to concentrate in spite of distractions.'

Ben looked at Simon and his sister.

'We'll try,' he said.

By now the dog and cat had become indifferent to one another. Brier hoped they might one day be close friends. Ginger sat on the dresser, watching them eat, knowing that when they had finished he would benefit by anything the children had left. Roi was not given leftovers.

The dog's main meal was now in the evening after work. Nothing at breakfast time.

They went outside. It was the second day of April. The weather had relented and the sun was shining. The change lifted everyone's spirits. Walk past the children, again and again, the dog's nose intent on that goodie, sure he would be given it when he had done right. As yet, he was not sure what he was being taught.

The liver titbits worked. As Brier took one from the bag Roi's nose came round to her hand, and he nibbled at her fingers, trying desperately to grab and eat.

Ginger strutted through the open door. This was now his home. He spent much of his time with Kate, who cooked wonderful things that sometimes fell on the floor. Years of poor feeding had made him a very greedy animal, anxious to avail himself of the smallest morsel. Dana did not like his habit of bringing home dead mice, but loved to stroke and pet him so long as he had no kill in sight.

He sat and washed himself, darting small glances at the dog, hoping to attract his attention. This might just result in a chase, with the dog being called to order. The children were sure that the cat did this on purpose and enjoyed hearing Roi called away from him.

The black and white coat was glossy with health, the once scrawny body sleek. Simon too had put on weight. Kate's careful feeding had given colour to his cheeks. There was a new sparkle in his eyes.

Ginger stretched, very slowly, one leg after the other, his eyes still on the dog. Roi turned his head.

'Roi, pay attention.' The liver titbit was still there and as the dog turned towards her, Brier rewarded him. It had been weeks since Helena trained him and this was a remembered delight.

At the end of half-an-hour, Brier began to have hopes that she could conquer the dog's attachment. Ben and Simon, she knew, no longer played games that might upset Roi's training. She wished she could be sure of Dana, who had a strong streak of wilfulness in her and hated being told what to do.

Roi was behaving well now during his formal training, and Brier began to relax. The other dogs were improving too, but there was still much to be done. The hours flew by, ever more swiftly, and tension rose. Who would pass? Who would fail? Would any of them pass? The queries on Josh's ever-growing list seemed to multiply daily. Derek was too stiff with his dog. How did you make a man relax and play the fool with an animal when he used formality as a defence against the world?

Tony, quicksilver-tongued, swift-moving, apt to speak before he thought, was too impatient. He was worried about his wife, the anxiety growing as each day passed. Jacko, now responding to the name Jago, was the most placid of the dogs, chosen because he did not easily excite, but this very characteristic annoyed his handler. Given Derek's exuberant Spike the partnership would have foundered, but Tony couldn't understand that.

Loki clowned at the wrong moment and had been allowed to do so for so long by his previous owner that Gwyn had problems with him, especially on windy days. Gwyn, more placid than the rest of the team and used to dogs, found that even his patience was being worn down and he wanted to snap at the dog, which, with Loki, would have been disastrous.

His first owners had mistreated him and Gwyn had a great deal of work to do to teach the dog that humans could be trusted. He worried at times. Suppose they went on street duty and came up against the wrong kind of person? Loki might prove dangerous. There was no sign of that, but early abuse could bring unexpected reactions, even years later. Gulley was hopeful, but the buck would always stop with Josh.

Pete and Rob might get by so long as nothing went wrong with either dog, and that was always a hazard. Lameness, upset tummies, or a bout of kennel cough could ruin all his plans. Brier was edgy, which affected Roi, so that he did not always perform as well as he might.

The morning sessions with Gulley started earlier and Josh covered pages with his doodles as he pondered. Dogs' heads and wild roses. Well, well, Gulley thought as he tidied up. Don't know if he even realises where his thoughts are leading him.

Most of Josh's thoughts were anxious. He was the teacher, responsible for mistakes, and time was short. There were too many interruptions. If only they had another dog trained to detect bombs. Only Lim was available. Another few weeks before their second dog was ready. If only the hoaxers would ease up and the bombers go away.

He dreamed, in the little spare time he had, of long weeks in the sun with nothing to do and no phone ringing. Sometimes he had Brier beside him. He sucked his empty pipe.

'Not to worry,' Gulley said to them each morning, bringing endless cups of sweet coffee and tempting cakes that Brier often refused, afraid they would give her a weight problem. Alice was becoming more and more imaginative, tempting them with goodies, aware of the stress piling up on all of them.

By now everyone knew that working with a dog was far from easy. On some days the animals were as excited as Friday afternoon schoolchildren. They bounced and were slow to obey, and each handler had to work twice as hard as usual.

The weather had reverted to gales and pelting rain. The ground was mostly mud. It didn't help tracking practice.

'Crooks don't choose fine days,' Gulley said, but that consoled no one.

'Worst year we ever had.' Josh became morose as rain lashed the ground and handlers worked with dogs whose soaked fur clung to them and they stopped often to shake themselves free of the clinging wet.

Mud made clothes hard to keep clean; mud clogged footwear; rain drenched all of them and meant more grooming and drying than ever before. Gulley worried about chilled dogs, and then as Rob, Pete and Derek in turn succumbed to heavy colds, about handlers with pneumonia.

The dogs were unaffected by the weather. Whatever the day, they were eager, often wild to work, beginning to understand what this new life was about.

Roi in particular had more energy at times than Brier could channel.

She woke, early one morning towards the end of the eleventh week of the course, to the sound of giggling, and the pad pad, pad of running paws on the stairs. She glanced at the clock. Five a.m. She slipped on her dressing-gown.

The three children were sitting, cross-legged, on Ben's bed. Dana looked up anxiously as her mother came in.

'We didn't do it. Roi did.'

The dog bounded up the stairs, carrying a cushion in his mouth. His eyes were alight with fun. He had woken early. He now slept outside the door of the boys' bedroom, as Simon's nightmares seemed to have ceased. She was unaware that the boy, if he woke, called Roi to him and buried his fingers in the long fur. Roi would look after him.

The floor was covered with cushions, with shoes, with socks, with Ben's jeans on top of the pile. Soft toys and the loofah, the sponge and two flannels, soap, and Brier's toothbrush.

Roi dropped the cushion and waved his tail, watching her, one cheek blown out, a trick he had when unsure of himself and waiting for her reaction. She stifled a wild desire to laugh.

'Are you cross?' Simon asked anxiously. 'Ought we to

have come to you to get him to stop it? I did try, only he wouldn't listen.'

'He's funny,' Dana said, wanting the game to continue.

'He hasn't damaged anything.' Ben knew that they shouldn't encourage Roi to play any games unless Brier had approved them. No retrieving, ever, lest they did it wrong and bored him, and then he'd refuse when she needed him most. Dana's retrieve games were a secret between her and the dog. Nobody else knew about them and she had no intention of giving up as Roi's tosses amused her.

Roi had been so good up to now. He had never before shown any sign of wandering until the alarm went. Always a first time.

'It is funny,' she agreed, 'but I don't think we ought to let him. He won't put them back. You'll have to.'

'Everything?' Ben asked, his voice forlorn. The mountain of trophies suddenly seemed to have doubled in size.

'Everything,' Brier said. She sighed. Roi had to learn, but the game had been fun. She took him outside and shut him in the empty kennel. He looked at her, sensing that this was some kind of punishment. He settled forlornly, nose on paws, hating his banishment from the house.

'I'll walk and groom and feed him from now on,' she said when she had dressed. Simon's eyes followed her.

'Look,' she said. 'Once the tests are over you can do it for me again. It won't matter quite so much then and he'll be much better trained. It's just while he's learning. OK?'

'He can still sleep upstairs?' Simon asked anxiously.

'Of course, though we must make sure he doesn't do this again. We can't afford to let him develop bad habits. We need to work together.'

'OK, Partner,' Simon said, his eyes hopeful, and Brier laughed and rumpled his thick hair.

She walked the dog down the silent streets. The world was only just waking. A few early workers waited at the bus stops. The postman and the milkman were busy, and lights came on in the houses as she passed.

Roi today was full of pent energy. He was much more active than any dog she had known. Fighting fit, she thought, and then hoped that that, at least, was not part of his make-up. He had shown no sign of disliking other dogs, but then he had mixed with dogs from puppyhood, which always made a big difference.

That was one of her bonuses. The other five had all been isolated, meeting other dogs rarely. They were kennel bred and not socialised, which was probably why they had gone wrong in the first place, and been handed over to the police.

Helena filled her home with people when she had new pups, so that the little animals learned that the human race was kind. Sometimes it was the wrong lesson to learn.

As she walked Brier tried to convince herself that she was lucky. True, the dog was only hers so long as Simon was nowhere near, but there was never a perfect dog. Compared to the other five, he was a paragon.

'I wish we could cure that stupid search problem,' Josh said, after one very bad session late on the Friday afternoon. 'On today's showing he won't even pass. What's got into the dog?'

Brier found no comfort at all in his words.

Roi had clowned with the first search article and had not found any of the others. He fooled with every article on the track and when Brier sent him out on the sendaway went in the wrong direction. A wandering black and white cat crossed his line of vision and he gave chase, convinced that Ginger had somehow reached the Centre.

The training that day had limped along.

Loki was a lazy searcher, often not finding. Spike was as near to a perfect search as any dog could be and Jago was doing well. Brier's failure had eased the atmosphere. Roi wasn't so marvellous, the men thought, and she wasn't such a brilliant handler either.

'Saturday morning,' Josh said. 'We'll put in extra time. We must get those dogs to a higher standard and I want to know what's going wrong with Roi.'

Derek glowered. He had planned a totally different weekend—with a little red-haired policewoman. At least she would understand he had no choice but to cancel the morning. Maybe they'd have the afternoon together. He must ask Gulley to look after his dog.

'Kate has the weekend off,' Brier said. 'Mother's judging at a Championship show, and Kate's her steward. Can I bring the children?'

'Why not? Gulley will look after them.'

'Be glad to,' Gulley said. And maybe I can find out what's going wrong, he thought. Children often gave away secrets that their parents sought to hide.

Saturday was a rare fine day, with a small wind tossing the tulips. There would soon be lilac on the trees and cherry and almond blossom in profusion.

They leaped out of the car. Gulley met them.

'Not a word, not a movement, or I go and scrub the kennels and you come and help. If you watch, you pretend you aren't there.'

Brier was first to work. Josh had littered the ground with odd objects. A sparking plug. A small roll of baler twine. A beer mat. A length of leather thong. A hypodermic syringe without its needle.

Brier released the dog and sent him out. He saw Simon and raced over to him, jumping at him eagerly, delighted to find the boy in his workplace. Brier had no titbits with her, and as yet Roi only ignored the children if she had his wonderful reward in her hand.

Josh, his face set, leashed the dog and took him back.

'I see,' he said, and Brier knew he did see and that the dog might well be retired.

She bit back her misery.

She walked with Roi on his lead, letting him take her

towards the search square. He picked up the leather and tossed it. She was startled by a desire to take hold of the dog and shake him in fury.

She took the strip from him, led him over to the beer mat and as he tossed it said sharply, 'No.'

'He doesn't like doing it that way,' Dana said. 'So when I play with him I let him do what he does like. He does it my way best. Your way is boring.'

Gulley stared at her.

'Does your mother know that you play that game with him?'

'No. She'd be angry.'

'We're going to have a picnic in the office,' Gulley said. 'Do you like doughnuts?'

The children nodded, their eyes glowing.

'It must be a secret. We don't usually have children here, so no one must know you came into the real police dog office or we'll have everyone at school wanting to come. Promise?'

Gulley took them inside, poured milk into three mugs and handed out doughnuts. Alice had filled them with jam and cream. He looked at the smeared mouths and brought damp kitchen paper to clean them.

'Those were gorgeous,' Simon said.

'I'll ask Mrs Gulley to make you some, specially,' Gulley promised. 'But just now we have to talk.'

He looked at the three watching faces.

'When's Roi going to be a real police dog?' Ben asked. 'Is it next week?'

'That's what we have to talk about. I'm not sure he can be, ever,' Gulley said. 'You see, he has to get very high marks in his tests, or he won't pass them. He keeps throwing up his finds and playing with them, instead of bringing them straight to your mum, and holding them properly in his mouth. The judge will take off all his marks if he does that. It's silly for a police dog to play like a puppy.'

He looked at the children.

'I think perhaps it might be better if your mum leaves Roi here every night and I look after him. If she can't trust you to do exactly what she wants, then you're going to spoil Roi's chances altogether.'

The children stared at him, looking as if the world were about to fall on them and crush them.

'I didn't know,' Dana said. 'I thought he just did it for me and did it properly for Mummy. It was my secret game! Nobody knew but me and Roi.' She looked very near to tears.

'You know now,' Gulley said. 'I know you'll be sensible, but if Roi fails his tests he has to stay at home or go back to your gran, and probably your mother will lose her chance of being a dog handler. I don't think Roi would make an easy pet. He needs to work and use his brains. You do want him to be happy?'

Dana nodded again. She blinked hard, trying to restrain tears.

'Can I pay that game with him if I do it your way?' she asked. Simon was silent, thinking hard, his eyes on Gulley all the time.

'I'm going to ask you to do something very grown-up,' Gulley said, after a moment's thought. 'Until the test, I think your mum ought to do everything for Roi. Suppose he loved you three so much that when he was chasing a criminal he saw one of you and let the man get away to come to you instead? What do you think the papers would write about him? Everyone would laugh at him.'

'Like they do at us at school because Grandee feeds us dog biscuits,' Dana said. 'Our teacher says it's awful. We can't make her understand.'

'Dog biscuits?'

'Not real ones,' Ben said. 'They look like dogs. They're shortbread really.'

'Ask your gran to give you some to take your teacher as

a present,' Gulley said, suddenly seeing another yawning chasm, into which Helena could easily fall through misunderstanding. The Social Services people would talk to the teachers. It only needed someone to say that Brier's mother was undesirable and fed the children as if they were dogs, and Simon would be cast into limbo.

He looked at the children. Dana spoke, her voice unhappy. She couldn't bear to think of losing Roi, and for the first time understood her game was spoiling her mother's training of the dog.

'I wasn't doing it on purpose. I didn't know it would make him muddled.' The small voice was contrite.

'Suppose Birdie told you that you need lots of milk to make you strong and your mum told you that milk is bad for you? You'd be muddled, wouldn't you? And that's what you're doing to Roi. You say something is right and your mum tells him it's wrong and he gets so confused that he becomes difficult to teach.'

'Can Roi and I be friends when he's a real police dog and not just learning?' Simon asked.

'You can still be friends. Just don't fuss him too much, and no games at all till after the tests. OK?' The children nodded. 'Now help me pour out coffee for everyone. Simon can put the coffee in the mugs and Dana can put milk in and Ben can take the sugar round. They'll be stopping for a break in a few minutes.'

The dogs were back in the vans, as Josh had decided the session could end. Even Roi had paid attention, once the children had gone inside, and had done as he was asked.

The children lightened the atmosphere. Dana walked over to talk to Derek, who was delighted by the small girl, laughing with her, relaxing, and astounding his colleagues. He had a small niece whom he saw too rarely.

Brier and Josh were deep in conversation.

'Somehow we have to detach the dog from the children,' Josh said. 'That's going to be hard.'

He turned, startled, as a small hand touched his arm. He cursed to himself, knowing that the children had heard him. He hadn't seen their approach.

'It's my fault Roi isn't working well,' Dana said. 'Mr Gulley told me.' She looked up at Brier. 'I didn't know it would spoil your training. It was just that Roi enjoyed playing the search game my way more than yours. He thought tossing was fun. So did I. I won't do it again.'

'When did you do it?' Josh asked.

'All the time, when Mummy wasn't looking. He picks up everything in my pocket when I drop it and brings it to me, and I laugh at him when he tosses the things. It's so funny. We all like playing with him. We did at Grandee's too, before he became a police dog.'

'Dear Heaven,' Josh said to Gulley, watching Brier and the dog and the children drive away. 'You plan and you scheme and you work, and then something happens to wreck everything, and often the something is as downright silly as this. I hope there's nothing more in store for us before the final tests.'

Gulley, looking up at an unusually cloudless sky, murmured a small prayer.

Twelve

Twelve days to testing time. Twelve days to discover whether the dogs were good enough for duty. Twelve days to find out who had passed and who, if anyone, had failed. They had worked their guts out.

Weeks of lectures. Only Gwyn and Brier had been prepared for the floods of information that had to be learned, had to be remembered, had to be acted on. The use and care of equipment; the care and management of the dog; the daily examination—for thorns, for grass seeds, for any sign of strain or injury, and the thorough grooming.

Lectures on temperament. They had enough different temperaments between them to be able to see the need for that. Loki was apt to clown at the wrong moment. Spike was too eager to chase and bite and difficult to stop. Jago, now answering to his new name, was at times wary and likely to sulk if scolded. Storm could still be aggressive towards any dog that came too near him.

Roi's chief fault was over-enthusiasm, wanting to do almost anything before the command was given so that Brier had to work very hard on control. Jago was inconsistent and at times was slow to obey, and Tony frustrated easily.

More lectures. Dog anatomy. Dog physiology. Dog psychology. Feeding the dog. Hygiene. Worming. Flea control.

There was so much to learn, as well as all the practical work.

Josh watched zealously. Everything must be done by firmness and kindness, never by brutality. There were still lessons to be taught, some of them more important than others. During the weeks Gulley had suspected Tony of venting his anxiety on his dog.

'Not a patient man,' he said. 'The dog is beginning to cower if I lift his lead. Needs a word.'

Josh knew he should have given this particular session before, but there had been so many interruptions. They were permanently stretched, fighting a war that no one acknowledged. During the course there had been two genuine bomb alerts. The bombs had been defused. There were also several hoaxes. Nobody dared ignore those, but they wasted so much time. Activists of all kinds threatened stability.

He lined them all up, without their dogs.

'Down on all fours,' he ordered.

They stared at him, but obeyed.

'Where are your horizons?'

From that position, the small bushes were large obstacles, the wall a barrier, with who knew what dangers beyond it? Nobody could see.

'There might be tigers beyond that wall; or a man with a gun or a knife. There might be a quarry, or a sheer drop to the sea. Your dog can never know. You have to think for him. He has to be able to trust you implicitly. You must never let him down. Never scold him without reason. Never lose your temper.'

It was uncomfortable to stay on all fours, bare hands on cold wet ground. Did the dogs feel this through their paws? Brier wondered suddenly.

'One day your lives may depend on your dogs. If they don't trust you they may not bother to defend you. We have to learn that, whatever we do, we must never let them down. Think about it. We all make mistakes; we aren't saints, but we must make sure the dog realises that our anger is short-lived and to the point, and never out of place.'

He stared down at them, towering above them, Brier's eyes level with his knees. A dog's eye view. People must look like enormous giants to a chihuahua, she thought, a sudden understanding of Josh's purpose giving her an illuminating insight into the world as her dog saw it.

Josh stood by Brier, looming above her, brandishing a lead. She almost fell flat as he yelled at her.

'Bad dog. Horrible dog.' The lead swished down, missing her, and slammed into the ground. 'I hate you.' Brier had never heard him bellow before. 'You never do anything right.' Down slashed the lead again.

Brier, convinced her instructor had taken leave of his wits, stared up at him.

'Anyone treating a dog like that in my team goes out, at once,' Josh said, his voice ominous. 'I mean it. I won't have it. Not for a moment. One whisper that any of you is unkind to his animal away from here, and that's the end of the road. You'll be out and back on the beat so fast you won't know what's hit you. Understood?'

He walked down the line, glaring at them, and then returned to Brier and knelt beside her, stroking her hair.

'Good girl, beautiful girl. My clever girl. Who's worked her heart out for me?' The voice was a croon, the hand soothing, and for a moment Brier longed to lean against him and derive comfort. 'Oh, Tom, Tom,' she thought, suddenly aching for her husband's arms around her, and the quiet evenings when both of them could talk and unwind.

Gwyn, who was next to her, butted Josh's knee, and whimpered like a dog.

Josh stared at him. Gwyn begged, and whimpered again.

'It's not fair. I want to be told I'm beautiful, too. Why pick on her?' he asked. There was a gust of laughter, as everyone stood up. The laughter carried them through the coffee break and lightened the next two hours.

Ten more days.

The theory of scent. How to track. Criminal work. The history of the dog and the bond between man and dog. How to use a dog in police work. Work during the day. Work at home—half-an-hour daily while the children watched. Lie awake at night, going through each lecture point by point, remembering the day's mishaps and trying to work out how to cure and avoid faults tomorrow.

'They're dog handlers at last,' Gulley said as he and Josh went over the notes on the work each had done the day before. 'They are beginning to think and work out what is wrong and why it is wrong and even suggest how to right it. There's hope yet.' By now they were all bonded to their animals. Even Derek had begun to find comfort in his dog, and to rejoice when Spike rewarded him with good work.

Revision. They walked around muttering to themselves. Gwyn and Brier had brainstorming sessions, firing questions at one another.

Police orders relating to dogs. Operational dangers. Crowd work. Keep up the training all the dog's life.

Eight more days.

That afternoon they tracked on roads, the most difficult work for the dog, as hard surfaces did not hold scent as did farmland. It had been raining, and none of the dogs did well. Josh wished he had planned something different, but there was a hard surface track on the test. No use ignoring it, even if it had diminished morale.

Home for the handlers was a brief interlude, to revise, to learn, to sleep. Up early to walk and groom the dogs. To make notes. Home for Josh was a chance to review his men and his dogs, and to worry even more than usual.

The dogs were animals, not angels, and sometimes raised problems outside working hours.

Jago, released from the van, unleashed, at their home, chased next door's prize Persian cat, although he didn't catch it. Tony thought it funny, which did not help his somewhat tricky relationship with their neighbours. Josh had a formal complaint and an argument to settle. Be more careful in future. Always leash him before taking him out of the van.

Spike refused to come when called unless Derek was wearing his uniform. Derek had to make sure he had a uniform jacket under his raincoat whenever they went for a walk.

Loki, bored one afternoon, ate all the buttons of Gwyn's best uniform jacket, which he had unwisely left on a chair for his wife to press. The buttons, fortunately, were all eliminated without causing a problem, though Gulley insisted on a visit to the vet. More expense, Josh said sourly, always conscious of his inadequate budget. Shouldn't have happened. Think!

They learned to keep the training period brief; to give the dog a very short track, as a sweetener, when he had struggled on a long one. The dog must be successful or he will lose heart and won't try. Reward him with a game.

The dogs learned that a command given must be obeyed at once, and not when the dog felt like it. Control, control, control. 'I'll stand up in my coffin on my way to my funeral and yell "control",' Josh said wearily on the last training day of the twelfth week.

They never knew where they were going. Deserted building sites, disused warehouses, and sometimes warehouses that were in use; an old army site, parks and playgrounds and the edge of the motorway, beyond the hard shoulder and over the banks.

Tracks on plough and furrow, on grass and on gravel, on sand and on mud.

Jumping hurdles, as they might have to jump fences. Over the long jump, as they might have to jump small brooks or other obstacles. Over the six-foot A frame, which represented a wall. Sendaway to a mark, as they might have to intercept a running man, making for safety, with a gap in the fence through which a dog could race, and keep the villain there till his handler reached him.

'The dog is your eyes and your ears, your legs and your safety,' Josh said. 'Cherish him.'

Only a few more days and they would all be operational, working police dog handlers with working police dogs. Or would they? The dogs needed experience. That could only come with age.

Seven more days.

They had been tested on week eleven and all had passed, though Derek had only just scraped through. He learned through his mistakes, and improved immensely for week twelve. Now they knew their deficiencies. Gwyn had been first in week eleven; Brier topped him by two marks in week twelve. Nervousness needled all of them. Brier, driving home, longed for peace and quiet.

The evenings were lighter now and the days warmer. Today the sun had shone, the sky was blue and it had been good to work with the dogs. There were flowers rioting in the gardens.

Brier was jaded after the long day and was thankful to find a silent house. Kate often took the children over to Willowbank Farm, so that she could eat her evening meal in peace and unwind before they hurtled into the house. The children were being very careful not to entice Roi away from her. Helena, told of the problem, had shown them how to ignore the dog's overtures. For all that, Brier felt a stab of guilt.

The phone rang just as she had finished changing. She intended to take the dog for a long walk. A walk on which she could relax, with no need to work or think.

'Gracie?'

'The case conference on Simon is the day after test day. His father is protesting and two of the committee seem unable to understand what all the fuss is about. It could go either way.'

'They wouldn't send him home?'

'Hopefully not. But the Social Services don't always seem blessed with sense. Don't hope too much.'

'I'll fight them,' Brier said. 'It would be a crime to let him go back, or to send him to strangers. He's been with us for weeks now. He thinks of it as his home.'

'I know, girl,' Gracie said, his voice gentle. 'Had to tell you. I'm gunning for you, too.'

He rang off, and Brier whistled to Roi, and shut the door behind her, wishing she could shut out all her problems as easily.

Along the lane and down the steps that led to the canal towpath. Roi was any dog, sniffing the grass, bounding forwards and returning to her, called to sit at heel whenever they met other people passing by. The boats had begun to ride the water.

There were flowers in the hedges, and birdsong. It was weeks since she had strolled slowly, day-dreaming, forgetting everything that bothered her. A woman and her dog, out on their own, all care forgotten.

The Stagecoach Inn had been prosperous in the days when narrow boats plied on the water and the men stopped to rest the horses and called in for a drink. She sat on a bench by a low wall, watching a sleek white cruiser tie up alongside.

The girl was slim and young and aware of her charm. The shorts and brief shirt barely covered her. Long legs and long blonde hair and a pert nose. Brier sipped at her orange juice. Roi lay beside her, nose to tail, watching quietly, his ears alert.

The man had been drinking for most of the day, Brier guessed. He watched as the girl steadied the plank which stretched from boat to shore. She darted across it, long hair tossing, and vanished into the Stagecoach.

The man tried to follow.

Two steps, and he swayed.

A moment later he was in the water.

Brier ran.

He was thrashing uselessly, drifting away from the bank, shocked into sobriety. Before Brier had time to think, Roi was in the canal, swimming.

'Hang on to the dog's collar,' she yelled.

Two men who had been sitting at a nearby table joined her, watching as Roi reached his target. Desperate hands gripped him and the dog began to move slowly towards the bank.

Two rescuers reached out to drag the man to safety. Brier, pulling at Roi's scruff, helped him haul himself onto the bank. He lay soaked and panting, looking up at her. She hadn't enough words to praise him, but he waved his tail, knowing he had done well.

'If it hadn't been for your dog . . .' The man looked at her, as he stood up, water dripping from him.

'One of us would have jumped in. Roi saved us a wetting,' Brier said. 'I need to get home.'

She had been out for longer than she had intended, and had not left a note for Kate, who worried about her.

Roi, trying to dry his own coat, shook himself and showered everyone within range.

'Shows what he thinks of us,' one of the onlookers said. He had followed her. 'I know you, don't I? You're Tom Morrey's wife.' He hesitated, about to substitute 'widow', and changed his mind. 'Is that a police dog?'

Brier nodded, her thoughts on home and the need to dry Roi and groom him. She didn't want a chill from the wetting, with the test due so soon. A newly risen cold wind made her wish she had worn a jacket.

Roi bounded ahead of her.

She stood outside the kitchen door, drying Roi, who seemed to think this was a new game, and that the towel was the canvas training sleeve that they wore on their arms to protect them when the dog chased and caught them. He tugged, refusing to let go. The children, seeing her, rushed out, bombarding her with questions. How had Roi got so wet? Had he been swimming?

Brier laughed and told them how their dog had saved a man from drowning. There was no way they could ignore him. They praised him and fussed him, and Roi, who had completely forgotten the episode, basked in their attention. Ginger, jealous, came up to him and rubbed against the dog's leg. Roi put his nose down and for a moment the two animals were face to face. Later, when Roi was in his bed, Ginger joined him and lay there and diligently washed him, managing to purr at the same time to the children's mystification.

Kate put the children to bed, and went to her own room to write a long overdue letter to her daughter. She had brought her own furniture and sighed as she looked at the photographs of her wedding day, and of Matthew just before he died. They stood, framed in silver, on her writing table.

Brier sat alone downstairs. Roi came to her and leaned against her, looking up at her, as if trying to fathom her thoughts. That night Simon slept without waking, and in the morning Brier found the dog lying across her own doorway, instead of the boys'. It was hours before she realised the significance of his presence.

Thirteen

Four more working days. Brier couldn't sleep. The thought of the tests worried her. They needed more work. She dressed and crept downstairs, praying the children wouldn't wake. Roi followed her happily, always delighted to be noticed.

Six o'clock. There was a small chill wind and the ghost memory of a full moon. There was dew on the ground and birdsong just beginning, and peace. The trees, in vivid young leaf, were shivering silvery shapes under a sky that presaged a fine day. If only the test days were fine.

She called Roi, to practise his heeling. She was sure he was less accurate and working badly. Maybe it had been silly to get up early. He would be tired before they reached the Centre. Overtraining was as bad as too little.

The dog butted her hand, trying to rouse her. Night was yielding to a grey dawn, the sun as yet a hint on the horizon.

'Oh, you,' she said, as he bounced round her, eager to be working. She had to concentrate her mind on him. 'We're going places, you and I.'

Simon came out of the door, fully dressed.

'I was worried,' he said, 'because Roi wanted me more than you. I have tried not to take any notice of him, but it's difficult. You won't send me away? Gracie says that it all depends on the Social Service people. You do want me?'

Roi barked. Brier was conscious of the child's dark blue eyes looking imploringly into hers.

'I do want you,' she said, and hugged him close to her.

'Can I live with you always?'

'I hope so.' She would try to keep him. Maybe she could

adopt him. She couldn't bear to think that she might lose him. 'I don't see why they should refuse to let you stay here. Let's go in and get breakfast,' she suggested, aware that time had passed, that the sun was now bright and the hours were flying by after their nightlong lagging march. She had dreamed of Tom, and woken desolate. 'I can't really make much difference by extra work now.' She was afraid to test the dog to see if he would work while Simon was close.

The mood she was in, she would never pass.

An hour later, her mind was milling as she drove. Tom had been alive in her dream, laughing, calling to her as they swung hand in hand down the Long Hill, one of their favourite walks. She had not been back, not since Tom died.

Tony glanced at her as she walked onto the grass, and then looked more sharply.

'Night on the tiles?' he asked. 'You look like something the cat wouldn't even want to bring in.'

'Thanks a bunch. That makes me feel lots better.' Brier resisted an impulse to hit him, and another to burst into tears. She turned and walked across to the office.

Josh looked at her, one eyebrow raised.

'Are you OK?' he asked.

'I dreamed of Tom. We were walking on Long Hill. He loved that walk and the view from the top. I keep dreaming the same dream.'

Gulley had come into the room while she was speaking. He vanished and returned fast, his usual remedy in his hand.

'Just poured it for myself. Haven't touched it. Drink up,' he said, and spooned sugar into it. He put down the cup and went out again, closing the door firmly behind him.

Brier drank and then looked at Josh, her expression rueful.

'I didn't mean to go all feminine and stupid,' she said. 'Sorry.'

'I still dream of Ellie,' he said.

'Does it get easier?'

'In some ways.' He was suddenly aware that he wanted to put his arms round her, to hold her and comfort her, to ease the bleak expression on her face. 'I take the dogs up to bed with me. Then I don't wake in a silent room. Their breathing helps.' He grinned at her, a sudden lopsided smile on his face. 'Don't you dare tell that to the men. I'd never live it down.'

Brier in her turn had a sudden startling urge to lean against his shoulder, seeking comfort. She stifled the thought.

'I promise.' It was only a faint lightening of her expression, but at least she looked as if she could now cope with whatever the day sent. He knocked on the window and gave Gulley a thumbs up sign. Ready to start. Gulley called to the men. He watched as the dogs were put in the kennels. They were bouncy, fresh with the day's energy, eager and alert.

The men were also in a lighter mood, Pete jostling Rob as they came into the room. They were laughing at something Gwyn had just said, and it was a moment before they settled.

Josh began the day's talk. A reminder about the need for control, for fast, accurate responses. No use a man surrendering if the dog failed to obey and ripped him. Call him off, at once. Practise, practise, practise. No dog was born trained. Young dogs took time to learn and even when taught needed experience.

Brier willed herself to concentrate. She was thankful when they broke for elevenses.

Gulley brought her black coffee loaded with sugar. Alice had made chocolate éclairs. They were carefully packed in a big cardboard carton. He handed them round.

'Alice's special carbohydrate fix,' he said, with a grin. 'Anyone who's not worried at this stage ought to be. Last-minute nerves. I remember how I felt before each race, even when I had the best dog. Even with Miracle, and he was a dog that won more than any I ever had.'

'Catches us all,' Josh said, grinning at a sudden thought. 'I remember some years ago when I had Star. We were in line for the Championship Certificate at a civilian trials. I wanted that CC so badly that when I went to send the dog away, I fluffed it and gave him the wrong command. I used hand signals. Instead of pointing in the direction he ought to take, I moved my hand in the way that meant "over".'

He paused to look round at them, and sipped his coffee. He laughed at his long-ago self. 'I really did mess it up. The poor dog looked around for a hurdle, found it, shot off and jumped it and lay down. Lost me all my sendaway points and the CC. My own fault, not his. All of us suffer. Doesn't do to want anything too badly.'

The story was no consolation at all. If Josh could go to pieces, so could any of them. Had he meant to unnerve them? Or to reassure? Brier was uncertain.

The ringing telephone startled all of them.

Gulley lifted the receiver.

'For you,' he said to Brier.

Worry flared as she heard Birdie's voice. She never rang her at work unless there was an emergency.

'Just thought you'd better know. Dana fell in the school playground. She's broken her wrist. Helena's looking after the boys if I'm not back by four. I don't know how long we'll be at the hospital. Just off there now. She's not bad otherwise; a bit shocked. There's no need for you to come home.'

Brier thanked her and rang off.

'Dana's broken her arm,' she said. She wanted to be with her, to go to the hospital, to comfort the child. 'Kate's taking her to the hospital.'

'Want to go to her?' Josh asked.

'Maybe just go over and see her . . . I don't know. Kate's like an extra grandmother to them all . . . she did say not to come.'

'If you do go, Kate may feel you don't trust her,' Gulley said.

Tony raised his eyebrows, giving himself an even more satanic expression. His dark, angular face was sombre. She looked round at her other companions, suddenly hypersensitive. What were they all thinking? Unnatural mother? She felt trapped by her dilemma.

'Gulley can drive you to the hospital at lunchtime, if they aren't home by then,' Josh said. 'I doubt if there's much you can do, but it would set your mind at rest. Kids are pretty resilient.'

It was a welcome solution.

Josh produced lists: the order in which they would be working. Less than a week. So much depended on this for all of them. Brier wondered if the men felt as nervous as she did. Josh had suggested a weekend with no training at all. 'Relax,' he said, as if any of them could.

Gulley passed round the photocopied sheets. WPC Brier. Obedience 11.00 a.m. Criminal work 12.30 p.m. She was the last before lunch. Rob, Tony and Gwyn all worked before her.

Pete was last of the day. Brier was glad that she at least did not have to wait until 2.50 before working her dog. Even so there would be time enough for nerves.

'What are the judges like?' Rob asked. There were two of them, a different one each day. None of them knew them. One came from the Midlands, the other from the South.

'The first day judge is a stickler for accuracy,' Josh said. 'I like to have a stiff test; if you pass, then my mind is at ease: I know that no one got by because of the judge's leniency. His fetish is control, so watch it; even between exercises, he'll be watching and deducting marks for any sign of a dog being out of hand.'

'Give them wine at lunch.' Derek said, unexpectedly.

There was a soft ripple of laughter, but Brier knew that everyone was as much on edge as she.

'Mellow them a bit and maybe they won't notice our faults!' he added.

'Good idea,' Gwyn said. 'Maybe give them so much they revise all the morning marks as well, in a flare of good humour.'

Brier looked down the list of exercises and their possible marks: 200 total for Obedience; 300 for criminal work. Overall control: there were 35 marks for that and that was where they might all lose. Roi needed a very firm hand when he excited, and the chase excited all of them. Spike was the most likely, still, to riot at times, and Jago was occasionally slow to obey commands. Their weakness was her strength, as her weakness was theirs. She needed to do brilliantly, to show that women had their place in the dog handling sections, to prove that she was as good as, or better than the men. She had a sudden memory of a farmer friend of her father's working a bitch that behaved like an angel in training, and let him down, time and again, in sheepdog trials when it really mattered. 'Only thing predictable about Nature,' he said one day, 'is that animals are entirely unpredictable.'

She kept the memory to herself.

'A woman in a man's world,' Helena often said. 'We always have to be twice as good or we aren't even noticed.'

Sixty marks for courage, testing the dogs with a stick and a gun. Loki, who had been beaten as a youngster, might shy off the stick, although he showed no fear of guns. Roi regarded both as toys that he wanted to possess. He adored any sort of game in which he had to fetch. He now knew he must not toss the search articles, and rarely forgot. If only he remembered when being tested. Dana had valiantly kept her word.

Crowd control; that excited Spike, who refused to stop barking when told. Derek was going to have problems.

Chase and attack. Sixty-five marks. Roi might excel there.

Four more days to practise. Four more days to worry. The weekend to endure. And then it would all be over. Only the parade when they had passed, in front of the top brass. All of them wearing their smartest uniforms, shoes and buttons polished till they reflected the sun, dogs groomed to perfection, swanking in front of the crowd. The reward of hard work. Then they would be on their own, fully operational with dogs that needed to be taught much more and that were still only dogs, and young dogs at that.

She was thankful when it was time for lunch. Gulley drove fast and competently. He walked with her into the Accident and Emergency department. Kate and Dana were just coming out of one of the cubicles.

'I've got plaster, Mummy,' Dana said, exhibiting her arm as if it were a trophy. 'Gulley can write his name on it and be first.'

Gulley wrote with a flourish.

'Kate and me are going to have fish and chips all by ourselves. The boys will be eating school dinner. I can have all the chips I want, and mushy peas, and we'll have it in the café part, and I don't have to go back to school this afternoon, so I'm going over to Grandee and she said I can have lots and lots of dog biscuits.'

Kate grinned at Brier, knowing how worried she had been.

'They bounce back,' she said. 'But you'll work better this afternoon for seeing her.'

'I suppose I was a fool,' Brier said, on the way back. 'Why are we going this way?'

'Just a mother. Wouldn't have thought much of you if

you hadn't worried. Dana triggered my taste buds. Best fish and chips in town here.'

He drew up outside and vanished, reappearing shortly afterwards with a bulging carrier bag.

'We'll go down Lovers' Lane. Eat it there in peace, or everyone will be jealous,' he said with a grin. 'Play hooky and have our own picnic. I got plastic forks so we needn't get greasy. I hope you're hungry.'

Brier felt as she had as a child when she and her cousin stole out of bed and helped themselves to goodies from the fridge for a midnight picnic.

'I enjoyed that,' she said, half an hour later, wiping her mouth on a tissue. 'I can't remember the last time I ate fish and chips out of the paper, sitting in a car in a leafy lane.'

'Soon be summer,' Gulley said, looking at the vivid springtime green of the trees. 'Last time I ate fish and chips with a pretty woman beside me in the car must have been when I was courting. And that's more years ago than I care to remember.'

Brier laughed.

'I hope Alice won't be jealous,' she said.

'Not she. She'd be the first to approve. She'll be sorry for that little lass of yours. Time to get on, or that dog of yours will never be ready.'

Back to work. Brier, coming in slightly late, was aware of a change of attitude. They were all now on their toes, determined to do well, maybe for their own sakes, maybe to show her that men were better than women.

Chase and attack. Search to find a hidden man and arrest him and escort him back to base. Gulley, acting as criminal, gave way to his gifts for mimicry and had them all laughing as he complained bitterly about the way he was treated.

As Gwyn walked him back, supposedly under arrest, Loki at his heels, he cringed and whined.

'Only resting after a night out,' he said. 'Not fair, hounding a man. The radio was lying in the road, see. Bringing it to you, wasn't I? And the diamond ear-rings fell into me 'ands out of a window. 'Aving a row they were . . . and she chucked them away. Not illegal to keep them, is it? And keep that dog off me. Bitten me three times and I've rights . . . I want a lawyer. I'll have Diamond Jack . . . gets everybody off, he does.'

Diamond Jack was the nickname for one of the town's cleverest lawyers, a big man who wore an enormous diamond ring and had the reputation of being able to defend a man he had seen commit a crime and get him acquitted. He was unpopular with the police.

Gulley produced a different and more absurd story for each of them.

Brier was sure she would say, 'I want a word with you,' in her dreams.

The afternoon went by.

Alice had made cheese scones and shortbread biscuits.

'We'll celebrate after the tests with a proper party,' Gulley said. 'Alice is busy writing out lists and thinking up treats for you all. The dogs are on top form, so see you all do them justice.'

There was still time for slip-ups. A lame dog, or a sick dog. Or a sick handler. Josh watched Brier whistle to Roi. Dana's accident was unfortunate, but from Gulley's report the child was rather pleased with herself. She felt important.

'OK?' he asked Brier, as she put Roi in the van and swung herself behind the driving wheel.

She smiled at him.

'I'm fine now.'

He watched the van turn out into the road, and vanish round the bend. He felt a sudden driving need to follow her, to call to her, to talk to her, to cherish her. Gulley, watching, guessed his thoughts, but said nothing.

Josh whistled his dogs, sighing. For the time being he

had to keep his feelings secret, and above all the men must never know, or there might well be problems beyond any he had ever experienced with his team.

Fourteen

Only three days left. Three days to perfect his dogs. Three days to cram in work that needed to be done. Five days to work on faults, as the weekend intervened. He knew no one would be able to refrain from training.

Josh was lost in a nightmare when the phone rang. He was listening to the judge telling him he was very sorry but not one dog was up to standard. Nobody had passed. He surfaced, thankful to realise it was only a dream. He woke, heavy eyed. One a.m. What now?

Reported bomb in the railway station.

He swore steadily as he dressed.

Out into the rainy night, the street lamps reflected on the wet road, the longing for more sleep deep within him, the two dogs in the back of the van. Little Lim was in the firing line again.

Cars, headlights, men waiting for them. He released the Spaniel and watched the small joyous body as Lim raced round the place, his busy nose working, his stump tail whirring with delight. He adored the hide-and-seek game, sure that Josh had hidden his favourite goody for him: half a sausage. That was in Josh's pocket and he watched, his mouth dry, as the little dog searched.

Lim stiffened and turned his head. A find. His tail circled, his eyes asked for approval. He had won his game, had found his trophy and done well. Oh, damn people, Josh thought. At least the little Spaniel had no idea of the menace that threatened all of them. He wished he were a dog. If only humans could live for the moment, enjoying the sheer delight of being alive. Lucky Lim.

Chris Martin, whose duty it was to defuse the bomb, walked across to them. Together they stared down at the biscuit tin. An ordinary square biscuit tin, from the inside of which came an ominous ticking. The fluffy kitten in a wicker basket pictured on the lid mocked them.

His job was done; Chris's was due to begin. Luckily the railway station was isolated and no houses were near. Chris opened the tin.

He stood up, holding a ticking alarm clock that proved as innocent as the day it was made, and a large piece of paper on which was written, 'Ha, ha. Ever been fooled?'

'Some bloody kid,' Chris said, his voice savage. 'Putting us all through this . . . I'll kill him if I ever find him.'

Me too, Josh thought, driving home through deserted streets. The rain had eased. The moon, almost full, lighted the world, a world that slept while he was awake. A world that trusted him and his colleagues to keep them safe. He turned into his drive and killed the engine.

He opened the back door and let the dogs into the garden. It was a routine, always, when they came home. A moment later, Spark squealed, a nerve-racking pain-filled sound that went on and on. Josh flashed the giant torch that stood on the shelf by the back door. The dog was standing, staring at him, blood pouring from his leg. Broken glass was scattered all over the grass. Some joker had been there in his absence.

The intensity of his anger shook him.

'Stay.' He prayed that neither dog would move. Lim froze on the spot, watching him. He picked up the little dog, his feet crunching on more glass, and put him inside, shutting the door. He lifted Spark. A great gash ripped across his leg, just above the paw. One pad was almost severed. There was glass everywhere.

Fury sent him into overdrive. Tourniquet. Both dogs into the van and use his radio to talk to the duty sergeant.

'Bloody hell. That's bad.'

Words were inadequate. His colleague's voice was angry. They all knew Spark. He was part of the Force. 'I'll ring the vet. He'll be ready for you.'

And not pleased either, Josh thought, sure that Paul Matthews would be woken for nothing as he'd arrive with a dead dog. He hoped that Spark wouldn't worry with his teeth at the tourniquet. He was afraid it would not hold and he knew it couldn't stay on long. He put his foot down, praying that none of his colleagues were about.

Rage governed him. He longed to find out who had spent the night hours so viciously. The bomb hoaxer? Probably. It was too much of a coincidence. And that meant someone very nasty indeed. He'd be checking the garden for poison and warning the other dog handlers.

Paul was waiting at the surgery door, lights blazing. He looked at the dog in dismay. He and Spark were old friends. The dog gave a feeble tailwag.

'Nasty,' he said, looking at the mess. He bent to put his arms round Spark's neck. 'We'll do our best, old fellow. Soon have you a bit more comfortable than this.' He stood up and turned to Josh, who was sure he would never see Spark alive again. 'Operation. You'll have to leave him. Marian's getting ready to help. Useful to have one's wife as partner.'

Within minutes Spark was on the table, a needle already sinking deep into his skin.

'He'll be OK?'

It was dreadful to lose a dog, appalling to lose him through malice.

'I'll do my best. He's lost a lot of blood. Ring first thing. Off you go now. Nothing you can do and there's no time to waste.' Spark lay there, as quiet as if he were dead. Josh stared at him, watching the deep chest. A shuddering breath shook it and he sighed with relief.

Marian was beside him, her hand on his arm, commiserating.

'Don't worry, we've saved worse.'

He knew that but it wouldn't stop him worrying. He drove home, aware of the empty compartment behind him, aware of Lim, lying forlorn. Aware that he had to scrub away the blood before starting the day. Hoping that nothing more would happen tonight.

Damn everybody. He wished he could put a curse on the glass breaker, give him as much pain as he had given the dog, and far more inconvenience. He did not feel tolerant, professional, or kind.

He would be in the worst possible mood, just when he needed to be able to encourage his team, who would all be suffering from pre-test nerves and would need his backing. Spark would take days to get over this and he was now a dog short. They had few enough operational as it was.

Policemen were supposed to be superhuman, Josh thought, as he went indoors. He needed something to eat and a drink. Toast was simple. Coffee? Would keep him awake and so would tea. He made himself a cup of instant soup. It would warm him. No use going to bed. He'd lie and toss and turn.

He switched on the gas fire and watched the artificial flames leap. Lim came to him, nudging his knee, walked over to Spark's empty bed and nosed it, puzzled, then lay against Josh's leg, heaving a deep and unhappy sigh. He thinks Spark's dead, and maybe he is, Josh thought, feeling more forlorn than before.

He stroked the dog, finding comfort in the feel of soft fur, in his warmth and deep breathing.

'It's all right, old fellow. He'll come back,' he said, wishing the dog could understand, and doubting his own words.

Spark was only just coming into his prime. Was one of the best dogs they had. It would be such a waste. He thought of Brandy, who had died under an anaesthetic, five years ago. It wasn't a consoling memory. A lovely dog, not yet two years old. It was always the best that went too soon.

There were so many dogs in a police handler's life. They were retired at eight, if they survived. He had had seven in his time. Shane had been killed on duty. Sol had been the first, and had lived to twelve. For the last few years of his life he had been a valued pet, greeting Josh with joy when he came off duty.

They passed through his mind, all well loved, all well trained, though some had been better than others.

Suppose Spark died before they could operate? Suppose he were crippled? Suppose . . .

The phone rang.

He listened, and was at once aware that he faced disaster. He hadn't got a dog, and this was life or death. They had tried all the other handlers. It was a busy night, with every lunatic on the patch out committing mayhem. His was the only dog not in use; and his dog was on the operating table three miles away.

Fifteen

Brier was sound asleep.

The ringing phone startled her.

She switched on the light, answering softly, saying that she'd go downstairs, where she could talk without disturbing everyone.

'Brier?' Josh's voice was anxious. She glanced at the clock: 3.30 a.m.

'Can you bring Roi? This place has gone mad tonight. Three break-ins, two stolen cars, a near-riot outside the disco, a report of a bomb at the station . . . and the damned thing was a hoax . . . Spark's being operated on at this moment. A nasty gash on his paw from glass . . . and now an old lady had gone missing from Saint Margaret's.'

His voice went on.

'She wandered away in her night clothes. The night nurse discovered it when she did her rounds. She's confused and she's diabetic. I haven't a dog free. Roi might just do the trick. It's a chance, but we have to take it. I don't think any of the others is as good as he.'

Brier raced upstairs to dress. Ben and Simon were on the landing.

'It's not dangerous?' Ben's voice was forlorn. He worried about her far more since Tom's death. Simon stared up at her, his eyes desperate.

'It's just an old lady who has wandered away and got lost. Nothing to worry about, so long as we find her.' She gave both boys a quick hug.

'There's no one but me and Roi,' she said.

'Let's go and make some cocoa,' Birdie said, emerging

from her room, her hair on end, her woollen dressing-gown tied tightly round her waist. She was used to night-time emergencies.

Guilt needled Brier as she walked downstairs. At least Dana was still asleep. Suppose she failed tonight? That would mean that she would fail next week. She remembered childhood superstitions. If I can do all the crossword, I know I'll pass my exams. If I can find three daisies in two minutes, I know I'll get my hockey colours. If I don't tread on any lines, I'll be house captain.

If only life were full of such small ambitions, she thought, smiling ruefully at her long-ago so innocent self.

Roi was waiting by the door, eager for action. He was always willing for what he considered fun. He would never understand what lay behind their expeditions.

Out into the windy night, the rain starting again. Not even a ghost moon. She tried to shut the front door quietly behind her and looked down the street, conscious of people sleeping. Some upstairs windows glowed. A sick child, an old man dying; a woman wakeful, sighing for a lost love. A large van passed her gate. Always someone abroad.

She thought suddenly of Tony at home alone, waiting for news of his wife and baby. He had been unusually silent for the last few days, trying to rally when he went to see Sheila.

Please God, let his wife and baby be fine, she said to the stars, as she unlocked the van door. Roi jumped inside.

Then nothing but darkness and the headlights illuminating new-leafed hedges that bordered the little lane that led to the old people's home.

She braked as a fox ran across the road, a rabbit dangling from its jaws. The animal paused, turned and looked at her, one paw raised, then loped on. A vixen, heavy in cub.

The nursing home was a converted small manor, standing in large grounds. Between stone pillars, each topped by a sitting lion, on to the long drive, already busy with police cars. Lights everywhere, and men searching the shrubberies. Acres of parklike gardens and a still lake that reflected the moonlight.

Matron, weary and overworked, met Brier. The woman's grey hair was untidy. Her red wool dressing-gown was clutched round her.

'Nobody saw her leave. Sister found her bed empty when she did the second round of the night. She was in her bed at midnight. We searched everywhere indoors while we were waiting for the police. Amy is a worry. She's gone back to her courting days and is sure her boyfriend is waiting for her, where they used to meet, but we don't know where that is. Her husband has been dead for over twenty years. She'll be ninety in a few weeks' time.'

Brier knew several of the men.

'We've not looked beyond the grounds. If she's gone outside, you ought to have a clear trail,' Bob Langley said. He was always aware that the dogs could have little chance if there were too many people walking over the ground.

Brier glanced at her watch. What idiot wrote about the wee small hours? An owl hooted from a faraway tree and was answered from almost over her head.

Where would an old lady go? Through the woods, or along the gravelled path, on to the footpath that led along the canal? Where would lovers meet, long ago?

Idiotically the tune of 'Where have all the flowers gone?' buzzed in her mind.

Roi began to search the ground as she spoke to him softly.

'Seek, good lad. Seek.'

Head down, he nosed the path. They might be tracking one of the men; they might be tracking a member of staff who had recently walked along this way. They might be tracking rabbit or squirrel, or stoat or fox or weasel.

She could only follow the dog blindly and trust that he was on a human trail.

It petered out at a high fence. No old lady could climb that.

Think.

Seventy years ago there had been no road here. There had been country lanes, and the fields beyond, and the old house that had stood derelict for more than a half a century. There was a story about the house. A feud and a wedding that healed a family rift. The trysting stile where the lovers met became a symbol of luck and other lovers met there for years afterwards.

Out of the gate and along the footpath. Through the kissing gate on to the muddy track, and Roi had his head down and was almost pulling her over. Time was vital. The old lady, they thought, had nothing on but a nightdress and the wind was cold and the rain persistent.

Alone in the dark, just her and the dog. The rain blowing into her face, the path slippery under her feet, the torch showing her obstacles to avoid and Roi, oblivious to everything but the scent on the ground, flying along at a speed that, if he did it next week, would lose her a multitude of points.

A muddy footprint. Bare feet.

They were on the right track. The dog eased his pace and yickered, the odd keening note he had made when he found Simon. Amy was lying in a huddled heap by the stile, her eyes terrified.

'Oh, love, you're so cold,' Brier said. 'And so wet.'

What a place to fall. She suspected one of the old lady's legs was broken. It was at a very odd angle. Nothing she could do except ask, fast, for help.

Roi, his job done, lay down, waiting for further action. Had he been dry she would have cuddled him against the old woman, but his coat was soaked and he was covered in mud. Brier spoke hastily into her radio, giving her location.

'I think she has a broken leg.'

They would alert the ambulance service.

She stripped off her coat and took the pathetic body in her arms, wrapping the jacket round both of them, holding the shivering old woman tight. Amy was bird-boned, her grey hair and her nightdress soaked.

'John wasn't there,' she said. 'He didn't come. Why didn't he come?'

'I expect there was a good reason,' Brier said, soothingly. No use telling her John would never come. He had vanished from the world many years ago.

'Are we on a boat? Will it sink? It's so wet.'

Oh hurry up, Brier prayed silently to her absent colleagues.

'We'll soon have you in bed and warm,' she said aloud.

The minutes were endless, but at last men were with her, hands were helping her, wrapping their casualty in blankets, easing her on to a stretcher.

'You got to her in time,' one of the ambulance men said.

Back at last through the rainy dark into the sleeping house. She stared down at her dog. He was covered in mud and soaking wet, and he had looked wonderful at bedtime. After five and no point in going back to bed. She yawned, wondering if she would fall asleep on her feet during the day.

Simon was in the doorway, looking at her.

'I was worried,' he said.

No use dismissing his fears. He looked so small in his pyjamas and dressing-gown. They had had to buy him new clothes as nothing fitted. He was a neat child, unlike Ben who could become untidy in two minutes.

He plugged in the kettle.

'You need a shower. I'll make you a drink. And I can dry Roi. I can today, can't I? He's not coming to me nearly as much now.'

Weary beyond imagining, Brier nodded.

'Where did you go? Was Roi good?'

'Roi was splendid.' Brier yawned. 'A very old lady

thought she was a girl again and went to meet her boyfriend by the trysting stile.'

'Is she all right? Did you find her?'

'Roi found her.'

'He's great, isn't he?' He had seized the kitchen towel and was rubbing the dog. Brier looked at the mud. Oh, well, washing machines took most of the work out of that chore.

The shower warmed her. By the time she had dried her hair Simon had made a cup of cocoa. She loathed it. It was the children's drink, but she drained every drop, aware of the grave, anxious eyes. He was so much more mature than Ben, who had been sheltered and loved and protected. Yet they were almost the same age.

She sat down in the big armchair, intending to rest for ten minutes, and fell asleep.

Simon roused her at seven, a cup of tea in his hand.

'I've brushed Roi. I can get breakfast. Birdie's still asleep. I didn't like to wake you. Ought I to have done so before?'

Simon's face was anxious. His dark blue eyes had disturbing depths to them, hiding thoughts that often baffled her. He had sat beside her, watching her, judging the time to perfection. Roi would have to do without his extra training this morning. He had had plenty of tracking practice the night before, and he too was tired.

She hugged Simon.

'I don't know what I'd do without you.'

The blue eyes glowed.

'Next week Roi will be a real police dog.' Simon stroked the dog, who waved his tail, his eyes on Brier's hand which was holding a piece of toast.

She shared it with him.

If only it were true.

Sixteen

Brier was exhausted before the day began, her eyes gritty with tiredness. She had an overwhelming desire to keep on yawning. She felt slightly sick, and her mouth was dry. Her nerves were taking over and she felt as uneasy as she had long ago at school when exam time drew near.

Those dreadful mornings when she woke sick and shaky after dreaming that she was sitting at her desk, unable even to write her name. Suppose that paralysis numbed her brain next week, just when she needed it most?

If only she could pretend it didn't matter, but it did. She wanted to work with her dog more than she had wanted anything for a very long time. The dog was an added dimension to her work, easing it, giving confidence. Roi was extra eyes and extra ears; extra arms, and added protection.

Faster than any human, he would be swift to come to her aid. If she had to give up and return to work alone again, she would begin to hate her job, and know fear again. Especially when a friend was injured. Her brain seemed to have switched into overdrive and the lagging minutes were destroying confidence.

Roi, Roi, she thought. You don't know how much I depend on you now. If only she didn't let him down. She rallied herself. Think positive. They had done a good track. The old woman was alive and recovering—thanks to Roi.

The dog had known, and had done all that was asked of him. Her training had paid off.

Gulley paused beside her, offering the inevitable mug of coffee and an intriguing little iced cake with a cherry on top. It was flavoured with lemon. She couldn't eat. She sensed tension in the man, and put it down to the fact that he cared so much about his dogs and their handlers. Gulley did not tell anyone that he had rung the surgery to ask about Spark and been told there was a major problem. The dog had lost too much blood. They were trying a transfusion. He hadn't yet told Josh.

Gulley was so angry that it was hard to hide his feelings. Josh was unable to use his garden until he had cleared up all the glass; and suppose there was a tiny splinter hidden in the grass, waiting to injure the dog again, or harm Lim? If he got his hands on the joker . . .

Josh came in late, unusually for him, his face thunderous. Gulley brought hot, sweet coffee at once. Josh helped himself to three of the tiny cakes, eating them without noticing what he was doing. Gulley spoke to him in a very low voice, not wanting to broadcast his news.

'Paul rang. They're doing a transfusion.'

'Will he make it?'

'Too early to say. This lot are nervy. Go easy.'

Josh rallied himself. He needed to ease the tension for all of them, to lighten the atmosphere. No amount of fine tuning now would make much difference. He didn't want overstretched handlers and dogs bored to lethargy by too much training.

Everyone was relieved when Gracie's car drew into the yard. Gracie came in, taking the steps two at a time, giving a breezy welcome.

'Wanted a word about Spark,' Gracie said. 'We're all blazing mad. Need to find out who did it.'

'Spark?' Gwyn voiced everyone's concern.

'Someone chucked broken glass all over my garden. You all need to watch. He looked last night as if he'd lose most of his paw. Paul's doing his best, but even if he recovers, he probably won't be able to work.'

Josh could feel their sympathy and was aware that no one knew what to say. They appreciated the disaster more than they would have done at the start of the course. Every dog was now a vital part of his handler's life, both as a companion and a workmate.

The phone rang again.

'The hospital want Tony. They're about to operate.' Gulley glanced across at the man, whose face had tightened as he spoke. Brier, who was sitting beside him, could feel his tension.

'Off with you,' Josh said. 'I don't expect you back today. Gulley will take care of Jago.' They all approved of the change of name. Jago was far more dignified that Jacko.

'And Gulley will drive him,' Gulley said. 'No use going off feeling sick with worry. That's the way accidents happen. Come on, son.'

'Never rains but it pours,' Rob said, feeling someone ought to say something, as the door shut behind them.

'Pray for them too.' Josh finished pouring boiling water into a mug and handed it to Gracie. 'For heaven's sake, think of something to cheer us up.'

'I can do that.' Gracie sipped, and helped himself to one of the day's ration of Danish pastries. 'I met up with Tiger yesterday. We both had a day off, and went fishing. He had a track and half with his dog some weeks ago.'

He grinned with reminiscent enjoyment.

'There was a break-in at a luxury food centre, way back in January, when it was snowing hard in his neck of the woods. The men stole one of the vans, wrecked it, and started off on foot, carrying frozen smoked salmon, lobsters, guinea fowl, and quail eggs.'

He looked round at the listening faces.

'It would have made a good Laurel and Hardy film. They dropped the eggs, which proved too much for his dog who stopped to feast and had to be dragged away.'

They were all aware that frozen eggs would not make a good snack for any dog.

'The pair took off down a footpath and across a newly

ploughed wet field, leaving footsteps so distinct that Tiger could have followed without the dog.'

They could all see the snowy fields, a bright moon overhead. 'Tiger found one of the men who was crouched in a dry ditch, shivering violently, as he'd tucked the smoked salmon into his jacket.'

Gracie grinned again.

'Tiger couldn't believe his eyes. Smoked salmon packets dropping out of his clothes, his body packed with them, so that he'd turned himself into a walking ice man. Daft. He was drunk. Celebrating coming out of jail four days before.'

He chuckled again, looking at the grinning faces.

'Couldn't wait to get rid of his haul. Heaven knows what he was going to do with it. Flog a packet here, and a packet there, I suppose.'

'What about the other man?'

'Tiger handed the silly fellow over and set off again. The second man was standing beside a stile, frantically pulling packets of frozen food out of his own clothing. Teeth chattering, hands blue with cold. Seemed positively pleased to be nicked.'

'Police canteen served smoked salmon?' Rob asked wistfully. 'Just think of it. Hardboiled egg; brown bread and butter and smoked salmon. Lobster thermidor. Smoked chicken.' He licked his lips.

'Don't suppose we can eat evidence,' Pete said. 'Anyway it would be partly defrosted; if they froze it again there could be trouble.'

Josh was thankful for the distraction. He was distraught and finding it hard to hide the fact. He was aware that Gulley had not told him the whole truth, and that worried him even more. The dog might die . . . he rallied his thoughts, aware of Brier watching him, a slight frown on her face.

'You did a good job last night,' he said. 'Matron asked me to thank you.'

Brier yawned suddenly, feeling as if her jaw would break.

'Lunch at the Swan. I thought we'd give Alice a break from providing sandwiches, as she's off to a dog show tomorrow. Got to bath her Tibbies,' Josh said. The bright little terriers always amused him when he called. 'We'll take it easy today. Join us, Gracie?'

Everyone was glad of the distraction. No one could chase away thoughts of Tony, waiting at the hospital, and Spark, poised between life and death.

The little pub was crowded. Brier was thankful to flop into a seat and for once be waited on as Gwyn went across to the counter to order for both of them. Josh was deep in conversation with Gracie, who wanted to know as much as possible about the night's events, in the hope he could find out who had planted the glass. Rob was silent. Gwyn chattered, his Welsh accent stronger than ever, but Brier was too tired to join in.

Josh slipped away to telephone the vet again. The dog might make it, after all. Ring back at six tonight. They'd keep him in until they were certain he would survive. Josh felt savage. He ordered a beer and then a whisky. Gwyn, standing beside him, tried to think of comforting words, but none came to mind. He sighed and went back to Brier, who was drinking pineapple juice.

Back in the office, Josh was about to start the afternoon's talk when Gulley came in, grinning.

'One piece of good news,' he said. 'I stayed with him. Not fit to be left, poor lad. It's a little girl. Seven pounds and screaming lustily. Sheila's fine. The doctors reckon that maybe Tony and Sheila can't have live boys, but that whatever gene it is that bedevils them doesn't apply to girls.'

He put down a carrier bag on the table.

'Tony has stood us all extra doughnuts. They won't be as good as Alice's, but that shop isn't bad. Don't think he knows what's hit him.'

Josh looked at the smiling faces. One worry the less. Tony ought to have come down off his cloud by next Monday, and maybe he would pass after all. Josh had had little hope if the baby were not yet born.

Gulley drove off fast at the end of the day, intending to search Josh's garden before the light went. He collected a yard broom and a bucket from the kennels, and called in on the way to borrow an industrial vacuum cleaner and a long extension flex.

He was just about to stop his self-imposed task because of the failing light, when Josh drove in and parked in front of his garage.

Gulley walked over, anxious for news.

'We'll know for sure tomorrow,' Josh said, grim-faced. 'I called in on my way. Paul had to almost reconstruct his leg and isn't sure about the nerves, which were cut too. Could make it. Might not. Shock, loss of blood and it's one hell of a gash.' He glanced into the bucket, at the jagged spikes of glass that glinted in the light of the street lamp, which had just come on.

'I feel murderous,' he said. 'If they come back and I catch them I won't be responsible . . .'

Gulley covered the bucket and put it inside the garage.

'Come home for a meal,' he said. 'Do both of us good. No use brooding. It won't worry Alice. She's all ready for the morning, and there's always plenty in the freezer.' He lifted Lim. 'He can join us, can't you, little feller?' The stump tail wagged merrily. Heaven alone knew how the little dog had escaped injury. 'He gets on well with our menagerie and doesn't bother the cats.'

Alice could never resist a kitten.

'How many is it now?' Josh asked.

'Six. Had a new one last week. It was going to be put down as they couldn't find it a home. You know Alice. It's a wonder we can move around our house.'

Josh knew that for the rest of the evening his mind would

be on his dog, but it would be better to have company than to sit by himself, anger dominating every thought.

By the time Brier reached home she was exhausted. It was all she could do to keep her eyes open. Dana was flourishing her plaster, now also adorned with Gracie's signature. So he had called in.

'Any news?' Brier asked Kate, once the children were in bed.

'Gracie says it all depends on the case conference. Next week. After the tests.'

'I wish I knew now.'

'It'll be all right,' Kate said, her fingers crossed behind her.

She switched on the television set, but Brier was almost asleep, worrying that perhaps she ought to take Roi outside and do some work. Maybe that wasn't such a good idea. She ought to have called in to see Helena, but there was never any time . . . only two more days. She drifted into a doze and woke, startled. She must get herself to bed.

'Please God it's a quiet night. No calls, no nightmares, no children feeling sick. I could sleep for a week.'

On the Friday she woke with a taste in her mouth and the knowledge that she was starting a really vicious cold. If only she could stay in bed, but Simon was beside her, with his anxious little face and a cup of tea that had too much milk and also had sugar, both of which she detested.

She roused herself, shivering, and sneezed. She took the cup.

Looking up at him, she saw desperation in his eyes.

'What is it, Simon?' she asked.

'I dreamed about my dad again. You won't let him take me back?' he asked.

'I'll do my very best,' she said.

'Gracie said the hearing's next week.'

Oh love, love, she thought helplessly. She put her arms round him and held him close.

'Try not to worry, sweetheart,' she said. 'We're all praying for you to stay.'

She sneezed several times as she dressed. Her throat felt scratchy, and her nose seemed to be stuffed with cotton wool. One more day and then the weekend. Time to get over the worst of it. She couldn't track with a handkerchief in her hand. Her voice sounded husky, and Roi might not recognise her commands.

Though he knew what training was about. She could use hand signals and maybe the words weren't so important.

She looked unhappily at the breakfast table and the food that Simon had prepared.

'He loves doing it,' Kate said. 'He won't let me.' She looked at Brier anxiously.

'You all right, love?'

Brier sneezed again.

'Anything but all right. I only hope I can keep going today.'

'Take some Lemsip,' Kate advised. 'It might ward it off for today, but I don't think you're going to get rid of it that easily.'

Wind rattled the windows and rain streaked out of a lowering sky. They would all be soaked to the skin. Winter seemed to have returned.

Seventeen

The morning started noisily. Tony was still bubbling with happiness and everyone was laughing and teasing him. The little girl had been named Hannah Mary.

'You wait till she comes home,' Pete said, wise with all of eight months' experience of fatherhood. 'You won't know what's hit you.'

'My mother-in-law, probably,' Tony said. 'She's come to stay and help Sheila over the first month. Not too happy about the dog. She reckons dogs and babies don't mix, and a police dog, of all animals . . .'

'He can stay with me,' Gulley said. 'I've a big indoor kennel. Then she can relax.'

Gulley appeared to be hiding a secret. He had arrived that morning carrying a large cardboard box. Brier watched him go into his little office, Bess walking importantly behind him.

'Maybe he's got an extra fine feast in there,' Gwyn said, licking his lips.

'His glad rags for test days. Gulley always dresses nattily for special occasions.' Pete grinned as he spoke.

His suggestion was greeted with a roar of disbelief. It was impossible to imagine Gulley without his overall.

'Gulley's sick of us all and going to blow us up. Box is full of dynamite,' said Gwyn, since he wasn't allowed to have his food.

Josh arrived and ended the speculation. They were swept into the day's work. He drove them hard, scolding them for letting the dogs get away with the tiniest faults in performance. They had to be perfect.

'I want them up to the standard of the Area Trials,' he said. 'And then we aim for the National. So keep working. I've not had a dog win the National yet but maybe this time . . .'

Spark was still in the vet's little hospital. There was a slight improvement on the day before, but it was too early to say. Suppose those wounds infected?

The more Josh thought of the broken glass, the more vindictive he felt. And that wasn't good for him or anyone else.

Without Spark, he felt as useless as if he had had a leg amputated. He guarded Lim when he ran free. He couldn't bear to have two dogs out of action.

The National. The top handler and dog in Britain. They were all dreaming. He was pushing them beyond the tests, setting their minds on yet higher achievements. Making them all think like winners.

Maybe Roi, Brier thought.

The day passed at last. Time to relax after the children were in bed. Roi lay at her feet. She sat quietly, listening to Brahms. Peace and an early night.

She was thankful for bedtime. Simon now rarely had nightmares. She drank Kate's over-the-counter remedy and was asleep before she had time to think. She dreamed of a pealing bell that nobody would switch off. She woke. One a.m. and the phone was ringing.

Dog handler needed. No one else was available.

Not again. Not again. Not again.

'I'm sorry,' Josh said. 'I've no choice. Would you like me to handle him for you?'

She was suddenly wide awake. Roi was her dog and it would be good experience.

'No thanks,' she said.

She was in the van within minutes.

'On my way.'

Down the lane, headlights picking out hedges laden with

blossom, flashing briefly on a cruising owl, shining on puddles left over after a late shower.

Wet fields. Rain misted the windscreen and she set the wipers working. Into the main road, a few hundred yards to the roundabout, on to the motorway, the van eating up the miles. She was thankful for the bright lamps that edged the road and saved so much energy when driving at night.

Very little traffic and thank heaven for that. Flashing lights and a small group of cars and men.

A taste of the future, she thought, as she made her rendezvous. Thank heaven Kate's remedy had cleared her head.

A Traffic Patrol car had chased a silver Porsche which had been stolen earlier that evening and used for a break-in. A safe had been blown and the wages taken.

The stolen car had been abandoned.

'They went off across the fields,' a voice said.

Roi was bouncing, pleased to be out working instead of going to his bed.

A high moon and a star-bright night. At least it wasn't raining now. A small chill wind blew into her face. She sneezed. There would be men behind her, following, listening to her as she described her route.

Roi knew his job. Down went his nose. Across the first field. Shortish grass. Molehills, and the memories of cattle. She slowed the dog. Couldn't do with a broken leg. It happened. A rabbit hole, a snaking bramble, out to trap, and there was another handler out of action.

She hoped Roi was tracking her quarry and not some joker who had decided to walk home through the fields instead of along the roads. The line was tight, telling her that he was working and not fooling.

An invisible ditch, shadowed by a high, thick hedge. No use using a torch as that would alert her quarry. She cursed as she slipped calf-deep into water.

'Gap in the hedge. Going through,' she said, and heard the acknowledgement.

A bank beyond and another small ditch. This time the moon glinted on water, warning her, and she and the dog jumped, Roi sliding. He turned up the field, zigzagging. A clever crook, out to foil the dog. He wouldn't succeed, not with this one. Suddenly an enormous wave of elation over-took her. Roi was tracking well, was working well, and had no eyes for anything but his job.

The ground was uneven, the going diabolical. Moles had been busy. How far had the fugitives walked? She felt as if she had been struggling for ever. She had only been out for twenty minutes.

'Over the stile,' she said. Easier said than done. Roi baulked and she had to encourage him to discover how to negotiate it. It was a ladder stile, of a type he had never met before.

It delayed them five minutes, and then they were in a rutted lane, puddled with rain from the day before. Roi pulled hard, towards a group of terraced houses. Beyond them was a main road. They waited for three lorries and a couple of cars to pass before crossing. Time wasted.

Across the road, the dog almost running, Brier holding on to him, hoping they had not far to go . . . 'miles to go before I sleep.' How stupid one's brain could be, tossing out irrelevant data. Her father had loved the poem. Simon loved poetry too and read it to her, when there was time.

Roi was on a speedway. She tried to slow him. The track was fresh with plenty of scent and he knew that there would be success at the end of it.

She was aware of the murmur from her radio, of men behind her, ready to back her up. They were a team, with one objective. There was a rumour that her quarry was armed.

'Take care,' said a voice that she thought might belong to Bob Langley.

They crossed the road, Roi tracking along the verge. She hoped he was right. Would they risk being seen from cars? She cursed under her breath as the dog baulked at a field gate, and indicated a need to go through. He leaped it effortlessly when told, and she clambered over, fouling her tracking line so that she had to stop and sort it out.

Behind her she could hear the sound of feet. She glanced round and was reassured to see three uniformed men.

The track led along the hedge and then, infuriatingly, into a field of bullocks, all curious, all anxious to inspect her and the dog. She stopped, afraid they might charge Roi.

'OK?' asked a voice.

'No. Have you a torch?'

'Sure.'

'Can you walk back into that far corner? It doesn't lead anywhere and I don't think our quarry'll be there. Shine the torch and see if the cattle'll come to it. Otherwise I'm stumped. They won't let Roi get on to the track and they're destroying any scent that may be here.'

She had heard that cattle would pack and trample dogs. Suppose they attacked her?

The cattle followed the light. Brier, sighing with relief, led the dog over the fouled ground, and let him hunt. A moment later he was on course through never-ending fields. One after another, stumbling into molehills, caught by seeking brambles, over gates and twice through hedges. Her quarry must be young and very fit. She glanced at her watch. Nearly 3.15 a.m.

Through a kissing gate, Roi puzzled by it, across yet another field, newly sown with a fresh crop springing. The farmer would love that. Out at another gate to find two parked police cars, the men standing by them.

No sign of anyone, though their quarry had been reported as coming this way. Her route had been noted, and the squad cars had driven along the road to meet her.

'They've far too much energy,' Brier said irritably, stopping thankfully to breathe. She poured coffee into the flask top, and gulped it, grateful for the thought. It spilled as Roi lunged and almost pulled her over. Someone grabbed the cup and they were off at such a speed that Brier was soon breathless.

It was hard to talk into her radio, but she kept the report going.

'At the edge of the main road; turning into Shadow Lane; down the steps to the canal, right along the bank.' Don't lose me whatever you do, she thought, giving yet another direction as Roi dived under the viaduct, pulled her up the steps at the end of it and crossed the road towards the railway station.

On to the line; along the track; pray no trains were coming. Off the track; up the bank; through a gap in the fence. Must know this well, she thought.

She paused, as Roi cast and cast again, baffled.

'Two men running towards the hospital grounds.' The voice sounded in her ear.

Damn them. They'd back-tracked. How had she missed them?

Clouds chased across the moon. She needed the light. Don't cloud over, she begged, aiming her thoughts at the sky.

The men might return to the canal path, unaware that they were being tracked by a dog. She sheltered under a humpbacked bridge, leaning against the damp stone. Light reflected on black, rank-smelling water.

There were footsteps above her. A man walked down the steps towards her. She stiffened, and Roi growled, but they both relaxed when he spoke. It was Bob Langley.

'Thought I saw you come down here. No sign of them anywhere.'

'I might pick their trail up again if I go back to the other side of the railway line. Maybe they separated.'

'No. A patrol sighted two of them, on the skyline in the Hollerton fields. I walked along the canal bank, up to the viaduct. No sign of them there.'

Brier sighed. Roi had been following Bob's track, not that of the two men. Back to the far side of the viaduct and see if she could pick up the trail again. It was a forlorn hope, but she didn't want to give up. This could be important to her future.

There were steps at the side of the viaduct. Roi pulled towards them. Up the steps; across the lane; through a gap in the fence. She was in the hospital grounds. He tugged her towards the entrance. Two shadowy figures crouched between the parked cars.

'Hospital car park. I need assistance, fast,' she said.

'Come out, or I'll send the dog,' she warned.

Nobody moved. Maybe they thought a woman wouldn't have a dog. They'd soon learn. She let the dog go.

Roi flew down the line of vehicles, and barked.

'Call him off,' shouted an agonised voice.

'Roi, stand.'

She was unable to see him, hearing only his deep, angry bay, hoping he had done as she told him.

She shone her torch into the faces of two slender youths. About seventeen years old, she guessed. As she did so, she heard a siren. The car drew up beside her.

She was glad to surrender her quarry. But she was arresting officer and it wasn't over yet.

'Need a lift back to your van?' Bob Langley asked, when her task was completed.

Wearily she climbed into his car, the dog beside her. She was exhausted and conscious of her wet feet and legs. Her cold was worse.

At last she was free to go home.

Nearly 5 a.m. She yawned.

The rain that had threatened for the last hour drove from a sky now laden with scudding clouds. Bob drew up beside her parked van. The rising wind flicked Roi's fur the wrong way, so that he turned and shook himself. She was too tired to savour success.

'Need some sleep?' Bob asked.

She managed a grin.

'I'll say. My legs won't work much longer and my feet are soaked. I wish the villains needed sleep as much as I do. Be nice to know we could stay in bed all night.'

'We can dream.'

'Only day-dreams.' She looked at the drawn curtains and dark houses that surrounded them and thought with longing of a world where even the police could sleep at night without worry.

She yawned, feeling as if her jaw would break.

'At least it's Saturday. I can stay in bed. If nothing else happens.' It was a thought to cherish.

My choice, she thought, as she drove home. She envied Roi, asleep behind her, able to forget everything at the end of his work. Her mind would whirl for the next few hours, reviewing what they had done and whether she could have avoided going off on the wrong track.

She walked into the sleeping house. Bed. She must be up in time to be with the children. Saturday was their day, a day set aside for fun and games.

'Oh, you,' she said to Roi, suddenly elated, and knelt and hugged him. 'You're wonderful,' she told him and the long tail waved from side to side and he butted her hand.

She slept and dreamed of an endless trail that led nowhere, and woke feeling as if she had not been to bed at all. She felt shivery and her throat was sore. Would she be fit by Monday?

Eighteen

It was over. The end of the course. Josh looked at his breakdown list, and couldn't believe they had covered it all. General obedience; agility; quartering to find their criminal. Gun and stick training. Grass and hard surface tracking. Building search for a hidden person. Search for lost property dropped during a criminal offence.

Not to mention cleaning of kennels, grooming and feeding and care of the dogs, their health and management. Thirteen weeks, during which he had had more problems than ever before, had left him feeling as if he had been ill for a month.

He collected Spark from the vet's during the morning. The dog was apathetic, a shadow of his usual lively self. The gash had infected, and he lay, looking into the distance, and barely responded when Josh spoke to him. He felt bereft without the dog he had spent so many years training, who had become a valued and dearly loved companion.

The highlight of the course was always the final parade, when those who had passed were on show, their dogs walking proudly beside them. For the first time in his career he would be unable to lead the parade with his own dog beside him. The fear of losing Spark was almost more than he could bear. Lim had to be kept from trying to play with his kennelmate. The little dog was puzzled, unable to understand why his big companion, usually so active, had little interest in either food or games.

Josh spent the day aimlessly, trying to read the newspaper, but failing to remember one single word. Gulley was unavailable, busy, he said. He had mystified everyone by bringing in his large cardboard box the previous day. Gulley's office was sacrosanct and no one went in except by invitation.

The ringing phone at four o'clock was a welcome distraction. He almost wished it was a call-out for Lim. Anything to occupy himself, and not to have to watch his dog lying so still, almost unaware of his surroundings.

It was Helena.

'Josh, Kate told me about Spark. I am so very sorry. Is he fit to put in the car? I have a problem and you may be able to help. Take pity on me and come and have a meal tonight.'

The invitation was so welcome that he could have kissed her, had she been standing in front of him. He did not want to drop in on Gulley. Alice was celebrating her first Championship Certificate and Best of Breed with her young Tibetan Terrier, Dynamite. He didn't want to spoil their pleasure and knew he would find it hard to pretend cheerfulness.

He drove to Willowbank by way of the shops and chose a congratulations card with a Golden Retriever on it. There were none with Tibetan Terriers, but Alice wouldn't mind. Gulley hadn't told him, feeling the timing was inappropriate; he had heard the news from Gwyn. He wrote a note inside and his name, and dropped the card into the post box. Alice would receive it on Monday.

Once in Helena's kitchen, he eased Spark onto the rug in front of the fire. Lim nosed the dog, and then looked at Josh as if asking him why Spark did not take any notice of him.

'I wonder if they suffer as much as we think through their lack of understanding?' Helena asked.

She looked at him, seeing a very weary man who needed comfort. 'Is there any news of the culprit who threw glass into your garden?'

'None whatever. I'd like to get my hands on that devil.'

Anger flared in his eyes. 'Maybe it'll be as well if we don't catch him. They expect us to be saints, and forget we're human too. People who hurt children and animals are beyond the pale.' Helena's big kitchen-cum-sitting-room was sanctuary. He dropped gratefully into the big armchair and leaned against the cushions, his feet stretched out to the blaze.

Firelight flickered on the model china dogs on the dresser, on the rosettes that were pinned to the picture rail, all round the walls, on a picture of two Shire horses ploughing, and the many framed photographs of past dogs. A lifetime of memories. Brier smiled at him from a photograph taken with her father, both standing beside a Jersey bull. The cup they had just won stood on a small table beside them.

Helena saw his glance and sighed.

'Willowbank Hero. George was so proud of that bull. He was the best we ever bred. I had to sell him, as I needed the money. I felt disloyal. I was there when he was born. Like selling my own child.'

A black and ginger kitten sat at Josh's feet, mewing, plainly asking to be picked up. He grinned and lifted the little animal and listened to its sudden, throbbing purr. It cuddled against him. Spark did not even notice. His eyes were unfocused, staring into the distance, as if he saw visions outside this world. Lim, jealous, pawed at Josh's leg.

Helena laughed.

'Marble's trying to find himself a new owner,' she said. Lim pushed his nose against the kitten, intending to oust him.

Marble swore at him. The spaniel's ears lifted outwards from his head, and his eyes sparkled with mischief.

'Lie down,' Josh said and the dog obeyed, but he watched every move of human and kitten. Spark lay with his nose on his paws, staring into the flames.

'Whisky?' Josh's thoughts had been miles away. He shook his head.

'I'm too tired and I have to drive home. No desire to be done by my traffic colleagues.'

Helena poured a glass of apple juice. As Josh took it, Marble jumped to the floor, skirting the dogs warily. Helena had put her own dogs and the young Burmese tom outside in the kennels, lest they disturb Spark. She looked at the dog, frowning.

The mother cat curled on the sheepskin rug, and held her struggling kitten down, washing him so enthusiastically that he squalled, pulled himself free, clambered over Spark, his claws digging into the dog's fur, and leaped back to Josh's knee. Spark sat up, startled. Jealousy triggered him to movement and he limped across the rug, and pushed Marble to the floor.

'Well, well,' Josh said, and Helena laughed as the dog settled himself against his master's leg, daring the cats to come near.

'Maybe he needs the kitten to bring him out of his depression,' she said. 'It's wonderful what a spot of jealousy can do to an animal.'

'Beef and marrowbone broth.' She poured it into a bowl and watched Spark lap it, showing the first sign of interest in food that Josh had seen. 'Works wonders.'

Spark lapped thoughtfully and then more eagerly, finishing every drop. Lim licked the empty bowl, making sure nothing whatever was left.

'I'll give him more before you go. Make some for him when you get home,' Helena said. 'My grandad used to call it corpse reviver. I've spare bones.'

Josh stroked the soft ears, and Spark settled himself, relaxing. He licked the caressing hand.

'He's on the mend.' Helena balanced herself on the edge of the table.

'Josh, are you going to have to retire Spark?'

'Almost certainly. Paul says he'll never be able to jump again. Not much use if we're out and he meets obstacles. At least they let us keep our old dogs now, but where in the world do I find a replacement?'

'That's what I wanted to talk about. The Breed rescue kennels are full and asked me to take on a twelve-month-old dog, since I bred him. He's very trainable. He's had a near-perfect home, but they've been hit by bad luck. They lived in a lovely house with a lot of land. Poor Khan. He's lost in kennels and I can't bring him in. My old girls won't tolerate him.'

She turned her attention to a saucepan cooking on the stove, and stirred the food.

'It's the usual story today. Husband redundant, firm bankrupt and no redundancy pay. They've sold the house and moved into a rented flat, and they can't keep Khan. They asked me to find him a really good home and I promised to keep him until one came along. He's part trained. The husband was going to do Working Trials with him.'

'Can I see him?'

'Sure, but let's eat first. This is ready.'

Helena dished out curry and rice, watched with avid attention by Lim, and by the cat and her remaining kitten. Marble still had designs on Josh's knee, but Spark watched, and he knew better than to try.

'So many people have been caught like that. It accounts for more than half the dogs in Rescue.' She put the two plates on the table. 'It's been a long time since I last saw you.'

'So busy.' Josh sighed. 'I only hope no one calls me out tonight.'

He walked over to the table, and Spark followed him with his eyes, but decided not to move. Lim sat at his feet.

'Anyone would think I gave them titbits from my plate. Lim's always hopeful.'

'There's always the odd pea that bounces to the floor.' Helena looked at him, her eyes thoughtful. Josh thought she was about to speak, but she said nothing and picked up her knife and fork. He ate in silence, savouring the food. It was a long time since any woman other than Alice had offered to cook him a meal. A long time since he had sat and talked with a willing listener other than Gulley.

'Brier said you've had a lot of call-outs for Lim.'

'Half the bomb scares are hoaxes, but we still have to go. There aren't nearly enough sniffer dogs. If we had more, I suspect that more bombs would be found before they went off. We're stretched to the limit.'

Helena passed him the casserole and he refilled his plate. He hadn't bothered to eat at all that day. Breakfast had been a hasty slice of toast, eaten without enjoyment.

'Do you eat enough?'

'Alice Gulley fills us up with wonderful cakes and pasties and makes our lunchtime sandwiches. They're good.'

'Too much junk food. You'll all get fat.'

'With all the exercise we get? Some hope.'

'I'm getting lazy in my old age,' Helena said. 'Everything I do is beginning to feel like a major effort. I need help here, and don't know where to get it from. They say there are a lot of people out of work, but I can't find them. I end up with youngsters they send under the employment schemes who are not in the least interested, or are even afraid of the dogs.'

'Maybe Alice would help you. She's just won a CC with Dynamite, but from what Gulley says she has plenty of spare time on her hands. She does a lot of work at the Rescue Kennels. Even a few hours a week would make a difference, wouldn't it?'

'A big difference. Alice is reliable. I hadn't thought of her. I'd pay her too; I don't suppose Gulley earns all that much and pensions don't run far these days.'

'I'll have a word with Gulley.' His mind reverted to the

dog outside. 'I suppose Khan isn't the same breeding as Roi? I could do with a few more like him.'

'No. My own bitch, but I mated her to one of the Crutchmore dogs. A nice fellow with a wonderful temperament. I gave him Best Puppy two years ago.'

'I'll give it a whirl,' Josh said. 'I can take him home and see what happens. Keep him in reserve and train him. Even if Spark gets back into harness, he won't be there for ever.'

'I wish you could come more often,' Helena said, sighing. 'No one round here ever wants to talk about dogs.'

'I know the feeling.' Josh detached the kitten, who was determined to climb his leg and eat from his plate. It stalked away, tail high, offended. 'I often long for someone I can talk to, other than Gulley. I can't monopolise him. He has his own life.'

Helena put the two empty plates in the sink and returned with a blackcurrant cheesecake and a tiny jug of cream.

'I'm worried about Brier. She isn't usually touchy but she's had a rough time, one way and another. She ought to be getting over Tom, but she isn't. I thought Roi would help, but I suspect that the children have been causing problems.'

'I think that's been sorted,' Josh said, hoping fervently that he was right.

The cheesecake was too good to spend time in conversation. Helena made coffee before she spoke again. She helped herself to sugar.

There were tiny cakes to eat with the coffee, almond-flavoured, melting in the mouth. Josh wondered suddenly if Brier could cook as well as her mother, who was in the same class as Alice. They sat on either side of the fire, completely at ease. Marble jumped to Helena's knee. 'Would you like him? He needs a home.'

'I've enough to do with my two dogs. More if I take on Khan. Gulley has just taken on their sixth cat. Can't offer him another.'

'What about an office cat?' Helena laughed as the kitten rolled on his back and kicked furiously at her hand. 'Marble's used to dogs. Thinks he is a dog. You can have him around when you're training and get the police dogs used to cats, without any hassle at all. He can sleep in the office, and come home weekends.'

Josh lifted the little black and ginger animal. The kitten snuggled into his shoulder and purred loudly.

'I seem not only to have found myself a cat but another dog as well. You ought to be a saleswoman, Helena.'

She laughed.

'What do you think I've been doing all these years? Selling puppies! But a cat would be fun, and you do need another dog. I'll fetch Khan.'

He cuddled the kitten against him.

'You've solved one of my main worries for me. I couldn't imagine where on earth I'd find another dog. I can see where your daughter gets her determination from,' he added.

'Not me. She was born on a Thursday. You know the old rhyme: "Thursday's child has far to go." Simon was born on a Thursday too, oddly enough within two days of Brier's birthday.' She grinned suddenly, looking Brier's age instead of her own. 'Me, I'm a Sunday baby. "The child that is born on the Sabbath Day is blithe and bonny and good and gay." Brier always says you could have fooled her.'

Josh laughed. He felt more relaxed than he had for months. The future, instead of being something to fear, endless days without Spark, was suddenly alive with possibilities. A new young dog to train. He loved the training. Another life about his house. A new character to study and learn from. A new wife? He thought of Brier with sudden fierce longing.

He looked at Helena.

'Twenty years younger and I'd be proposing to you,' he said. 'You don't look your age.'

'Age is what you feel. But I'd never marry again. And I'm not looking for a toy boy.' She grinned at him. 'I enjoy freedom too much.'

She was suddenly serious.

'Brier misses Tom. She needs a man in her life,' she said.

That was a subject he did not want to discuss.

She went out into the dark. The security lights lit the yard. The dog, unhappy in his unfamiliar surroundings, greeted her with fervour, jumping at her, licking her hands, and crying. Josh heard the sounds and came out.

Josh whistled. Khan, who had been bonded to his master and preferred men to women, trotted across to him, tail waving eagerly.

'Come on, son,' Josh said, leading the way into the kitchen. Spark and Lim, both used to other dogs, watched without moving, obedient to Josh's signal.

He knelt and stroked the dog, looked into his eyes, which met his happily. He was coloured black and gold, with a greyer saddle than Spark's which was inky black. Khan, who had been a house dog and companion for all his short life, was delighted to be noticed and out of the kennel. He leaned against Josh and licked the man's chin. Josh looked at him, his eyes thoughtful.

'Well made. Strong bone. No sign of nerves or aggression. Looks a smart dog. Alert.' Josh didn't need time to make up his mind. He could see at a glance that Khan had the makings of a good police dog. Maybe not one of the top flight, but steady and solid and what he needed. 'Can you keep him here till the middle of next week? I'll pay for his food and kennelling. With luck, I'll have Spark back on his feet. The course will be over, and the tests. No time now to think of a new responsibility. I need all my wits about me for Monday and Tuesday.'

'Worried?' Helena asked, as the dog dropped beside her, his head on her knee. Lim nosed him, and then rested his head against the dog's flank, accepting him. Spark was watching him, expecting a command to get up and go home.

'I have nightmares every time. Anything can go wrong. A man ill, a dog ill. A vile day for the tests and a gale blowing that fouls up the scent. Some lunatic planting a bomb somewhere ghastly, like a power station, just as the judging starts.'

'I can only console you with Kate's favourite phrase: Don't worry, it may not happen.'

Josh laughed.

'In our line of work, it so often does. Train crashes. Plane crashes. Motorway pile-ups. I sometimes feel like Don Quixote must have done tilting at his windmills.'

He yawned.

'I'm off. Pray tomorrow's a quiet day and everyone is rested by Monday. You've cheered me up and given me another dog. As well as giving us Roi. I can never thank you enough, Helena.'

She watched him go, and thought that he would make a very good son-in-law. She sighed, wishing she could rearrange the world. Two more hours before she need start the last round of the kennels. There were only four boarders, and her own dogs were easy.

She switched on the television set.

Nineteen

Saturday for Brier was in ruins. She felt extremely ill.

'Don't you dare tell mother, or Josh,' she said.

Kate took matters into her own hands when she realised that Brier was flushed and feverish, and plainly suffering from a very bad cold indeed.

She rang Alice, who promised that Gulley would come and take Roi for a long walk, and say nothing to Josh. The children were put on their honour to be quiet and leave Brier alone, and Brier herself was scolded back to her bed.

She was not sure that that was a good idea. Suppose she were still unfit on Monday morning? Could she cope? Kate brought her hot drinks and aspirin, a hot water bottle, and magazines to read, but the words refused to make sense and she was unable to concentrate.

She put the magazine aside and began to review the thirteen-week course, her mind spinning. How could they ever have crammed so much into so little time? How could anyone expect the dogs to do well, when they had been pushed to their own limits?

She wished she had no time to think. Tom looked at her from the photograph beside her bed, and she longed for time to go backwards, to the days before he had been killed, when life had seemed secure and they were so happy.

She wished that Gulley would return with the dog. He needed exercise and would have been impossible all night without it, but she needed his company.

She re-read the sheets that Josh had given them. Starting time 10 a.m. each day. Obedience and Criminal work in the grounds of the local training college. Here would-be chefs were learning their skills and it was possible to buy a three-course lunch very cheaply. But nobody could work after such a meal.

A sandwich and a coffee was all she would allow herself, if she could eat it. If she hadn't made such a hash of her test that she felt sick with misery.

Gulley, returning a couple of hours later with the dog, looked in at her bedroom door.

'He's had a good long walk and about twenty minutes' free running. I pinched your tube. Took him on the common and we had an audience. Nearly charged them, they got so much entertainment,' he said, laughing.

'Thanks, Gulley.' Brier sneezed. 'Better keep out of my way. How on earth am I going to work on Monday?'

'You will. Wonderful what a couple of days' rest can do. Have a lazy day tomorrow and you'll be on top of the world and do us all proud.'

Roi settled quietly beside her bed, as if knowing she felt ill. His presence was reassuring, and she lay and watched him stretch out with a sigh and fall asleep.

Sunday passed quietly. Gulley took Roi out again, and returned with Alice. They lunched with Kate and the children and spent the afternoon playing Monopoly with them.

The rest had done Brier good. A brilliant April day, almost summer warm. She took a very short walk with Roi. The distant foothills were blue and hazed, the young leaves reflected the sunshine and there were swans on the canal, brilliant white against the murky water.

She woke on Monday to find Simon beside her bed, a cup of tea in one hand and a tiny parcel in the other.

She opened it. Inside was a little black cat, carved out of slate.

'It's from all of us,' he said. 'For luck. Kate says not to worry you, so I won't.'

The face that looked back at Brier from the mirror had

lost its wanness. Her cold was so much better that she knew she could cope with the day, however it went.

Kate had pressed her uniform and her shoes shone. Her hair was newly cut and sleek. She used very little make-up: she didn't want the judge to consider her femininity. She could pass on her merits as a dog handler, or not at all.

Simon had groomed Roi and then glossed his coat with the hound glove. He shone in the sunlight that came through the kitchen window. She ate a little toast and drank her coffee, hardly hearing the children's chatter.

They waved to her from the door.

'Good luck, good luck!' Their shouts echoed after her.

She drove to the Centre, Roi behind her. She and Gwyn travelled together to the venue. They sat in silence, neither of them able to make conversation.

They had been given a small sitting-room in which to wait. Rob appeared to be reciting to himself and Pete was yawning as his small son was teething and they had been up for half the night.

'It would have to be last night,' he said. It was the first that had been interrupted by the baby for some weeks.

Tony, who had given up smoking some months before, had bought a packet of twenty and lit one from the other.

'Last time. Wouldn't be good for the baby.' He grinned happily. 'Give it up for ever on Wednesday.'

'How is she?' Brier asked, grateful for anything that took her mind off the approaching ordeal.

Tony's face relaxed into a smile. A different man, Brier thought.

'She's doing fine. She's the prettiest mite, and she can grip my finger already.'

Gracie put his head round the door, wished them all luck and vanished. The sight of him brought the thought of the case conference to her mind, but she pushed it back again.

Get today over. Get tomorrow over, and then worry.

A fine day, after rain in the night. Sunlight shining on

the parklike grounds of the college. Tomorrow they would be out in the country, tracking.

Waiting was agony. She wished that she could be alone. Nerviness was catching.

An hour to go. Her mouth was dry and her hands, she was horrified to see, shook when she picked up her coffee cup. Better not drink it. Gulley had brought flasks, and was plying them all continuously.

'How's Spark?' asked Brier.

Gulley shrugged.

'Surviving. But that gash is septic. He's on a heavy dosage of antibiotics, but he's not responding. Paul says it's touch and go.' Spark was back in the vet's hospital, having been put on a drip.

He walked away from her, a worried little man.

Josh was outside, watching the tests from a discreet distance. If Spark died . . . Brier knew how he would feel and was surprised at the sudden awareness of how much she cared. Josh had become important to her, more important than she had realised. Only she couldn't let him guess. She was one of his team to him and that was all.

She realised that Gulley was trying to attract her attention.

It was time.

She was an actress, on stage, hiding every personal feeling. Hiding worry. Hiding fear of failure. Confident, head up, think yourself into the part, woman. Her brain gave orders to her body. How to greet the judge? With a smile, or would that seem overconfident? Would he read something into it she hadn't intended? As the only woman, how would he react to her?

She glanced at the assistants, who were all fully qualified dog handlers. She felt that they always had a certain reserve in dealing with her, as if sure no woman could do the job, especially when it came to criminal work. Maybe she was wrong. Maybe just being female made her hypersensitive in a world where men predominated. And where had that thought come from? Fear of the judges' opinion of a woman dog handler? Maybe the result was predictable before she began.

'Go to it, girl,' Josh said softly in her ear as she passed him. 'Do me proud. You can.'

I can, she thought, if only . . .

The judge nodded to her, and checked her name and the name of her dog.

Above her the clouds played games with the wind. Not too much wind. Blue sky overhead and a brilliant day. She glanced across at the apparatus. If the pieces were set wrong and the dog had to jump into the sun. Everything was set right. She knew the judge had seen her glance. He noted something on his pad.

'Don't you let me down,' she said softly to Roi. The dog, attracted by her voice, looked up at her and waved a buoyant tail.

They were off and there was a job to do. Suddenly she forgot everything but the fact that she was working with an eager and willing partner, that the day was fine, and that Roi was responding to her.

The heeling pattern was a good one. Normal pace, slow pace, at a funereal walk, the dog beside her, never out of step. At fast pace she was afraid he might excite, but then, glancing down, was aware of Roi close beside her heels, blissfully unaware that this was the test to end all tests and that on it their whole future was to depend.

Lucky dog, she thought. You don't know that everything depends on what you and I do today.

The sendaway was next, and Brier's spirits lifted, as this was an exercise that Roi adored.

There was a tree on the horizon, which would make it easy.

'Send your dog towards that tree and drop him level with the corner of that building.'

The building was a ruined pavilion at the edge of the field. Beyond it the square college buildings were half hidden among thickly planted trees. The sun glinted distractingly on massed cars in the forecourt.

Brier sighted on tree and pavilion before sending the dog, working out when to command him. Roi would overshoot the mark if he were going fast. She needed to tell him to lie down when he was within ten yards of the target.

He sped towards the tree, and dropped at once as she called. She glanced across at the pavilion. He was right in line. No problem there.

'Send him fifty yards towards the pavilion.'

She put her hand in her pocket and touched the little black cat that the children had given her. Its body was smooth and hard. Bring me luck.

Redirection was never as easy. She realised, with a drop of her spirits, that she had always practised directing the dog along a fence. How could she have been so stupid? Dogs tended to form habits fast. Maybe he wouldn't go where she wanted without the barricade behind him. There was no fence here. Josh had warned her. But there was a boundary on Helena's land, where she often practised, and she had not thought ahead.

A minute hesitation, that would cost at least one mark, and then Roi understood and flew to her right. She dropped him, loving the way he flashed down fast with an air and a flair that the other dogs lacked. She glanced at the judge, who was smiling. He was a big man, his thinning hair turning from blond to grey, his face craggy and time-worn, with a nose that was the worse for having been hit by a jemmy in a confrontation with two burglars, many years ago.

Roi shouldn't have lost many marks there. No use trying to work it out. She'd know the worst, only too soon.

Roi was watching her. Time seemed to have changed its

ways, and every minute lasted an hour. Would he try to run to her too soon? No time to worry.

'Call the dog.'

She had to stop him before he reached her, the dog standing, facing her. A couple of steps after her signal. Not as accurate as he might have been.

The distant control was another exercise that she often practised just before bedtime, the dog being asked to go from the sit to the down, to the stand, twice, on the steward's commands, and never in the same order.

One tiny paddle with one front paw as he stood. A mark lost? It had been fractional. Maybe the judge hadn't seen it.

'Down your dog.'

Roi dropped on the spot, and Brier drew a deep breath.

'Sit the dog.'

Again he obeyed her. He couldn't have dropped many marks there, could he? It all depended on how severe the judge was on marking tiny faults. But this wasn't a competition to see who would win. It was a test to find out if the handler and dog would make a good operational team.

Brier took a deep breath. She wondered briefly how the other dogs had done, but time was running on and she had to concentrate.

'Call your dog.'

Roi flew to her and sat, his tongue out, his tail waving again. He always wanted to be with Brier. Even when off lead, he now watched her, ready to fly to her defence, knowing it was up to him to keep her safe.

One after another came the other exercises, so fast that she felt as if she had little time to breathe between each. He retrieved swiftly and accurately, homing in on her with his trophy as proudly as if he were carrying a fortune.

It wasn't an easy object to retrieve: the judge had chosen a washing-up-liquid bottle half-full of water. He had to get it balanced to carry it, and the water sloshing as he ran could have put him off, but he held on and offered it to her, waiting until she took it from him.

Now for the agility. At times he dragged his hind paws as he tried to clear the hurdle. She held her breath, praying hard. Don't do it today, boy. Look at the pole and make sure those legs are held high.

Over the hurdle, with an inch to spare, and drop to the ground. Success at times made him exuberant. Josh's voice in her brain. Control. Control. Control. He said it so often. The dog went down, the moment she spoke, and slowly confidence began to return.

The six-foot high scramble board was no problem at all. The dog loved that. His build aided him. Derek's dog found it an effort. Jago disliked it. Thoughts flashed unbidden into her mind and she dismissed them.

Concentrate.

Over and down to wait until told to return. Back with a racing run that ended in front of her, his eyes looking up at her, saying, Aren't I good?

'Oh yes, you're good. If only I don't let you down,' she said in her mind.

Over the long jump, front legs outstretched, hind legs tucked in, every movement graceful. Roi was, she suddenly realised, a very elegant dog. Spike and Storm were both large-boned and clumsy. For a moment she revelled in looking at him. Time was running on.

As she walked towards the steward, the dog pacing proudly at her side, she began to feel elated.

Success heartened her. All that mattered was now. She felt a sudden wave of affection for Simon, who had tried so hard to ignore the dog. He had done everything that Gulley had asked. Roi was now bonded to her.

'Speak on command.'

The deep bay sounded confidently across the field. She signalled for silence and he stopped at once. Thank heaven for those hours of practice with the children every morning for the last two weeks, and for the two boys, who could provoke a bark and stop it, just for fun. Roi had to bark if he wanted a treat from either of them. She had trained them as well as the dog, and they never let her down by being silly with him after Gulley's lecture.

Steadiness to the gun. They had practised that too, and normally he showed no sign of worry. But the judge might use a gun that made far more noise than that they had in practice. There were never any certainties.

Not a sign of fear as the sound cracked on the air, making her start slightly, although she had been expecting it. The dog hadn't, as his back was to the man who fired and she was walking away.

Brier's thoughts ranged as she counted the slowly passing seconds in the long down. Ten minutes seemed endless, the longest ten minutes that any of them spent.

The handlers had to be out of sight, not knowing what the dogs were doing. Brier had time to worry again. Suppose he came to look for her? The slightest movement, a wriggle, a scratch, a shift of his body, and he would lose marks. Not one mark or two, but all of them. He had to be perfect. He had to be absolutely dependable, otherwise he was useless. All six dogs were tested on that exercise at the same time.

She returned to see him lying still, not a paw out of place, and was unable to resist a broad grin of pleasure. Roi, Roi, my beauty, she thought exultantly. Come on, come on, we can do it, you and I. I don't care if we win or not, so long as we pass. No other dog had moved. Everyone grinned in relief.

And that was the control work ended and surely, surely, they had done well. She glanced up at the judge, towering above her. She felt like a schoolgirl, facing the Head.

'That's a good dog,' he said.

More waiting. More time for nerves to take over. More time to watch Tony pace and smoke and Derek chew gum. More time to listen to Gwyn's babble, talking about almost anything. Rob spoke rarely, sometimes giving wrong answers. It was affecting all of them, though not one of them would admit to nerves.

Criminal work. She tried to remember the order on the sheets. Temperament of the dog and demeanour of handler. Head up, look confident, don't let your dog down. She walked out, a neat figure in her blue overalls.

Then she forgot everything but the job in hand. Crowd control and chase and attack. Chase a man who asked her to call the dog off; Roi had to stop when commanded. Brier, overcome with panic, yelled her command more loudly than she intended. Roi, startled, froze, as if he had been shot, which was what was needed but had never happened before. He stood barking, a ferocious and terrifying animal, nothing like his usual placid self.

Search the 'criminal' who upset her gravity by winking at her, so that she found it hard not to laugh. Escort him towards the judge. The distance seemed endless. Once he tried to break, and Roi was up to him immediately, barking, challenging him, telling him not to dare.

Chase the criminal and stand away from him the second she told him. The chase was exciting. The dog might be too enthusiastic when he reached his target, dying to jump on the protective sleeve, that he regarded as a trophy to be won. If he didn't stop the second he was told, more marks would be lost.

The running man stood still, turning to look at the dog. Roi, Roi, don't let me down. The lack of movement was his signal, and he began to circle, barking his warning. Don't you dare even twitch a finger.

The judge nodded.

Brier walked over to the man and the dog, standing thirty feet away. Her own nervousness could blow this exercise.

'Roi, here.'

Roi came to her and stood beside her, watching his man all the time. She signalled to him to stay and walked over to the 'suspect', praying that this man wouldn't wink at her, or tease in any way.

A few questions, but this man was no criminal. He was an innocent passer-by, who had been in the wrong place at the wrong time. She smiled at him and let him leave the area. She called Roi to her and walked towards the judge. It had been a trick test.

They hadn't done badly, she was sure. Roi had been under her control the whole time and had not tried at any point to overstep the mark.

Then came the test of courage. Brier watched her dog as the 'criminal' raced on to the field, brandishing a stick and shouting.

The stick flashed towards Roi, who leaped and bit the attacking object, hanging on with determination. The man, fighting him, pulled it out of his mouth. How dared anyone try to hit him? It was plain in the dog's demeanour and even plainer as the stick lashed towards him and he grabbed at it, tearing it from the man's hand. He dropped it, and barked.

Brier called him to stand and be quiet. He turned his head to glance at her and then concentrated on his quarry.

Only the gun. Disarm the 'criminal'. The last exercise. He flew at the arm that pointed at him, angling round to take the man from the side. He held on to the protective sleeve, rendering the arm useless. The gun dropped to the ground.

As Brier left the field, she felt sure they had enough marks to pass. He couldn't have dropped many points. She knew that Derek and Tony would both lose marks for lack of control. Pete and Rob? She wasn't sure. Gwyn was her main threat. She wanted, more than anything, to show she could beat the men, that a woman could do the job and do it very well.

'OK?' Josh asked. Everyone had been watching from a distance. She had been unaware of the spectators until now.

Brier thought before she answered, weariness suddenly attacking her.

'I think so. I hope so.' She drank the coffee gratefully. Lunchtime already.

'I decided to give the restaurant here a miss,' Josh said. 'We'll all be happier in the pub. We'll save the three-course meals for afterwards.'

Once they were settled Josh joined the judge and they sat well away from the handlers, in earnest discussion. Everyone was aware of them, watching them, wondering anxiously. So much depended on those results. A whole future. Maybe a whole lifetime.

Brier ate, barely tasting the food, thinking back over the tests, trying to assess her marks. Had she been slow with her commands? Had Roi obeyed reluctantly? Had he picked up the retrieve article cleanly? Had he tried to chew it, while he was running to her?

Little faults could lose a great many marks, added up overall.

The afternoon passed even more slowly than the morning. Nothing to do but wait for the results. She spent part of the time watching, but decided that her cold justified her going to sit down indoors. The warmth induced sleep, and she was startled when Gwyn shook her.

'The hour of doom,' he said.

She stared at him, wondering what on earth he was talking about, and then realised it was time for the post mortem, for the day's results.

Josh handed out the sheets, his face impassive.

Brier looked at her total. 194/200. Six marks lost in all on the Obedience. She hid a grin. Who's perfect?

She turned to the criminal work sheet. That was where most marks would be lost. She looked down the entries. The judge's figures were large, black and bold. 298/300. Gwyn had 294. She had passed and she had beaten all the men.

But they were only half-way. There was always tomorrow, and no use pretending that that would be as good.

The judge was talking, but she was so tired that she barely took in what he was saying. Then it was over, and they were comparing marks, sharing the last flask of coffee, Josh and the judge in conference again.

She hoped for a word from Josh, but he sped off as soon as the judge had gone, just wishing them luck and warning them to be on time tomorrow. He needed news of Spark.

By the time Brier reached home her cold was bothering her again and she was thankful Gwyn had been driving. Even the knowledge that so far she was in the lead and that Roi had worked magnificently could not overcome her exhaustion.

Gwyn dropped her and her dog at the gate.

The door opened before she reached it and the children were there, waiting for her. Simon put his arms round Roi. Ben looked up, his eyes anxious. Dana was the first to ask the questions.

'Was it all right? Did he do well? Have you passed?' The three voices rang out. Kate was behind them, her eyes also questioning.

Realisation hit her. They'd done so well.

'Hey, hey. Let me get in. So far we're first. It's only half-way through, but we did OK.' Tomorrow would sort them out. Tomorrow would be far less easy. If the dog failed the track, then she would lose so many points that she would never stand a chance. No use feeling secure yet. Another night; another day of waiting; and anything could happen.

After the children had gone to bed she and Kate relaxed in front of the television set, but Brier was unable to settle. She must phone her mother. She felt suddenly guilty. Helena would be waiting for news, and desperate for her wonderful dog to do well.

'Get to bed. You're out on your feet,' Kate said. 'I'll ring Helena. You need to be alert for tomorrow. That's the day that's going to sort the men from the boys.'

And the woman from the men, Brier thought. She yawned. Life seemed full of promise again, even if she was so tired she wondered if she could crawl up to bed. Roi needed his last walk.

She glanced at the sheet of marks before she went to sleep. Josh would be proud of her. She needed his approval. She was suddenly more aware of him than ever before. No use daydreaming. The tests were by no means over. If only they could work as well tomorrow. If only it was as good a day. If only . . . She drifted off to sleep . . .

She was racing for a train she had to catch because her car had broken down, but the train never came. Walking with Roi, running with Roi, trying desperately to reach the venue in time.

Reaching it and finding Gulley there, wearing a butcher's apron, sweeping the grass with a broom, saying, 'You're too late. It's over. They've all gone home.'

Simon roused her, the inevitable cup of too-milky tea in his hand.

'Sleep well?'

Brier laughed.

'I had nightmares, Simon. I thought I had to catch a train, as my car had broken down. When I got there only Gulley was there.'

The dream vision came back absurdly, and she felt a small attack of hilarity.

'He was wearing a blue and white striped apron and sweeping the grass. He said everyone had gone home.'

Simon grinned at her, sharing the joke.

She went downstairs slowly, her stomach churning with nerves. Simon had cooked porridge, and added cream to it. Scrambled eggs on toast were keeping warm on the hot plate. She'd have to try and eat.

Kate watched her playing with her spoon.

'You'll be all right,' she said. 'Look how well you did yesterday.'

Brier bit her lip. 'I was nervous yesterday,' she said, 'but today I've woken up in a panic. Suppose we blow it all?'

'You can do it,' Kate said. 'So can Roi, and you've put in enough work to ensure he knows everything thoroughly. Relax.'

'Easier said than done.' She could never perform even half as well as she had the day before. Roi was over-eager, asking to go out, coming in again and barking at her for no reason, and then racing to the front door, as if saying, for goodness sake, let's be off.

That extra energy could be her undoing as he would be difficult to control and might anticipate everything.

The children were watching her. Kate gave her a quick hug.

'We'll be thinking of you, all day. And praying.'

'Birdie, we could still fail. Today is much more difficult.'

'You won't,' Kate said. 'Once you get started it will be OK. You'll see. Here's Gwyn.'

Simon followed her to the gate. His desperate expression was back. He had looked at her, worrying, all through breakfast.

He bent to caress Roi, hiding his face in the dog's thick fur.

She stooped and hugged him. 'Try not to worry, sweetheart,' she said, knowing that his anxiety was as much for the case conference as for the dog. 'He's doing splendidly so far.'

She waved to the small, anxious figure as they drove away. Wind harassed the trees and rain streaked out of a lowering sky. They'd all be soaked to the skin.

She hated working in the rain. So did the dog.

Twenty

Gwyn was no comfort at all.

'You need all your wits today,' he said, staring through the sweeping windscreen wipers at the wet road. 'Especially with this weather. And it's not yesterday's judge. He was a stickler, but you've seen nothing yet. Today's is supposed to be have taken lessons from the Star Chamber. Book you for thinking of a crime, or standing on a yellow line, never mind having a motor. Rumour has it that he takes off marks for having an inch too much tracking line, or the dog running widdershins in the search square.'

'Trying to cheer me up?' Brier asked.

'No. Just sharing my own fears.'

'You're all heart,' Brier said. 'Maybe I should drive. This is a thirty-mile an hour zone. Don't want to get nicked before we get to the venue.'

'I could get narked,' he said, negotiating a bend, and sighing as they drew in behind a milk tanker. A winding lane, and a double white line. 'As if I'd do that to you.' There was opposing traffic as far as he could see on the road ahead. The tanker was crawling. 'Oh, hell. I wish he'd turn off. Maybe I didn't have so much time after all. What time's your track?'

'11.30. When's yours?'

'After you. We can both relax.'

'With this weather and today's schedule? You must be joking.'

'Think of the passing-out parade, in front of all the top brass and your relatives.'

'My mother could come,' Brier said, realising it suddenly.

'She donated Roi.' She thought of their marks again. 'You could easily beat me today; only need a bit of bad luck . . .'

'I'd beat you hands down if I had Roi. He's a cracker. As it is, Loki takes some handling. I walked him for an hour before I picked you up in the hope of settling him down. If you win it's because of your dog. If I win it's because I'm a terrific handler.' He grinned at her, daring her to challenge him.

Brier was tempted to offer to swap dogs and prove her prowess. Was she always going to be accused of winning because of Roi and not through her own hard work? She stared out at the darkening day. Clouds shadowed the sky, threatening even heavier rain in an hour or so. The busy wipers barely cleared the screen.

Gwyn overtook the tanker and settled to a steady fifty miles an hour, watching the signs.

'Don't want to get lost,' he said.

Brier was suddenly light-hearted. She grinned.

'We could ask a policeman.' She reverted to her thoughts. 'I suppose I'll always be doomed to be judged on my dog and not me.'

'Not to worry. Josh knows what went into the dog. I could do as well with him as you, I think, but the others wouldn't. Poor Derek manages to sound as if he's swearing when he says, "Good dog", though Spike seems able to take it.'

'Tony is managing better than I expected with Jacko, I mean Jago. Not sure his first name isn't a better fit—he's an ass. Poor Tony. He didn't like the dog at all at first.'

'Tony has the makings of a handler, but he does get impatient; bad fault, that. And he doesn't praise enough. Whoever said "praise is the good handler's secret weapon" knew what he was talking about.' He turned off the lane onto a cart track, and then through a field gate, parking by the other vehicles on the grass. 'We're here, thank Heaven. Thought I'd taken a wrong turning back at the roundabout.' He looked at the soaked ground. 'Hope we can get off tonight; this field looks sodden.'

Brier glanced at her time sheet.

Track at 11.20 a.m., not 11.30. She was fifth to work, not fourth. Then a wait for her hard surface track. That was going to be dodgy if the rain went on. Tracking on roads or pavements was difficult at the best of times.

Her police problem was included there. That might sort them all out, especially as it had nothing to do with dog work.

Property search and the hidden person search at the end of a long day. In every case she was fifth on the list, with Gwyn working last. Tony was second each time. Just as well, maybe, though he became extremely testy while waiting for the next set of exercises to begin. He hated waiting for anything. Sort of bloke that wants results yesterday, Gwyn said, as they sat.

Derek was first and he seemed to be the one who suffered least from nerves. But there was always a wait before the next part of the test.

At last it was time. Brier wished she hadn't to wear her jacket, but the rain was heavy, driving into her face as they walked to the edge of the common. The visibility was poor, the distance murky, the ground sodden, with rough grass and thistle and furze.

She stared at the uninformative surface, hoping there might be telltale footmarks or disturbed grass, but there was no sign at all. The ground looked as if no one had ever walked there. Sometimes in the early morning you could see footsteps in the dew. Up to her dog now. Nothing she could do. The tracklayer might have walked anywhere. The rain might have washed all scent away. There might be animal trails that would lure Roi away from the human scent.

How could one man, just walking over that ground, ever be traced by any dog? It was a question she often pondered.

Today's judge was not as big a man as yesterday's. He had much colder eyes and a face that looked as if it didn't know how to smile. A man who didn't much like women, or at least, not as rivals, she guessed, and hoped she was wrong: it might prejudice his marking.

Time to start. The judge nodded. The steward spoke, and she was off, her mouth dry. Roi hunted the ground, his nose down. He started off, and she realised with a sinking heart that he was back-tracking, picking up the trail of the man where he had walked away instead of going forwards. She stopped him and sent him out again.

He seemed bewildered, and looked back at her, as if questioning her judgement. He had been on a track. So what was he doing wrong? Nothing, old son, nothing at all, Brier said in her mind, praying he would understand what was needed.

Elation leaped in her as down went his nose. He was off, driving away, pulling into his harness, with such speed she almost fell over. Too fast—he'd miss the turns.

A word and he slowed his pace, but he was intent, satisfying the curiosity she had built into him over the weeks. Where had this man walked, what had he dropped on the track, where were they going? Out into the country for miles, she thought, as the dog lost the scent, and stopped briefly to shake rain from his head. Damn the weather.

Four things to find. Half-a-mile, and, like the ten-minute down, it was a far longer half-mile than any she ever walked normally. So much could go wrong. A rabbit crossing the trail which the tracklayer had laid for her two hours ago. Just a man walking. She hoped she had a heavy man. He'd leave a heavier spoor on the ground.

Roi might scent the rabbit and go off in a false direction. And she wouldn't even know. Would he be docked because the rain was bothering him? He shook himself again. It was driving at them. Maybe it had washed all scent away.

The dog circled, nose down, knowing that he had to go

on, that the scent he was seeking was somewhere here. Brier gave a deep sigh of relief as the line holding him tightened and they moved forward. He was on the track again, forging onwards, his whole body eager.

He stood still, turning to look at her, telling her that here was something she ought to investigate. She looked in disbelief at the wallet. It was well filled with banknotes and credit cards. They must be crazy, but come to think of it, it was very near the start of the track. Perhaps it was nothing to do with the test. She picked it up and pocketed it.

She raised her arm, signalling to the judge. A find.

'Track on, boy,' she said, and the dog surged forward. A corner, a moment's doubt, and they were off again, Roi sniffing every inch, pulling her along, though he stopped several times to shake rain from his face. Don't do it, son, she thought. You could be losing me a cricket score.

The rain seeped under her collar. She should have tucked a towelling scarf in, as the jacket was slightly on the large side and didn't fit well at the neck.

They had never before tracked in such appalling weather. Brier's hair clung to her neck. She wiped her face with tissues that were soon soaked. The dog's fur was plastered to him, so that he looked unfamiliar, a lean animal, his shape outlined. He paused yet again to shake the rain vigorously from his fur.

Nervousness flared to worry. He must be losing marks every time he stopped to shake himself, but the amount of rain falling was exceptional. If only it didn't stop for the others, so giving them an unfair advantage. But that was mean, and she checked her thoughts and watched Roi closely, noting every tiny deviation from the straight line he ought to be following.

They turned another corner. The wind was now behind them, driving into their backs. It was so strong that Brier was sure the dog was on a parallel track, after a turn, far away from that laid, due to the strength of the gale. He might miss the other articles that he had to find. They couldn't afford to lose any more marks.

Another stop, and this time she was holding a cartridge case, which seemed a more likely object. Nobody would lay down a wallet full of money. Someone must have lost it accidentally. Roi needed to find three more objects.

They must still be on course, unless someone had been shooting here and the cartridge case was another accident.

Turn again, sharply this time, and the dog was off, pushing into the wind, as if scenting something at the end of the trail. It must be almost the end. She had forgotten she was under trial, forgotten everything but the need to watch Roi and make sure he really was tracking, not just out for a game, having scented rabbit in the hedge.

One object. They must surely be near the end of the track. Had he missed one? Had he missed three? He halted again. A piece of leather. Collect and signal. On into the rain.

Another halt, this time to pick up a spark plug. So they were still on track: no one could drop that in a field by accident. Or could they? People did the oddest things.

He stopped again, and this time she knew it was the end of the trail. She picked up the object that lay there, a small packet of white powder. Sugar? Meant to indicate a little parcel of dope. The end of the track. The end of the test. No chance now to redeem any mistakes.

Back to the judge.

'You can throw away your first article. There was nothing there for the dog to find,' the judge said, as she approached him.

She held out the wallet.

'Are you sure?'

The tracklayer, who had been watching her, walked over to her, and stared in disbelief. He felt frantically in his pocket.

'I must have dropped it as I started out, feeling for the cartridge case. I didn't even notice,' he said. 'Reckon the dog needs a bonus. Gee, I'd be in a mess if I lost that.' He grinned and rewarded Roi with a pat on the head.

The judge looked at his score sheet.

'Given me a problem,' he said. Brier knew he would have deducted marks for that; maybe he would now restore them.

Time. Waiting time. Endless time. Nailbiting time. Time to worry, time to think back. If only I had done that. If only I had realised . . . Watching at a distance. The other dogs would do far better than Roi.

Had she blown it? Time seemed to stand still between the tests. If only they could run them all off for each handler, without the dreadful hanging about waiting for time to pass and to be under scrutiny again.

She was aware of time as never before. The waiting was worse than anything she had ever experienced.

The hard surface track was laid on a disused road that ran alongside the venue. The most difficult thing the dog would have to do, and heaven alone knew if there was any scent left in all this rain.

Roi put his nose down, and Brier followed, feeling the tug on the line that was attached to his tracking harness. Along the road, behaving as if, by some miracle, the ground was telling him that scent lay here. He was slightly off the line. She saw the tiny card that lay at the end, some inches to his right.

Was it the end of the track, or had it been dropped, or blown in the wind? It was encased in plastic and heavier than she expected.

There was a tiny lead fishing weight in the back of the plastic case. Nobody would put that there—or would they? A fisherman?

The name and address on the card meant nothing to her. A business card. She picked it up and took it to the judge. Roi had no further interest in the ground, behaving as if the track had ended there. She had to rely on him. Nothing to see.

The judge gave her no indication as to whether she was right or wrong. Not finished yet. The tests seemed to be going on for ever.

'I can't stand the waiting in between,' Tony said, starting on a second packet of cigarettes.

'None of us can.' Derek walked away, irritated.

'I don't know if it's better to watch everyone, or to go right away and see nothing,' Gwyn said. He produced a packet of extra-strong mints. 'Have one. They blow your head off. Stops thinking.'

Brier laughed. Nothing would prevent her busy mind replaying every minute, wondering desperately how they had fared.

She was dreading the police problem. Once that would have been set for handler and dog. Now it was to make sure the handler was an efficient officer. Surely she was that or they would never have accepted her for the dog team? Surely she couldn't fail that? Should she take Roi with her or hand him to Gulley to hold?

No one had told her how to handle this. She decided to keep the dog beside her.

She walked towards the judge, wondering how this would be done. A man was lying on the ground beside him, one leg crumpled under him, blood on his head. She stared at him, shocked, thinking she was about to be faced with a genuine emergency, and then realised that he was acting.

She looked down at the man.

'He needs an ambulance,' she said. 'Injured leg, maybe broken, and a bang on the head. I'd send for that at once.'

The judge nodded and made a note.

She dared not move him, and there was little use in taking off her soaked coat to make him comfortable. She had to act as if this were a real-life situation, or she might make a mistake by failing to take the man's injuries seriously, knowing they were faked.

'What happened to you?' she asked.

'He chucked me out of the car. Pushed me out at thirty miles an hour or more, the swine.'

'Why did he chuck you out?' She hadn't expected that answer.

'Had a row, didn't we?'

'What about?'

'I said to split fifty-fifty. He said he'd done all the work and it was forty to me and sixty to him. And now he's got it all.'

'Got what?'

'We did the Building Society on the High Street in Dorsington. And now he's got the lot.'

'What was he driving?'

'Blue van. He'll have ditched it now and pinched another.'

'The van was stolen?'

'Be your age, missus. We wouldn't use our own wheels, would we?'

There seemed so many questions before she could unravel the story. When she thought she had covered every detail she left the man, to have a look at the terrain. A lane leading to the main road: the other man could have escaped in one of several directions. Alert other units. Let her dog search the area, just in case. The busy pencil was unnerving.

Roi sniffed at the 'victim' and then put his nose down and began to nose the ground. A few yards from the junction with the main road he stood, turned his head and looked at her. 'Got something here,' his eyes said. 'Come and see.'

He was uncertain as to the exercise. Should he retrieve, or was he tracking? Brier wasn't sure either. She walked up to him. He was standing by a gun. She was well stocked with tissues and took out several from her pocket and picked it up carefully. She also had a plastic bag, though not as part of the tests, but in case Roi had an accident.

She hoped the judge wouldn't realise that and would think her very efficient. She put the gun in the bag.

So the judge had tried to trick her. It was only chance that had led her to ask Roi to seek.

The dog hunted around, but found nothing more.

'What's this, then?' she asked the man, showing him the gun.

'Threw it out as he turned onto the main road, didn't he?' he said in disgust. He was enjoying his role. 'Didn't use it; just threatened with it.'

At last she could think of nothing else to ask. She had no idea how she had fared. The judge had an interesting clipboard, a plastic domelike cover enabling him to keep the paper out of the rain. It intrigued Roi, who could not take his eyes off it.

Time to break off.

Lunch included hot soup. The little pub was expecting them. An intelligent landlady had taken pity on them, knowing how much the test meant, and sympathising over the weather.

Brier was content to eat and relax, to listen to the men. Gwyn thought he had done fairly well. Tony was aggrieved, blaming the rain. Rob and Pete thought they might have a fair score. Derek was silent, glaring at his food as if it had done him an injury.

Josh again ate with the judge. He had spoken to them briefly, his mind on Spark. The dog was very far from well and was still on the drip. Worry flared at inconvenient moments, so that he had to concentrate hard on what was being said. Gulley, as anxious for the dog as Josh, was still angry. It was unlike the kennelman to snap and Brier wondered if she had upset him.

Josh, anxious as a hen with chicks, cursed the weather,

and brooded over his team, encouraging them, making light of the conditions, trying to give them all a positive feeling, needing their success. He couldn't afford to lose even a single dog or handler.

He was worried about Brier. He wanted her on his team. He wanted to see her daily, to grow to know her better and maybe, one day, when Tom was a loved memory and the bitterness had died . . .

It was one of the worst test days he had ever known. It could make or break. They would have to work in all weathers, but then they would be operational and not under test. It was a very severe trial, much stiffer than on his other courses, with this amount of wind and rain. So much depended on the judge, on the standard he demanded and the way he marked.

The result could be disappointing. Today was critical, and he knew this judge marked very stiffly indeed. Also, he did not like women in the Force, let alone in the dog section. Josh began to feel more nervous than his handlers, watching each of them, desperately anxious for all to do well. If only he didn't paste Brier. That wouldn't be fair. But the judge's decision was final.

Derek, unexpectedly, appeared to be without nerves. His dog never minded bad weather. Gwyn was uneasy, watching his dog, knowing that Loki detested rain and would spend much of his time shaking himself.

Tony was buoyed by the thought of his small daughter, who was thriving. He had raced home the day before with an armful of flowers for his wife. Today nervousness was taking over. Jago had already lost too many points and was likely to lose even more. The dog seemed to have developed a will of his own.

The day dragged on. Waiting time seemed endless, though most of the tests flashed through, over too soon. Did they all feel as she did? Brier wondered, or was this a peculiarly stupid feminine trait? She had become an automaton, familiarity carrying her through every action.

The search. The moment of truth. Had his training really paid off, or would he revert to tossing every item as he picked it up? She held her breath as he raced out into the square. His nose went down, catching the scent on the wind. Four items to find. Four chances to revert to that game he had played with Dana. Four chances to wreck the day.

He brought the items in proudly, swaggering, holding each firmly, pushing it into her hand. A broken watch strap. A clothes-peg. A cleft piece of stick. That couldn't be right, and then she noticed that in the cleft was caught a small piece of tweed. A metal key.

She wanted to hug him. She glanced at her watch. They were within the time allowed. No penalty there.

He hadn't tried even one single tiny toss.

Time to drink Gulley's strong, sweet coffee, to try and eat the doughnut he insisted would give her energy. Jago had brought in four articles, but Storm had only found three. Major had found all four fast, working brilliantly. Loki hated metal. Now, as she watched him drop the key, she knew that it was no longer important to beat the men, only to pass the tests, and pass them well.

Now it was Roi's turn to find the immovable object. That was another of his obsessions: what he found he was sure he had to fetch to his handler. He could waste time and lose points trying to drag an anchored object out of deep undergrowth.

She was thankful for the hours she had spent with the children, hiding all kinds of ridiculous things for Roi to find. The dustbin. A large plastic bag filled with sand. The children's bicycles. He still tried to carry them, quite certain that that was what he was really supposed to do.

They went out into the field. It was a long time since anyone had cultivated it. Vast masses of briar and bramble covered outcrop rocks. The old farmhouse in the next field was a ruin. Last year's high grass had died and stood straw-like, almost over Roi's head.

He vanished, and she could only tell where he was by the movement in the stems. The dog found the hidden property without any difficulty, though he did try to retrieve the motor bike, grabbing its handlebars. Brier could hear him panting and heaving, and wondered if the judge would dock him.

It resisted him, and he realised he had to stand and bark. Another test over. She began to feel as if time had imprisoned her and the day would never end.

By mid-afternoon Pete and Rob seemed to have lost the power of speech. Both men were worried. Rob maybe had more reason. The day before Storm had not completed the sendaway, refusing to redirect, which would lose him valuable points.

Gwyn could change Loki's mind; Rob, frustrated, could make Storm behave more stupidly, as the dog became anxious and then confused by his handler's inconsistency.

Jago, unexpectedly, worked well on the hard track which was one of his worst exercises. Tony, buoyed by his dog's performance, developed a new confidence.

Roi should carry Brier through. She looked increasingly weary during the afternoon and Josh was worried about her. He hoped her tiredness wouldn't affect her dog. One never knew.

Roi had performed well, of that she was sure, though she was sure of nothing else. She was tired of standing in the rain. She went back to sit in the van, shivering, her teeth chattering. She switched on the engine, running it until it was warm and she could put on the heater.

'Can you last out?' Josh asked, putting his head in through the window which she had opened when she saw him.

She looked up at him.

'Stay me with flagons, comfort me with apples and pray for my soul,' she said.

I'd like to do a lot more than that, Josh thought, and hid his thoughts behind an even sterner expression than usual, so that Brier felt she had done badly and that he knew it.

'We'll all be glad to get warm and dry,' he said.

Even his stiff manner could not dampen her spirits. They might not have won, but surely they had passed.

'I'll be more than glad to. I'm cold, wet, feel slightly sick and I'll be thankful when it's over. For better or worse. No, that's the marriage ceremony, isn't it?' She began to wonder if she were light-headed. Her tongue seemed to make the most ridiculous remarks.

Josh stared at her, and then stood up and walked away, so that she wondered if she had upset him.

Gulley seemed to fill every moment of waiting with coffee and food. Alice had made a feast, hoping that frequent snacks would help to keep them calm. His busy little body seemed to be everywhere, encouraging, commenting, making Tony laugh by a brief remark that Brier didn't hear.

'What's funny?' she asked.

'Jago picked Gulley's pocket and whipped his wallet while we were standing watching Storm track. I never even noticed. Gulley took it from him. Suggested I went on race-course duty and we went into partnership. We could clean up.'

'New version of the bent copper,' Brier said. 'It's different. What would the charge be? And who would be charged, you or the dog?'

It was an idiotic conversation but it passed the time. Derek joined in unexpectedly with suggestions of other tricks they could teach the dogs, such as shoplifting.

'Never knew I was training a bunch of crooks,' Josh said, overhearing them as he passed. The judge had stopped for a coffee and what appeared to be a feast of cakes and scones.

'Sweeten him,' Gulley said, as he passed them with the

tray of empty dishes. 'Loads of sugar in that. Alice suggested lacing everything with brandy, but we thought maybe that wouldn't look too good.'

They all grinned. Nice to know Gulley was on their side, and thinking of them, even if his methods were unlikely to affect the results in any way.

It was over at last.

Back to the Centre to change, coaxing a lift from one of the visiting dog handlers. Back to being dry. She wondered at her mood swings. One moment confident, and the next sure she'd failed. If only she knew. Now.

'Come on.' Gulley had returned a few minutes before her. A moped was not much fun in the rain. 'Let's get some warmth into our bones.' Brier followed him inside. The other handlers had not yet returned.

He put the little heater on in his office, and sat her in front of it, with the inevitable mug of hot, sweet coffee.

Brier glanced at the cardboard box. There was a sudden flurry of squeals and she went over to it and looked inside.

'So that's your secret. We all wondered. Bess has had pups!'

'Wanted a son from her, before it's too late,' Gulley said. 'Couldn't leave them at home as Alice is too busy. She's going to help your Ma as well as doing some time still at the Rescue Kennels. One of these is for your children. Might give young Simon something to think about instead of Roi. They're nice temperament, though they're Jackies. No problem in finding homes.'

'Gulley, you're an angel. The children would love a pup. Have you asked Kate, though?'

'Asked her before I asked you. No use if she wouldn't look after it during the day. She had lunch with Alice a few days ago, and they discussed it then.'

She watched Bess feeding the pups. Their eyes were not yet open. Four or more weeks before the children had their own dog. Time to make plans.

The rain, perversely, had ceased after the last dog had worked. Josh had booked the snug in the Swan. The landlady provided them with hot soup, sandwiches and tea so strong the spoons almost stood up in it. Never was food so welcome.

The judge was summing up. Criticising.

'I haven't deducted any marks from anyone for dogs shaking off the rain,' he said. 'It's been one of the vilest days I've seen and I'm pleased with the way your dogs performed. Operationally, they'd all get by and nobody failed any of the tests. The wind presented tracking and searching problems, in that the scent was blown so far, but again I have made allowances for that.'

He looked across at Brier.

'Your new woman police dog handler was the only one of you who thought to use her dog to search the territory round the man. There was a gun hidden in the grass just before the road junction. Her dog found it.'

He smiled at her, his whole face altering suddenly so that she began to like him.

'Never take anything for granted,' she thought, as Josh handed out their sheets.

It was a minute before she summoned up enough courage to look at hers: 452/500.

And 492/500 yesterday.

A total of 944/1,000.

She'd passed. They were in. She wanted, still, to be first, but she'd dropped so many. How had Gwyn done? She turned to him.

'Nine hundred and thirty,' he said. 'You've pipped me. I never thought to use Loki in the police problem.'

Brier grinned at him.

'Never take anything for granted.'

The judge walked over to her.

'You did well,' he said. 'Not easy to work in the weather we had today. That was very rough luck on everyone.

That's a fine dog. Somebody did the Force proud when they donated him.'

'My mother gave him to us,' Brier said. 'She bought him as a stud dog, but he got infected and became sterile.'

'Lucky for us. I'll watch out for you both.' He nodded and went over to speak to Gwyn.

Josh came across and sat beside her, stretching out long legs.

'I'm proud of you. Proud of all of you. Well done.'

'Could have done better,' Brier said, judging herself harshly, as always. 'They were my points lost, not the dog's.'

'Weather was against all of you. Derek's through, in spite of Spike going off at the end of the track in the wrong direction. Just scraped that. So I've six new dogs and six new handlers.'

Gulley came into the room. He had rung the vet to ask after Spark. He came back in time to hear the words. He grinned.

'Spark's going to be OK. He's off the drip and he ate a little food.'

Josh drew a deep sigh and then smiled at them.

'I hope you'll understand when I say that that news has made my day, though I'm delighted with all of you. I didn't think he'd make it. If your dog doesn't get to you, then you need to wonder why you're in my section. Sorry if I've been short with you . . . couldn't get the dog out of my mind.'

He stood up.

The judge was packing his briefcase, nodding to them, as he prepared to drive home.

'It's been an interesting day,' he said. 'I congratulate all of them. I've never judged in such appalling weather. It was a very severe test of stamina, let alone anything else.' He smiled, shook hands with Josh, and was gone.

'I've several nights' sleep to make up. You probably have, too. We'll celebrate tomorrow. Tonight you'll all want to get home and get the chill out of your bones if you feel anything like I do.' Josh's warm smile embraced all of them. The worry had gone from his eyes.

They'd all passed and Spark would live to work again. They watched as Josh and the kennelman went out. Brier thought of her own dog, and knew that losing him would be one of the worst things that ever happened to her. And lose him she would, probably while still in the dog section. Few dogs worked beyond eight years old. No one would realise the terrible gap left unless they too had owned a dog.

'Tough,' Gwyn said. 'And he never even let us guess how he felt. Hell of a guy, that one. Worked his guts out for us all. Ready for off?'

They were all elated, a babble of conversation and laughter. The dogs had to be taken home and dried and fed and groomed. Simon would do that for her, Brier thought, and uttered a small prayer that the authorities would let her keep him. She couldn't bear the thought of what might happen to him if he had to go elsewhere.

The journey home seemed endless. She couldn't wait to tell her news. Gwyn dropped her and roared away, eager to reach home himself. There seemed to be lights in every window in the house. The hall was filled with people as she opened the door, all of them standing silent, looking at her.

Kate and the children. Helena, her eyes anxious. Gracie and Meg.

This was success. This was elation. This was the climax of weeks of work, of planning, of worrying, of training. Roi bounded in, and pranced in a circle, unable to decide who to greet first.

'Meet Police Dog Roi. Top of his class. Isn't he wonderful?' She wanted to hug everyone. She wanted to dance and sing. She looked across at the photograph of Tom, and discovered that the bitterness had gone.

I did it, she told him, hoping that perhaps he was somewhere near and could hear.

They were all around her, Helena hugging her, Simon grinning all over his face, Ben stroking Roi, Dana dancing.

'Roi's a police dog. Roi's a police dog. Roi's a police dog.'

Ginger, appalled by the noise, retreated to the top of the dresser and curled himself up, looking down at them, his eyes revealing what he thought about all these insane people.

Roi raced from one to the other, overcome by all the fuss, not understanding why they were so effusive, but only too willing to be star of the show.

'My lovely boy,' Helena said. 'That's made it all worthwhile. Now I want to see him Police Dog of the Year.'

'Don't aim low, whatever you do,' Brier said, feeling as if she would never stop smiling.

'I never do,' Helena said. 'Why sell yourself short?'

Brier took off her jacket and walked into the dining-room. She stared in disbelief at the table, which was spread for a feast.

In the centre was a huge iced cake, a picture of a dog on the top of it, and the words 'Congratulations Brier and Roi'.

'I don't know how you dared,' Brier said, bemused.

'Easy enough to take icing off, but I knew I wouldn't have to.' Kate was looking as smug as if she alone were responsible for their success.

And maybe she is, Brier thought. I could never have done it without her.

'Congratulations,' Gracie said. 'I knew you'd do it. And there's more good news. The case conference was today. I couldn't tell you, didn't want to add to your worries, so I pretended it was tomorrow. It's OK. Simon can stay with you as your foster child.'

There could be other decisions later, Brier thought, but

this was not the time to cast doubts on a permanent future.

'And this is for Simon,' Kate said, bringing in another cake, heavily iced, with the words 'Welcome home Simon,' written on it.

The boy raced at Brier and buried his head in her chest.

'I can stay for ever and ever and ever and ever?' he asked.

'That's a very long time.' She laughed. 'Maybe until you want to leave home and get married or live your own life. But there'll always be a place for you with us.'

She looked across his head at Dana and Ben. Ben lifted one thumb, a huge grin on his face. Dana smiled and said, 'Good.' She wished she had a sister instead but knew it was better not to say so. She was growing up.

Kate lifted her coffee mug.

'To Roi,' she said. 'To Simon. To all of us.'

Everyone laughed and took their own mugs from the tray.

Roi, bewildered, went from one to the other of them, unable to make out why they were all chanting his name.

'Gulley wants to give us one of Bess's puppies,' Dana said, creeping up to her mother and leaning against her. 'We can have it, can't we?'

Brier hugged her daughter, conscious that she was not drawing away. Dana had changed in the last few weeks.

'Of course you can. Gulley told me. What are you going to call it?'

'Treasure,' said Dana.

'That's silly. Lucky's a better name,' said Ben.

'Pirate,' said Simon. 'They'll all be like Bess and have a patch over one eye.'

'Gulley says we can choose one when we come to the parade to watch you and Roi. We can come, can't we?' Ben was looking at her, his eyes eager.

'It wouldn't be a parade for me without all of you there. Perhaps Gulley can help find a name. Meg, are you coming?'

'Just try and stop me. By the way, no one seems to have remembered to tell you that Josh phoned to say he has Spark home from the vet and the dog's beginning to make progress. He stole Lim's supper.'

It added a gloss to the evening. Brier went up to bed that night feeling absurdly happy. Roi followed her and settled down outside the door.

Excitement kept her awake for some time, but at last she dropped off into a deep, contented sleep.

The ringing phone shattered her dreams. She glanced at the clock. Not again. It was 2 a.m.

'Brier?' It was Josh's voice. 'I'm sorry, but Gulley and I drew up a rota, taking your names out of a hat to see who worked first. It was you . . . and we didn't feel we could change it, although you've already been out twice. Break-in at the golf club.'

'I'm on my way.'

'That's my girl. Brier . . .' he hesitated, almost telling her he loved her.

Now wasn't the time.

'Good luck. They're waiting for you.'

She was dressed and downstairs, Roi at her side. The kitchen light was on, and Simon, rumpled from sleep, stood anxiously beside the table, holding out a thermos flask.

'Black sweet coffee. Kate said it's an "in case you go out" flask. She forgot to tell you it was ready.'

'I couldn't do without you, Simon.' She ruffled the blond hair. He grinned up at her, suddenly confident and aware of his own place in the family.

There was a new moon, lying on its side, a star above it. A symbol of fresh beginnings.

Roi leaped into the van, eager for action.

This is it, she thought as she drove towards the golf club. This is what we trained for, this is our destiny. We're a link in a small chain, keeping crime at bay.

Later that night, returning home, their mission successfully accomplished, an odd thought crossed her mind.

Up to now it had been memories of Tom that had buoyed her, a longing to earn his approval, even though he was no longer there.

Tonight, as she handed over her captive, she had had only one thought in her head:

'Josh will be proud of us.'

The thought remained with her when at last she fell asleep. She dreamed that she was walking with Josh in a deep wood. They came to the edge of it and the shadows were fading and sunlight lay ahead.